"Good night **leave.**

He reached for

"What?"

Placing his hands on her shoulders, he tilted her toward the porch light. "You have some soot on your face."

"Do I?" She dabbed at her cheeks, smearing rather than removing the soot.

"Here. Let me."

He removed a kerchief from his coat pocket and gently wiped her face. While pretending to scrutinize his work, he studied her eyes, which never veered from his.

Molly might have trouble expressing her innermost feelings, but they were clearly telegraphed in the tiny nuances of her expression. What Owen saw made his heart bounce wildly inside his chest. She didn't entirely object to his touch—even enjoyed it.

He took a leap, not caring about the consequences. "I'm going to kiss you, Molly."

"You are?" she breathed.

"Unless you object."

He waited for her to say something. When one moment stretched into two, he dipped his head and brushed his lips slowly across hers.

Since 2006, *New York Times* bestselling author **Cathy McDavid** has been happily penning contemporary Westerns for Harlequin. Every day, she gets to write about handsome cowboys riding the range or busting a bronc. It's a tough job, but she's willing to make the sacrifice. Cathy shares her Arizona home with her own real-life sweetheart and a trio of odd pets. Her grown twins have left to embark on lives of their own, and she couldn't be prouder of their accomplishments.

HEARTWARMING

The Christmas Agreement

Previously published as *A Cowboy's Christmas Proposal*

—————

New York Times Bestselling Author

Cathy McDavid

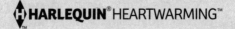

Recycling programs
for this product may
not exist in your area.

ISBN-13: 978-1-335-08177-3

The Christmas Agreement

First published as A Cowboy's Christmas Proposal in 2018.
This edition published in 2019.

Copyright © 2018 by Cathy McDavid

For questions and comments about the quality of this book,
please contact us at CustomerService@Harlequin.com.

HARLEQUIN®
™ www.Harlequin.com

Printed in U.S.A.

To Kathleen. You've given me so many incredible opportunities during my career with Harlequin, including this one. Thank you for the chance to continue writing the kinds of books I love and to find brand-new readers.
You are the best.

CHAPTER ONE

HEARING WHAT SOUNDED like a hammer banging against metal, Molly O'Malley tossed the covers aside and sat bolt upright. Her sister had beaten her to the shower. Again. Now she'd be late getting downstairs—the last thing she wanted today of all days. After endless planning, preparation and backbreaking labor, Sweetheart Ranch was finally opening for business.

Molly pushed herself out of bed, excitement and nervousness replacing the fog of sleep. Grabbing her flannel robe hanging from the bedpost, she padded to the closet, every third floorboard creaking in angry protest. A single tug on the antique glass knob and the closet door glided open. Thank goodness. It just as often stuck and refused to budge.

Like the faulty water pressure in the pipes and the creaking floorboards, no amount of tinkering had remedied the finicky closet door. Molly's grandmother, Emily, claimed the many quirks only added to the old house's charm.

Molly did agree the house possessed a cer-

tain appeal. People raved over the quaint and
rustic decor inspired by local history, nearby
cattle ranches and the herd of wild mustangs
that had once roamed the valley. At least, those
were the comments Molly had received from
guests who'd viewed their website and booked
a wedding, or a honeymoon stay in one of the
six cabins.

Five weddings were scheduled these last four
days of November and a dozen so far in December. Understandably, the holidays were a popular
time to get married. What better than to com-
bine two joyous occasions?

Only 50 percent of the ranch's cabins, however, had been booked. As head of guest relations, Molly worried. Grandma Em, their
resident wedding coordinator, had assured her
the situation was temporary. Lately, she'd issued
the statement with a twinkle in her eye.

That, too, worried Molly. Grandma Em had
poured almost her entire savings into the ranch,
converting her country home on ten acres into
what would hopefully be the most popular,
and most unique, wedding venue and bed-and-
breakfast in Arizona. She should be fretting and
pacing and biting her nails to the quick. Or, like
Molly, racing around in a constant state of agita-
tion. She certainly shouldn't be dismissing valid
concerns with a casual shrug.

Molly contemplated the three O'Malley women as she chose an outfit. They were a study in contrast, each of them dealing with stress differently. While Molly planned for every conceivable catastrophe, her older sister, Bridget, stayed up late testing recipes and developing menus. Grandma Em, perhaps the smartest of them, took things in stride.

Both sisters had worked in the hospitality industry since graduating college—Bridget as a pastry chef and Molly in hotel administration. When their grandmother had called last summer and invited them to share in her long-held dream of owning and operating a Western-themed wedding ranch, they'd jumped at the chance—for entirely different reasons.

Hurrying down the hall, Molly stopped at the bathroom door and knocked loudly.

"You almost done?"

"Give me two minutes," Bridget hollered above another pipe-banging symphony.

Molly groaned in frustration, more annoyed with herself for oversleeping than at her sister for dawdling. She'd stayed up late last night, too, envisioning every detail of their grand opening and mentally reviewing her lengthy to-do list.

While she waited, her glance traveled the hall to Grandma Em's bedroom. She'd apparently risen some time ago, for the door sat ajar and not a single peep came from inside the room.

Likely, she was downstairs, making coffee and toasting homemade bagels for breakfast. Molly was straining her ears for any hint of activity when Bridget flung open the bathroom door and emerged from behind a cloud of steam.

"Thanks for hogging the entire hot water supply."

"Get up earlier next time."

Molly huffed as she shouldered past her sister. Being adults didn't stop them from squabbling like they had when they were young.

"Whatever." Bridget darted to her room, tucking in the tail of the bath towel she wore on her head like a turban. Several red tendrils had escaped and lay plastered against her neck, forming a row of inverted question marks. Molly's own wavy hair would look the same when she stepped from the shower.

It was one of many similarities between them. They shared freckled cheeks, a cleft in their chins, a love of sweets and an unwavering determination to marry a man just like their late father.

They also had their differences. Big ones. While Bridget was an open book, messy to a fault, and tended to easily trust people, Molly kept her thoughts and feelings to herself, preferred her surroundings and every aspect of her life to be neat and tidy, and exercised caution in all situations.

She had good reason. Her twice-wounded heart needed protecting. Grandma Em's invitation, issued on the heels of Molly's latest breakup, had provided the perfect opportunity. She'd packed her car and bid Southern California goodbye without a single regret.

Molly showered in record time before the hot water really did run out—another quirk of the old house—then returned to her room. After throwing on her clothes, she ran a brush through her wet hair. She'd style it and apply makeup later, before the open house started at noon. There was simply too much to accomplish before then.

Of course Bridget had beaten her downstairs. Molly made straight for the kitchen, expecting to be assaulted by the aroma of freshly brewed coffee and toasting bagels. Instead, Bridget stood at the counter, dropping clumps of thick, chocolatey batter onto a cookie sheet. The coffeepot sat untouched.

"Where's Grandma?" Molly asked, mildly irritated. She desperately needed to fuel up on caffeine.

"I haven't seen her yet."

How odd. Maybe she was on an emergency

run to the market for some last-minute item. Though, on second thought, the town's one small grocery store didn't open until nine.

"Did you call her?" Molly asked.

"Been too busy."

Fishing her cell phone from her jeans pocket, she dialed Grandma Em. The call went straight to voice mail.

"She must have forgotten to charge her phone."

"Wouldn't be the first time." Bridget slid the cookie sheet into the oven.

Ignoring the twinge of anxiety winding through her, Molly set down her phone and filled the coffeepot with water. They did have a brand-new individual cup brewing system in the dining room, but that was reserved for guests.

"Do you think we were wrong to plan our grand opening in the middle of the holiday season?" she asked. "It's still technically Thanksgiving weekend. People are going to be out shopping or putting up Christmas decorations."

"We can't afford to wait."

"True." Expenses were mounting while revenues wouldn't pick up until after they officially opened. Molly knew that for a fact as she handled the ranch books.

It was then she spotted the small piece of notepaper taped to the refrigerator. Grandma Em's familiar handwriting jumped out at her.

"What's this?" With her free hand, Molly tore off the note and started reading. The next instant, her fingers went slack, and she nearly dropped the pot. "I don't believe it!"

"What's wrong?" Bridget glanced up from sprinkling flour onto a rolling mat.

"Grandma's gone." The words fell from Molly's mouth in a shocked whisper.

"Where? The café?"

"Try the Grand Canyon and then Nevada. In Homer's RV." Molly gaped at her sister, alarm battling with disbelief. "They've eloped. They're getting married in Reno and then taking a month-long road trip."

"No way!" Bridget wiped her hands on a towel and charged across the kitchen. She snatched the note from Molly and quickly scanned the paper.

"She must be kidding," Molly said. "Grandma wouldn't leave on the day of our open house for anything. Right?"

"I don't know. She might."

"What are you talking about?"

Bridget thrust the note back at her. "She made a comment the other day about really liking Homer."

That was news to Molly. Yes, Grandma and Homer were friends and went out to lunch sometimes. But eloping? Surely Molly would have noticed her grandmother falling in love. She wasn't *entirely* self-absorbed.

"You should have told me."

"Honestly," Bridget said, "I didn't think a lot about it other than if Grandma had a boyfriend, then good for her. At least one of us was dating."

"Apparently, he's a lot more than a boyfriend. They're getting married!" Without Molly and her sister and their family in attendance. She tried to ignore the sharp stab of hurt. "What about the grand opening? Grandma's our hostess. And who's going to marry people?"

Grandma Em had originally suggested they hire Homer to wed those couples without their own officiant. It had seemed like a sensible solution at the time. The O'Malleys were in need, and Homer was available since retiring from his position as minister at Valley Community Church.

"Grandma says in her note replacements for her and Homer are on the way. That everything's been handled."

"What kind of replacements?" Molly fought for control. She didn't fare well with blows from left field.

"Guess we'll find out." Bridget returned to the counter. "Look, I need to start the bread or it won't rise in time."

"Bread? Really? We're in crisis."

Molly dug her fingers into her forehead where an ache had started to throb. Grandma leaving hours before their grand opening and marrying a man no one had had any idea she was even serious about was nothing short of insane.

Setting down the coffeepot, she grabbed her phone and dialed her grandmother's number again, only to disconnect when the recorded greeting kicked in.

"They must be out of range." Bridget dumped an oblong of bread dough onto the mat and began kneading. "You should have left a message."

"And said what? The two of you had better get yourselves back home right now? We have a business to run. Guests to accommodate. Couples to unite in wedded bliss."

Photographers. Live video streaming. Floral arrangements. Music. Decorations. Molly realized with some dismay she wasn't as familiar with her grandmother's job at Sweetheart Ranch as she should be. In addition to the books, Molly oversaw cabin reservations, customer service, housekeeping, marketing and the various amenities they offered. That left her too busy to participate much in the wedding planning.

"Give her a chance to explain," Bridget advised. "Love makes people do crazy things."

"I think we should cancel the open house."

"Absolutely not! Our first guests arrive this afternoon, and our first wedding is at seven tonight."

"Assuming we have a minister."

"Relax. Take a deep breath." Bridget followed her own advice. "Panicking will only make matters worse."

How could her sister *not* panic? Their world was collapsing around them. Worst of all, Molly was about to fail at the fourth job she'd held in seven years. And this time she wasn't to blame.

"I'm serious. We should cancel."

"Grandma has too much money invested." Bridget rhythmically worked the dough. "And are you willing to tell the happy couple their wedding's off? They're expecting to honeymoon tonight as man and wife."

"But what if—"

"Have some faith. Grandma won't let us down. If we haven't heard from her by midafternoon, we'll hire Reverend Crosby."

"He charges a fortune."

"Better than turning the couple away on our first day of business."

Molly made a decision. "I'm calling Mom."

"What's she going to do?"

Nothing, as it turned out. She didn't know about Grandma Em's elopement, either, and had no advice for Molly other than to move forward as best as she and Bridget could.

"I'd love to help you," she said. "But Doug has a touch of the flu and can't fend for himself."

"Thanks anyway, Mom. I'll talk to you later."

Left with little choice, Molly buried herself in work, her usual coping mechanism. While Bridget continued baking delicacies for the open house and a cake for that night's reception, Molly arranged champagne flutes, crystal punch glasses, china plates and silver flatware in the parlor.

On impulse, she set out cinnamon-scented candles flanking the festive fall cornucopia in the center of the table, certain the delicious aroma would stir feelings of Christmas for their guests the same as it did for her. It was never too soon to start celebrating.

Fortunately for Molly and Bridget, the ranch's launch wedding was on the smaller side—only twenty-seven people including the bride and groom. The most their chapel could accommodate was forty-five. The veranda held thirty for those who preferred an outdoor ceremony. For larger weddings, folding chairs could be set up on the lawn.

Over the next hour, whenever the ranch phone rang, Molly dove for the polished mahogany counter in the foyer that served as her workstation and registration desk. She answered the callers' questions about the open house, praying that she and her sister could indeed pull off the event without their grandmother.

Expecting a delivery from the florist, Molly didn't think twice when the front door opened. Hearing the *tat-tat-tat* of running feet on the foyer's wooden floor and a child's squeal, she paused. This was no floral delivery.

A little girl no older than three burst into the parlor at the exact moment Molly entered from the kitchen. She was quickly followed by a boy of possibly five. Hair disheveled, cheeks flushed and clothing askew, the pair skidded to a halt and stared at her.

"Oh." Molly stared back. "Who are you?"

The next instant, the boy reached out with both arms and shoved the girl from behind. She tumbled face-first to the floor, landing half on and half off the braided rug. Instantly, a high-pitched wail filled the room. The boy, her brother given their resemblance, simply stood there, his expression a combination of victory, contrition and dread.

Molly started forward. She didn't have a lot of experience with kids, but she could tell the girl wasn't hurt. Not really. A bruised knee, perhaps. Molly and her sister had regularly engaged in these types of scuffles during their childhood.

"Are you okay?"

She was halfway to the girl when the arched doorway separating the parlor from the foyer and the chapel was filled by a pair of broad shoulders, a tall lanky form and a dark brown Stetson.

Molly came to a halt. She'd seen plenty of attractive cowboys since moving to Mustang Valley, but this one in his pressed jeans and Western-cut suede coat rated right up there. The fact that he balanced a third child in his left arm, this one a toddler, diminished none of his good looks.

Assuming they'd arrived early, Molly produced a smile and said, "I'm sorry. The open house doesn't start until noon."

"Actually..." He bent and assisted the little girl to her feet, restraining her when she would have shoved her brother in retaliation. "I'm Owen Caufield. And you must be Molly O'Malley, right?"

His name didn't ring any bells. "Am I expecting you?"

"You are." An appealing grin tugged at the corners of his mouth.

She grew suddenly tense. Something told her that she was in for a surprise and not the happy kind.

"I'm your substitute minister. Homer Foxworthy's my great-uncle." Owen set the toddler down to join her siblings. "I'm staying here for the next month, through Christmas, while he and your grandmother are on their trip. Along with my kids."

She stared at him, every particle of her being resisting. Please, someone tell her this wasn't happening.

"NO OFFENSE, BUT you don't look like a minister."

Owen didn't blame Molly for doubting him. He wasn't really a minister. And his three intent-on-misbehaving offspring were hardly aiding his image.

"I got ordained online," he explained. "A buddy asked me to officiate his wedding a few months ago. We had this bet and, well…"

"Is that even a real thing? Getting ordained online?"

He corralled his children closer. They'd attempted to wander off in three different directions, and the room had far too many breakables for his comfort level. "I guarantee you, I can legally marry people. In Arizona, at least."

"Do you have any credentials?"

"I didn't bring my certificate. I figured Uncle Homer had vouched for me."

"What's his cell phone number?"

Owen chuckled. "You plan on calling him to verify my story?"

"Yes." She squared her shoulders. "I do."

"That's funny."

"Oh?" She drew out the word.

"You said 'I do.' Like in a wedding vow. And I'm an online minister."

"Huh."

All right, not funny. Ms. O'Malley apparently lacked a sense of humor.

Then again, Owen was a complete stranger, and he'd obviously caught her at a bad moment, when she was overwhelmed and not expecting him. Anyone's sense of humor would desert them.

She lifted one side of the apron she wore and produced a phone from her jeans pocket. Swiping the screen, she raised her brows expectantly. "What's your uncle's number?"

Owen obliged her, and she quickly entered it. He might have spent more time losing himself in the depths of her incredible green eyes, but his son chose that moment to renew the squabble with his sister.

"Cody, that's enough."

Owen blocked his son's hand right before it connected with his oldest daughter, Marisa. Cody was strictly forbidden to tease or torment his little sisters. Unfortunately, that seldom deterred him, and Marisa was his target more often than Willa, the youngest.

In response, Marisa dropped to the floor and resumed crying. "I wanna go home."

Willa collapsed beside her sister, whining in solidarity, while Cody grabbed Owen's arm and, lifting his feet, dangled in his best monkey impersonation.

Owen attempted to quiet the girls and sent Molly an apologetic smile. This wasn't the auspicious beginning he'd envisioned.

The sad truth was Owen didn't know his children very well or they him. He'd been away more than he'd been home in recent years and was sorely lacking when it came to parenting skills.

One of the reasons he'd agreed to take a month off and cover for his great-uncle was the perks that came with the job. He'd been promised a cabin and plenty of free time to connect with his estranged children.

Never again would he pick them up for a scheduled visit only to have Willa not recognize him. The blow Owen suffered had been the motivator behind him turning a new leaf, and he'd vowed from that day forward nothing and no one would come before his children.

"Homer's not answering, either." Molly disconnected and repocketed her phone.

"I'm sure they'll call when they reach Flagstaff. Service is pretty iffy between here and there."

"Did your uncle coerce my grandmother?"

He thought at first she might be joking then realized she wasn't. "I doubt it. She seemed pretty eager when they came by my house on Thursday to ask if I'd cover for Uncle Homer."

Molly's gaze narrowed. "Just how well do you know my grandmother?"

"We've met twice. I'm all the family Uncle Homer has in Arizona. Which is why, I think, they chose to elope and take a long RV trip. Uncle Homer's son couldn't arrange time off work on such short notice to come to a wedding, and his daughter's scared to death of flying. He wanted your grandmother to meet his children and brothers and grandchildren, and they're spread out over six different states. Kind of romantic, if you think about it. Eloping and touring the country."

"Except my mom and aunt haven't met Homer, and none of us were invited to the wedding."

Owen heard the hurt in her voice she tried to mask and felt a need to ease it. "The way Uncle Homer put it, they were trying to be fair. His family couldn't come here and you're not able to leave. Eloping was a compromise."

Molly shook her head. "Grandma wouldn't

up and leave. Sweetheart Ranch is too important to her."

"I'm sure she put you and your sister in charge because she's confident in your abilities to manage the ranch without her."

"We need her. Today's our grand opening. The mayor's coming. And a reporter from Channel 5." Molly glanced over her shoulder at a clock on the fireplace mantel. "They'll be here in three hours."

Three and a half, to be exact. But Owen didn't correct her as his kids were again demanding his attention.

"Daddy, I'm hungry."

"Cody kicked me."

"Where Mama? Want Mama." Willa stuck her pudgy thumb in her mouth and sucked lustily.

Owen bent and scooped up his youngest. He simultaneously took hold of Cody's shirt collar before the boy made a run for it. With her siblings restrained, Marisa was likely to stick close.

"I know you're busy," Owen said. "If you can show us to our cabin, we'll get out of your hair."

"Your cabin," Molly repeated.

"Emily mentioned she'd reserved one for us."

"Right." Molly's shoulders slumped ever so slightly, another sign of how hurt she was by the elopement. "I should have guessed. She's been planning this for weeks. That's why she insisted our vacancies didn't matter."

Owen suffered a stab of guilt. Perhaps he shouldn't have encouraged Uncle Homer. "We can stay at the inn in town if it's a problem."

"It isn't," Molly said.

"You sure?"

"Positive. The cabin's empty anyway."

"Daddy," Marisa pleaded.

"I wanna eat." Cody twisted sideways.

Convinced his luck was about to run out, Owen said, "Let me get the kids settled and give them a snack. Then we'll be back, and you can put me to work." He flashed his best sales rep smile in an attempt to win her over.

"You'll help?"

"I'm capable of more than marrying people."

"We do need a minister," she mused. "And someone to move furniture."

"I'm good at heavy lifting."

She returned his smile, a genuine one this time, and Owen found himself quite captivated. Strawberry blondes were his weakness, and this one came with the added bonus of freckles.

He admired Molly for more than her looks, though. She was obviously overwhelmed from being thrust into a difficult and unexpected situation. Yet, that hadn't prevented her from doing her job.

A nose-to-the-grindstone attitude and the ability to navigate chaos were qualities Owen appreciated, and he cultivated them in himself. He attributed his success in two careers—professional cowboy and marketing—to those same qualities. He had every intention of applying them to repairing his strained relationship with his children.

Before any of them had taken a step, the front door whooshed opened. Molly went visibly weak with relief. "Finally! The flowers are here."

Owen wished his arms were a foot longer. The better to contain Cody who was intent on beating the rest of them outside.

"Slow down, partner."

Rather than the florist, a pinch-faced, pint-size elderly woman in a large, drab coat entered the parlor. Molly was about to be disappointed for a second time.

Except she immediately brightened. "Nora! Please tell me you're here to rescue us."

"What else would get me out of bed at this ungodly hour?"

Was eight forty-five an ungodly hour? Apparently for Nora it was.

"I assume this is Homer's great-nephew." Removing her coat, she gave Owen careful consideration. "He didn't mention you were easy on the eyes."

Owen grinned. "He didn't mention you were, either."

Her dour countenance magically transformed into a delighted grin. "And charming to boot. I do believe this next month is going to be quite enjoyable."

"For me, too."

She twittered. Owen didn't think he'd heard a woman twitter since he first met his former mother-in-law.

"Are you a witch?" Cody glowered at her. "I don't like witches."

Owen was tempted to cover his son's mouth before the boy embarrassed him further. "Sorry about that."

"No worries. Your children are adorable. Emily asked me to watch them while you're busy marrying folks. Got a half-dozen of my own grandkids, so I'm plenty experienced."

Owen thought her assessment of his kids was much too kind. "I'd be very grateful and will compensate you."

"Emily's paying my salary. Said childcare was part of her arrangement with you."

It was, but Owen didn't want to take advantage.

"Did Grandma tell you she was eloping?" Molly asked Nora.

"I'm her best friend. She called me last night."

Molly scowled. "She left us a note."

"Don't go getting bent out of shape. She didn't tell you because you'd have tried to talk her out of it."

"I absolutely would have."

"See?" Nora moved her suitcase-sized purse to her other arm. I'm also supposed to take over guest relations for you."

"What?" Molly drew back. "No!"

Nora shrugged. "Suit yourself. But it's either that or wedding coordinator, and I'm thinking you'll be a whole lot better at coordinating weddings than me, considering you have experience planning two of your own."

Molly ignored the comment and faced Owen. "I'll fetch the cabin key and meet you there. Number six. Drive around back. Farthest one on the left." With that, she left.

Owen watched her retreating back. Molly had been married twice?

"Touched a nerve, apparently," Nora said, erupting in laughter.

CHAPTER TWO

MOLLY WALKED TO the cabins, ruthlessly zipping her jacket against the late-November chill. She shouldn't care what Owen thought of her. She hardly knew the man. They'd met mere minutes ago. So what if he was good-looking. He had three children and was probably married.

Then again, would a husband leave his wife for a month and take the kids? She doubted it, and he wasn't the type. Owen Caufield had *responsible* written all over him.

Rather than continue fuming, she directed her anger where it belonged. At Nora for blabbing what was Molly's personal business to a complete stranger, and at her grandmother for leaving her and Bridget in this predicament. The Saturday after Thanksgiving, no less.

True, Molly would have tried to talk Grandma Em out of eloping, but that was no reason to hide her plans. As her trusted employees who were expected to cover for her, *and* as her granddaughters, Molly and Bridget should have been told. Had *deserved* to be told.

Despite what Owen said, his great-uncle must have convinced Grandma Em to elope. There was no other reasonable explanation. According to him, Grandma Em and Homer were trying to be fair. Really? There was nothing fair about excluding everyone from the wedding.

Twice Molly had come very close to walking down the aisle. Both times she couldn't have imagined the day without her parents, sister, extended family and friends there to share in the celebration. Not having loved ones present seemed almost...a sacrilege. It was certainly selfish, inconsiderate and hurtful to those not invited.

Love makes people do crazy things.

Bridget's words echoed in Molly's ears as she cut through the courtyard, bypassed the gated swimming pool and clubhouse, and skirted the storage room that contained bikes, hiking equipment, lawn games and a washer and dryer for the guests' use. She emerged on the other side at the same moment a silver pickup truck, Owen's she presumed, proceeded slowly along the dirt lane circling the back of the ranch house.

Ahead of Molly were six cabins, spaced approximately twenty yards apart. Constructed of pine to resemble the main house built in the 1880s, the cabins were new and blissfully without quirks. Rule number one in the hospitality industry: guests didn't like being disturbed by clanging pipes, the periodic flickering light and a furnace that grumbled like an old man.

The stables and carriage house were a short distance away. Also part of the original homestead, the twin structures had been refurbished by the same contractor who'd built the cabins. Two draft horses resided in the stables, their job to pull the wedding carriage on romantic rides through town—Sweetheart Ranch's signature amenity for the happy couple. In addition to the carriage, the ranch also had an old farm wagon used for hayrides.

Big Jim, a semiretired wrangler from one of the many cattle ranches in the area, worked parttime for the O'Malleys. He saw to the horses' care and drove the team. He was in the stables now, cleaning stalls in preparation for the open house, which would include tours of the cabins and the horse facilities.

Grandma Em had insisted on everything being spic-and-span. Except she wasn't here to see it.

Molly fought against the rush of tears threatening to fall. She wasn't about to let Owen Caufield see her cry. She was on the verge of enjoying her first successful job of a thus-far lackluster hotel administration career. Without her grandmother's guidance and support, history might well repeat itself.

Could this be a test? Was Grandma Em attempting to determine if Molly had the necessary skills to assist managing Sweetheart Ranch and potentially take over one day? For all Molly knew, her grandmother could return tomorrow morning after the open house had bombed and tell Molly her previous employers had been right to let her go.

Failures. Her life was full of them. Failed relationships. Failed engagements. Failed jobs.

"Not this time," Molly promised herself and headed toward cabin number six.

Owen had already parked in front of the cabin when she arrived. His son immediately jumped out of the back passenger seat and landed on his feet with a thud. He then bolted for the cabin's shaded front stoop.

"Cody, get back here," Owen hollered.

Molly suspected Cody misbehaving and Owen reprimanding him was a regular occurrence.

"I gotta go, Daddy. Bad."

Ah. A bathroom emergency. Molly hurried, the key jangling in her hand. Sweetheart Ranch didn't use plastic cards. Grandma Em had been firm on that issue. Keys enhanced the old-fashioned ambience.

"Hold on," Molly said, glad to set her emotions aside. Climbing the stoop, she nudged Cody's hand away. He'd been repeatedly twisting the uncooperative knob.

"If you wait a minute, I'll be right there." Owen had managed to lift the toddler from her car seat. His other daughter refused to stop fidgeting despite his requests, making freeing her difficult.

"It's okay. No rush." Molly opened the door. "I'll watch him."

Watch him like a hawk. She'd bet money Cody would find trouble if left unsupervised.

"You stay here," Cody demanded and charged inside. "Going to the bathroom is private."

"Of course." Molly nonetheless kept an eye on him as he stomped through the front room and down the hall.

A moment later, she heard footsteps behind her and turned to see Owen and the girls come inside, a cold gust following them.

"Nice." Owen paused and surveyed the room with its overstuffed sofa, oak coffee and end tables, lamps that resembled lanterns, antique oxen yoke hanging on the wall, and lacy curtains. "Very cozy."

"There's a kitchenette with an under-the-counter fridge, a three-burner stove, microwave and sink." Molly pointed out the various features with pride and satisfaction. The cabins were indeed nice, and she'd contributed significantly to their design. "The sofa is a sleeper with a queen-size mattress."

"That's good." Owen let go of the girls' hands, allowing them to explore. "I brought a portable crib for Willa. I'm thinking Cody and Marisa can sleep out here while I take the bedroom."

"I don't wanna sleep with Cody." Marisa made a face and glared at the offending sofa.

"But this bed's special," Owen said. "It pops out of the sofa like magic."

Marisa wasn't mollified. "I want Oreo."

"Oreo," Willa agreed and dropped onto her bottom in the middle of the floor.

"Their dog," Owen told Molly. "She sleeps in the girls' room on Marisa's bed."

"I'm sorry. Only service dogs are allowed at the ranch." Molly admired his patience with these three. They were a handful.

"Wow!" Cody exploded from the bathroom. "Daddy, come look. The tub is huge."

"Each cabin comes with a built-in two-person spa tub," Molly explained to Owen. "And an enclosed courtyard in back for privacy."

"I'm intrigued." His gaze caught hers and lingered.

Molly glanced away first but not before her heart gave an unexpected leap. Really?

She checked Owen's left hand for a wedding

ring before she could stop herself. There was none, not that she cared.

"Daddy!" Cody insisted. "Come look at the bathtub."

"I'm hungry," Marisa complained from the kitchenette where she was opening every lower cabinet and drawer within her reach.

"I'll leave you to get unpacked." Molly seized the chance to escape and inched toward the door. "Let me know if there's anything you require. Extra towels or pillows. Assistance connecting to the complimentary Wi-Fi."

"Can we ride the horses?" Cody asked.

Owen reached out and tousled his son's hair. "We noticed the stables."

Molly gave an apologetic head shake, neatly slipping back into guest relations mode. "I'm afraid Moses and Amos are for carriage and hayrides only. But Powell Ranch is a half mile up the road, and they rent horses by the hour for trail rides and lessons. There are also plenty other family-friendly activities in the nearby area. They're listed in the binder." She pointed to the coffee table. "Hiking trails and the Ody-Sea Aquarium. There's even recreational bull riding at the Poco Dinero Bar and Grill."

"I've heard about that," Owen said. "Maybe I'll take a spin."

"You've rodeoed before?"

"In my previous life. Before I became a marketing rep for Waverly Equine Products."

That was interesting. Despite his Western dress, Molly hadn't pictured him riding bulls. Must be the pressed jeans. She'd pegged him as more of a weekend cowboy.

"Daddy was a champion," Cody announced. "He has gold buckles and trophies."

"I'm impressed."

"I made a living at it." Owen shrugged. "For a while."

"What happened?"

"Complications," he said. "Mostly these three. Their mom didn't like me being on the road every week."

"Understandable."

"The funny thing is I wound up traveling just as much with Waverly. Which is why I quit. More time to spend with this motley crew. It's also why I agreed to help out Uncle Homer for a month. I plan on getting sick of their company."

"You're not working?" Molly immediately wished she could take back the question. "I'm sorry. That was rude of me to ask. And none of my business."

"It's all right. I'm not embarrassed. The fact is, I need to make some changes in my life, and now I have the chance. Don't suppose you've heard of any places in the area hiring a former senior marketing rep who doesn't want to travel much?"

"Afraid not."

"I guess the good news is I brought my laptop and you have complimentary Wi-Fi."

Molly reached for the doorknob, more eager than ever to be on her way. "If you'll excuse me, I have about a hundred tasks waiting for me at the house."

"We'll be along shortly."

She barely heard his reply as she shut the door behind her and trotted down the steps. At the bottom, she wiped her brow.

"That was close."

Owen was a charming man and potentially hard to resist. But going all soft inside at a man's admiring glance had landed Molly in trouble before, causing her to fall blindly in love and miss the obvious indicators of trouble brewing.

Besides, Sweetheart Ranch and its success were her priorities. She owed her grandmother that and more for giving her a second chance. Now wasn't the time to act on any romantic sparks. Especially with a man who had his own important priorities that included taking care of three young children and finding a new job.

MOLLY STOPPED AT the clubhouse on her return from Owen's cabin, making sure all was in order for the open house. When her cell phone suddenly started playing Mendelssohn's "Wedding March" on her way out the door, she jumped. Grandma Em returning her calls. Finally! With fumbling fingers, she whipped out her phone and answered.

"Grandma. Where are you?"

To her dismay, a sob caught in her throat—from relief and from sorrow at her grandmother's abandonment. Not that her grandmother had abandoned her exactly. In the same way her father hadn't exactly abandoned Molly when he'd died soon after her twelfth birthday. Still, she felt a keen loss whenever someone took off without warning and tended to react emotionally.

"In Flagstaff," Grandma said. "We stopped for gas."

"Okay." Molly's voice sounded small.

"I'm sorry, sweetie. Please don't think I bailed on you."

If she were a completely unselfish person, Molly would assure her grandmother that everything was fine, express her joy over the elopement, and wish her grandmother and Homer a safe and enjoyable trip.

But Molly was too overcome with hurt to be completely unselfish. "You left without saying goodbye."

"It wasn't an easy decision. Believe me."

"Then why?"

"I knew if I told you, you'd have probably hog-tied me to the nearest chair."

"You make me sound like a bad person."

"No, no, sweetie. You're a sensible person and any argument you made would have been too sensible for me to resist." Grandma Em sighed wistfully. "I never dreamed I'd meet a man and fall in love. Not after all these years. Homer's wonderful. Kind and generous and funny and thoughtful."

"Why couldn't he have waited a couple months until the ranch was up and running before insisting you run away together?" Molly closed and latched the pool gate behind her before turning in the direction of the house.

"He was more than willing to wait. I'm the one chomping at the bit."

"Grandma!"

"I know it sounds stupid, and there's a hundred reasons why we should have delayed. But I just didn't want to go one more week without being Mrs. Foxworthy. I'm in love, Molly. Head over heels. Fallen off the deep end. Whatever other silly clichéd saying comes to mind."

"This isn't like you."

"Actually, it is. At least, it's like the person I used to be. Many years ago."

"Irresponsible?"

"Impetuous and spontaneous and living for the moment."

Molly could hear her grandmother smiling, which made staying mad impossible. "Don't you want us with you when you get married?"

"Of course I do. Homer and I are planning on renewing our vows after we get home and throwing a huge party for family and friends. We were thinking of New Year's Day."

"I suppose that'll be nice. I'll clear the calendar." As of yet, no weddings were scheduled.

"You're young, Molly. I don't expect you to understand. But when you reach my age, well, waiting for the right moment wastes valuable time. Homer and I don't want to lose a single second of married life together."

Had Molly ever sounded this excited and happy when she'd been engaged? Her former fiancés had both been excellent matches with good jobs, bright futures and plans to start a family one day. Molly hadn't believed she could make a better choice for a husband. Choices, she amended.

Yet both men had dumped her before making it down the aisle, the second one a mere three days before their wedding. The excuses they'd cited weren't dissimilar, Molly was too uptight, detested anything spur-of-the-moment and refused to admit it when she was wrong.

Coincidentally, two jobs ago, her boss had cited her refusal to admit she was wrong when he'd fired her for consistently low scores on her customer satisfaction surveys. Molly had quit her last job, sensing termination was imminent and not wanting to further tarnish her employment record.

For someone in the service industry, she wasn't very…what were the words her last boss had used? Ah, yes, flexible and accommodating.

She'd been striving ever since to become a better version of herself. Hadn't she accepted Owen as his uncle Homer's replacement and seen to the comfort of him and his kids? She could have thrown a fit instead.

Here, she supposed, was another chance to prove she'd changed. "I'm happy for you, Grandma. Truly. Homer's a nice man."

"I was hoping you'd help me plan the party."

"Of course I will."

"Did Owen arrive yet?" Grandma Em asked, changing the subject.

"I just finished showing him and the kids to their cabin."

Molly headed for the kitchen door rather than track dirt into the recently vacuumed front rooms. She noticed Bridget through the kitchen window and hesitated, not yet ready to face her sister.

"He's very handsome, don't you agree?"

"Is he?" Molly was purposefully vague, refusing to reveal just how handsome she found him.

"He and Homer are quite close. I really want him and his children to feel welcomed and part of the family."

Was that a subtle chastising from Grandma Em or was she simply attempting to smooth what could be a rocky transition for everyone?

Uncertain how to respond, Molly said, "Nora's here, too. She says she's taking over guest relations. Are you sure that's a good idea? She can be grumpy." Except, apparently, when Owen sweet-talked her.

"She'll do fine. She was once an executive assistant for the president of A-1 Home Insurance Company. Part of her job was arranging corporate events—charity fund-raisers, holiday parties, annual stockholder meetings."

Nora? An executive assistant?

"Let her do the grunt work," Grandma said. "You handle the rest."

"She needs to smile more."

Grandma Em laughed. "She'll learn. You did."

Molly *had* learned, motivated greatly by having a vested interest in the business and a potentially long-term career for herself.

"Will you send us pictures of the wedding?" she asked.

"Prepare to be inundated."

Molly's mood lifted. Her grandmother had found the kind of contentment that thus far had eluded Molly. The least she could do was run the ranch with her sister to the best of her ability for the next month.

"I love you, Grandma."

"I love you, too, sweetie."

Molly entered the kitchen and held out her phone to Bridget. "It's Grandma. She and Homer are in Flagstaff."

With a squeal, Bridget scurried out from behind the counter, nearly knocking over a bowl of liquid in the process as she reached for the phone. "Grandma, hi!"

Molly helped herself to a cold drink, half listening to Bridget's side of the conversation. She was considerably more enthused for their grandmother than Molly had initially been.

"Hugs and kisses," Bridget said when she was done, then returned Molly's phone. "She sounds ecstatic."

"You don't think she and Homer are rushing things?"

"Dad asked Mom to marry him on their fifth date and look how that turned out."

Molly's sister made a valid point. If not for the driver running a stop sign, their father might still be alive today and their parents celebrating thirty-three years of wedded bliss.

Sadly, the driver *had* run the stop sign. And after sixteen years of loneliness and misery, Molly and Bridget's mother had recently married again and moved to Casa Grande.

Doug paled in comparison to their father. While not mean or abusive—Molly and Bridget would never tolerate their mother being mistreated—he was frequently needy and narcissistic and extremely stingy with money. The sisters suspected their mother was just as lonely and miserable now as after their father died. But she refused to divorce Doug, claiming men like her late husband were few and far between.

She was right, but that didn't deter Molly and Bridget from trying to find such a man and refusing to settle for less. It wasn't easy, their mother had been right about that. Molly need only examine her own track record.

Nora abruptly called from the foyer. "Florist is here!"

"Go." Bridget waved Molly away. "I need to start decorating the wedding cake."

The delivery man was setting the first arrangement on the table in the parlor when Molly got there. One look and she stopped in her tracks.

"Those aren't the right color roses."

He checked his delivery schedule, squinting

his eyes at the electronic device in his hand. "Ten dozen arrangements in glass vases."

Molly approached the table and fingered one of the blooms. "We requested pale peach. These are orange."

"Let me call the office." He pulled out his phone. "I'm at Sweetheart Ranch. The customer says the roses are the wrong color." After a pause, he passed the phone to Molly, who put it to her ear. "It's the manager," he said.

"Hi. Molly O'Malley here. The roses are supposed to be peach."

"Hold on a second while I pull up the record."

Molly silently fumed. She knew precisely what the bride had requested. She'd reviewed the order herself.

"According to my records, I spoke to Emily O'Malley on Thursday morning at ten twenty." The sound of flipping papers could be heard in the background. "I told her we didn't have the exact shade of peach you ordered, and she said the darker color would be fine."

"I see." Molly searched her memory. She'd been at the print shop on Thursday morning picking up their new brochures.

"Is Emily there?"

"No. She's out of town."

Grandma Em had probably forgotten to mention the call or note the change in the bride's file. Too many distractions, like her impending elopement and road trip. Molly couldn't hold the florist responsible.

"What would you like us to do?" the woman asked, a tinge of impatience in her voice. "We can substitute white or yellow roses."

Molly debated her choices while two pairs of eyes watched her, Nora's and the delivery man's. The bride had been specific about her wedding colors; white and yellow weren't included. Then again, neither was orange. Come to think of it, had the bride even been informed about the unavailability of peach roses? Hopefully, yes, but Molly didn't want to assume. And if Grandma hadn't informed the bride, news of the orange roses could upset the poor woman who was surely already frazzled.

Molly's first problem as fill-in wedding coordinator, and she was stumped.

"We could call your grandmother," Nora suggested.

Not happening, Molly decided. She'd deal with this on her own. "It's fine," she told the shop owner. "We'll take the roses."

Once all ten arrangements were brought in, Molly and Nora went about placing them in the chapel. After the service was concluded and photos taken, the roses would then be moved to the parlor for the reception.

"What do you think of Owen?" Nora asked.

Why was everyone eager to know Molly's opinion of him? "He seems nice enough. The better question is how good is he at marrying people?"

"Gotta admire a man who'd quit his job to spend more time with his kids."

Molly had been thinking he wouldn't be able to support his kids without a job or make the monthly payments on that slick new truck of his.

"I guess, but won't he need a job soon? Unless he's independently wealthy."

"Well, according to Homer, Owen took stock options at Waverly. They bought him out when he quit, and he's got enough to carry him for a while. Which is good because finding a job at his level and in the Phoenix area will be a challenge."

Nora filled a bowl with small packets of birdseed to toss at the bride and groom while Molly arranged candles on the altar.

Unable to resist, she said, "He seems kind of young to be the father of three kids."

"He and his wife married in their early twenties and had Cody within the first year. His wife was the one who insisted he quit rodeoing and stay home. Which was a shame, Owen loved it. He took the job at Waverly on the promise he wouldn't travel so much. That quickly changed, however, and, as you can guess, his wife wasn't happy. 'Course, she did like the nice things his salary bought them."

"Can you really blame her? Not about the money but him traveling extensively. They had three children."

Finishing in the chapel, Molly and Nora returned to the parlor where everything sat in readiness for the open house. Molly knew she should get changed soon. Instead, she listened to Nora go on about Owen.

"It was an excuse." The older woman made a sound of disgust. "The marriage had run its course. But rather than just admit they were better off apart than together like two sensible adults, she blamed him and his job and made him suffer."

"Did Grandma tell you all this?"

"She figured you'd be interested in him and wanted me to tell you."

"Interested in him?" Molly feigned shock as if nothing could be further from the truth. "Whatever gave her that idea?"

The next second, Owen and his three kids strolled into the parlor. Molly went still, wishing she could disappear. How much of her and Nora's conversation had he heard?

The last part of it, certainly, judging by the amused expression he wore.

CHAPTER THREE

"PLEASE, DADDY, can we stay with you?"

"Sorry, son." Owen gave Cody's shoulder a reassuring squeeze. He and his kids stood in the parlor, waiting for Nora. "I've got to work."

Not work exactly. It was, however, the simplest explanation and one his kids were used to hearing.

His attendance at the open house wasn't mandatory. The brochures on display in the foyer mentioned an on-staff minister as one of the many services offered at Sweetheart Ranch. No need for the temporary wedding officiator to make a personal appearance.

But after spending half the morning helping Molly, her sister and Nora finish readying the downstairs public rooms, he felt invested in the open house and wanted to see the outcome for himself.

With both of them wanting to attend, he and Nora had struck a deal. She'd watch the kids for the first half of the open house, and then Owen would relieve her so that she could enjoy the second half. She'd insisted she didn't mind, and Owen had begun to suspect the elderly woman had a real soft spot where kids were concerned.

"I'll be good," Cody whined, hanging on Owen's arm.

He'd heard that promise before. Most recently this morning on the drive to Sweetheart Ranch from their mother's house. Cody had started a fight with Marisa two miles into the trip. Owen couldn't risk another incident ensuing during the open house. Molly and her sister were stressed enough as it was.

At least the girls were behaving, Owen thought. They'd taken a shine to Nora rather quickly. Possibly because they were young, and she reminded them a little of their mom's neighbor who occasionally watched the kids.

No fooling Cody, though. He still suspected Nora might be a witch and shied away from her.

"We talked earlier," Owen reminded Cody, determined to remain patient. His children had been through a lot for one day. They'd been separated from their mom and beloved dog, were living in a new place, sleeping on an unfamiliar bed, and had been left in the care of a father they'd seen only four times in the last three months.

Everything would be different soon, and Owen had his ex-wife, Jeanne, to thank for that.

She'd been resistant at first, and he'd hesitated involving his lawyer to enforce their shared custody agreement. Taking a different approach, he'd convinced her the arrangement benefited them both. Owen got the chance to right past wrongs while Jeanne and her new boyfriend were able to have some alone time and go off on a short trip. Take-home lessons from Cody's kindergarten teacher for the missed week of school had sealed the deal.

Now Owen needed to make the most of the opportunity and not screw up.

"When I'm working," he said, "Miss Nora will watch you."

"I wanna go to the party." Cody screwed his face into a scowl.

Owen regretted describing the open house as a party. Cody was no doubt thinking games and prizes and cake and ice cream.

"The open house is for grown-ups."

"She's not a grown-up." Cody pointed to Nora's granddaughter Tracee, who'd been hired to serve refreshments and clean up afterward.

"She's fifteen," Owen said. "Plus, she's working. That's different."

"Not fair." Cody's voice had gained considerable volume.

Nora came to the rescue. "How about you, me and your sisters go to the kitchen? I happen

to know where there's a secret stash of fresh-baked cookies. If your dad says it's okay, you can have one."

Owen felt compelled to warn Nora about his kids on a sugar high. "You might want to take them to the cabin afterward. Let them burn off their excess energy."

"I was thinking along the lines of the clubhouse first and then an afternoon nap." She rested a hand on Willa's downy curls. "This one for sure is going to need some downtime."

"I'm too old for naps," Cody insisted.

Owen checked the arched entranceway leading to the foyer. No guests had arrived yet, which was a relief. His son was on the brink of throwing a fit.

"You don't have to lie down," he told Cody. "But you do need to behave for Miss Nora and can't make noise while your sisters sleep." He turned to Nora. "Their mom packed some games and movies and his truck collection."

"Come on." She captured the girls' hands. "First cookies and perhaps a glass of milk to wash them down. After that, if you're good, we'll play a game of Ping-Pong or how about croquet?"

"What's that?" Cody asked.

"You hit a ball with a mallet through little hoops."

The idea of hitting balls clearly intrigued Cody, though he stubbornly held his ground.

"I'll let you watch a movie while your sisters nap."

"Which movie?" Won over at last, Cody reluctantly followed Nora and his sisters toward the kitchen.

"What one's your favorite?"

"*My Little Pony*," Marisa squealed with glee and skipped ahead.

"No." Cody slapped his forehead in very adult frustration. "Not that one again."

The remainder of their conversation was cut off when they disappeared around the corner. Owen was thinking he could learn a lot from Nora when Molly suddenly entered the room. Good thing he was alone. That way, no one witnessed his jaw going slack at the sight of her.

She looked amazing. Not that she hadn't been pretty in her jeans and T-shirt. But the pale knit dress she wore and the way her soft, wavy hair framed her face elevated her appeal to a whole new level. She was, quite simply, lovely, and Owen felt his heartstrings stir.

Granted, Molly had a few funny idiosyncrasies. Like the way she flitted around the room, obsessing over the placement of coasters or holding her splayed fingers above her head to test the airflow from the AC ducts. Funny, but also amusing and sort of endearing. He could only assume those former husbands of hers were idiots for letting her go.

"Easy does it," he muttered under his breath. He was here to restore his faltering relationship with his children. Not find his next romantic interest.

Must be Sweetheart Ranch. There was something about a place where love abounded. Hard to steel oneself against the effects.

"Thanks for your help earlier."

Owen gave a start. Where had Molly come from? Last he'd seen, she'd been straightening pictures that didn't need straightening and refanning the precisely fanned napkins.

"My pleasure," he said, trying not to stare.

"And thanks for coming this afternoon. People will enjoy meeting you."

"Do I look minister-y enough? I wasn't sure what to wear. Marisa picked this." He tugged on the hem of his leather vest, a recent gift from his mother. The brand for his brothers' ranch was burned on the front. "Not sure I should rely on the opinion of a three-year-old."

"Three-and-a-half," Molly corrected him. "She was quite adamant about that when we were wiping down the folding chairs."

"Six months is important when you're her age."

"She's cute. All your kids are."

"Thanks, but I can't take the credit. Any good genes they got came from their mother."

Molly studied him at length, long enough for him to feel the effects. "I think they take after you."

"Is that a compliment?"

She didn't answer, fussing with an imaginary wrinkle on her dress.

Owen suppressed a chuckle. She liked him. Liked his looks, anyway.

"Having planned two of your own weddings must come in handy for being in a wedding co-ordinator." He admitted to himself that he was fishing for information.

Molly took the bait. "I've never been married."

"No?"

"I was engaged twice and, as Nora mentioned, I did the planning."

But had broken off the engagements, evidently. "What happened, can I ask?"

She drew in a breath. "No offense, Owen, but I have no desire to share details with you about our pasts."

"No offense taken." He agreed the timing was bad and shifted gears. "This house is incredible."

Molly visibly relaxed. "It was built in the late 1800s by my great-great-grandparents. They came to Arizona from back east and were one of the original families to settle in the Mustang Valley."

"You have deep roots here."

"Very deep. Growing up, Bridget and I spent every summer with our grandparents. They owned the local inn and put us to work as soon as we were big enough to push a laundry cart and kept us working part-time all through high school and college."

"Nothing like learning the business from a young age." Owen could boast a similar experience. He'd come from a rodeo family going back three generations. "Where'd you work before coming here?"

"For a couple different big hotel chains."

"Which ones? I've stayed in a lot of hotels."

"I like working for a family business much better. It's hard but the rewards are worth it."

She'd purposefully avoided answering his question. Owen was curious why but didn't press her.

"There's a lot to be said for being your own boss. Can't say the idea hasn't occurred to me." He'd spent a few interesting hours researching.

"What kind of business appeals to you?" Molly asked.

"Retail. Sales. Something along those lines."

"Because that's where your talent lies."

He winked. "One of them."

She glanced away, sending a very clear message. She didn't welcome his flirting.

Owen curbed his impulses. Being friendly was part of what had made him a top-earning salesman, but he'd gone one step too far with Molly.

"I tend to talk a lot," he confessed. "But I'm also a good listener. Two traits that might come in handy while covering for Uncle Homer."

"People do love to talk about their weddings."

The sound of the front door opening alerted them to the arrival of guests. Molly went instantly into hostess mode, rushing to the foyer to greet them and take their coats. Escorting them to the parlor, she pointed out the refreshments and introduced them to Owen, using his uncle as an ice breaker.

Here, he was in his element and easily launched into polite conversation. An hour into the open house, he was recruited to talk to the TV reporter. Having done interviews during his rodeo days, he was comfortable in front of a camera as well. During all the mingling and schmoozing, he kept an eye on Molly, watching her as she gracefully moved from person to person. No one went without beverages or hors d'oeuvres if she could help it. Judging by the many compliments he overheard, the open house was a huge success.

He was just thinking it was time to go to the cabin and swap babysitting duties with Nora when Molly appeared beside him.

"Have you practiced for tonight's wedding?" she asked.

"Not really."

"Do you think you should?"

"Do you?" In truth, he'd planned on winging it. That had worked just fine when his buddy got hitched.

"I watched the video earlier of the wedding you officiated."

"How? Where?"

"I Googled you. Your friends have a wedding website. The video's posted there."

"That's right." He'd forgotten.

"You were a bit…unrehearsed."

"We improvised." And they'd all enjoyed a good laugh afterward at those unrehearsed moments.

"I don't recommend improvising again. Not to nitpick, but this is our very first wedding. We have a lot riding on it."

"Uncle Homer left me copies of a few of his more popular ceremonies."

"Notes are okay. Just try not to appear like you're reading from them. Glance up at the couple and out at the guests. Make eye contact. Humor is great, too. A touch will help put the couple at ease. But don't go overboard, or you'll spoil the ceremony. Be earnest and sincere and, most of all, likable. This is a once in a lifetime experience for the bride, the groom and their families. Our job is to make it special and memorable and perfect."

"Yeah. Okay." Owen's stomach started to tighten. He hadn't been nervous until now.

"Don't forget to smile, though not too much, at the appropriate intervals. And stand up straight. You'll be filmed and photographed the entire time."

Owen squared his shoulders and drew in a deep breath. Had he slouched before?

"Remember to speak clearly and project."

"Got it."

He tugged on his shirt collar. When he'd officiated at his buddy's wedding, most of the guests had been his friends, too. People he'd known for years if not his whole life. The wedding, a casual affair, had taken place at a nearby park and the reception had been held in the couple's backyard.

No one had complained about Owen's posture or warned him not to crack too many jokes. Of course, they hadn't paid a fee for his services. His job at Sweetheart Ranch included compensation in the form of room and board and childcare, and he'd do well to take it seriously. Molly was giving him sound advice.

"Maybe we should try a dry run," he said. "Will we have time before the ceremony?"

"I won't." She debated a moment. "There's a full-length mirror in the groom's dressing room off the chapel. You might practice reciting your lines in front of that."

"Good idea."

"Be done by four thirty sharp. That's when the wedding party's arriving. Oh, and stick close after the ceremony to meet guests. Also plan on attending the reception if the couple invites you. You don't have to stay past the toast."

Any more requirements and he'd need a list to keep track. "Where will you be?"

"Hovering in the background in case there's a problem and praying everything goes well."

The load on her shoulders was growing heavier. He could say the same for himself.

Had he made a mistake by agreeing to substitute for Uncle Homer? In any case, it was too late now to back out.

"Hello! Please come in." Molly welcomed the bride and her entourage, ushering them through the foyer. "We're so happy to have you."

"We need to hurry," the bride exclaimed, her face flushed with excitement. "My fiancé's ten minutes behind us. I don't want him to see me before the ceremony."

"Follow me." Molly escorted them down the hall.

The bride, her hair arranged in an upsweep, juggled several bags and cases, including one for cosmetics and one for shoes. A middle-aged woman wearing a tasteful mother-of-the-bride dress carried a voluminous garment bag raised high so as not to drag on the floor. The maid of honor also carried a garment bag, hers considerably less voluminous but guarded with equal care.

As the group passed by the chapel on their way to the bride's dressing room, Molly crossed her fingers, willing the bride not to notice the orange roses.

"Mom, look at the flowers!"

Uh-oh.

"They're gorgeous," her mother gushed and everyone came to a standstill. "Absolutely stunning."

They were? More oohing and aahing followed, and Molly breathed a little easier.

"Just like you," the mother said, her eyes misting as she reached out a hand to pinch her daughter's chin. Molly doubted these were the first tears shed today, nor would they be the last.

At the dressing room door, she stopped and

handed the bride a small black pager. "If you need me, just press the green button." A matching device was clipped to her pocket.

"We hate to bother you right from the start…" The maid of honor tilted her head appealingly. "Do you have any food we can snack on? We're not particular."

"I haven't eaten all day," the bride admitted. "I've been too nervous."

Her mother laid a hand on her shoulder. "We can't have her passing out from hunger."

"No problem." Molly smiled graciously. "I'll bring something right away."

"Low-cal, please." The bride patted her waist. "I can't afford to gain a single ounce if I hope to fit into my dress."

Molly ducked out of the room.

There were plenty of leftovers from the open house. She'd prepare a selection of fresh fruit and yogurt dip and finger sandwiches. That should satisfy the bride.

Molly hurried through the parlor, now empty except for Nora's granddaughter Tracee who was pushing a vacuum. Every last trace of the open house had been removed and the buffet freshly set for the reception.

Right now, Sweetheart Ranch didn't offer catering services beyond a cake, nonalcoholic punch and a continental breakfast. If couples chose, they could bring their own champagne and hors d'oeuvres. One day, if the ranch did well and turned a decent profit, they hoped to offer light catering. Bridget was already planning ahead.

One step at a time, Molly told herself. For now, guests would come to the main house between 7:00 a.m. and 11:00 a.m. for some of Bridget's incredible homemade croissants, breads, pastries and jams. Yet another ranch specialty was a honeymoon breakfast prepared to order for the couple the morning after their wedding and delivered to their cabin as late as noon. Until then, they wouldn't be disturbed.

"Hey, the bride's here," Molly announced upon entering the kitchen. "She and the others are in the dressing room. The groom's on his way."

"Our first wedding. Now we're really and truly open for business." Bridget fussed over the cake, adding a tiny flower here and smoothing a patch of icing there.

Molly removed a clean platter from the rack and began loading it with leftovers.

"Hungry?" Nora asked.

Temporarily relieved of her babysitting duties, the older woman had returned to the house for a short break and a quick bite. She'd be back on the clock, so to speak, during the wedding when she'd resume care of Owen's children.

"This is for the bride and her entourage," Molly explained. "They're hungry and requested a snack."

"You must be happy. The open house was a huge success."

"Are you kidding? I'm thrilled. Not a single hitch." Molly couldn't believe their good fortune.

"You two worked your tails off." Nora tore off a piece of her quesadilla. "Have you talked to your grandmother yet? I bet she's bursting with pride."

"For two minutes. I promised to call her later when we weren't so busy."

More people had attended the open house than expected. Along with potential clients researching wedding venues, several locals had shown up to lend their support. There had also been a large number of curious folks who'd heard or read about the ranch and wanted to see for themselves.

During a free moment, Molly had sought out their neighbor, the owner of Powell Ranch, and proposed an idea of cross-promoting. He'd seemed interested and had told her to call him later in the week. The owner of the Poco Dinero Bar and Grill had heard them chatting and asked Molly to include her as well.

The best part had been the many compliments and well wishes. By the time the crowd had started thinning at around three thirty, Molly was walking on air. With everyone gone, however, exhaustion had set in. She longed to rest her aching feet but at the pace she was going, that wasn't likely.

She loaded strawberries, blackberries, apple slices and finger sandwiches on the platter while Nora prattled on about the open house. At the mention of Owen's name, Molly paused.

"He quite enjoyed himself," Nora said.

"He's prejudiced."

"Why do you say that?"

"The TV reporter made a big fuss over him. Did a whole seven-minute segment with him alone." Molly would have quite enjoyed herself, too.

"Can you blame her?"

"He's just the minister. A temporary, online minister at that. Bridget and I are the owners, and we only got three-minute interviews."

"You timed the reporter?" Bridget asked in amazement.

"I happen to glance at the mantel clock." Molly waved her sister away. "The point is we're Sweetheart Ranch. You and I. Owen is hired help."

"Maybe you got three minutes. My interview

was longer than that." Bridget disappeared inside the walk-in pantry.

Okay, now Molly was good and miffed. Apparently, she was the least interesting person on staff at the ranch.

"Owen's the kind of man who draws attention," Nora observed. "He has that quality about him."

"He is scrumptious," Bridget remarked, returning from the cooler. "With a great smile."

"Don't forget well built." Nora fanned herself. "My, my."

Molly huffed. "You two are being ridiculous."

"Am I wrong?" Nora appealed to Bridget.

"Not at all. If I was a female reporter, I'd spend more time interviewing Owen than anyone else."

"The purpose of the TV interviews is to promote Sweetheart Ranch," Molly insisted. "Not some *scrumptious* cowboy."

"Ha! Then you agree with us."

"I didn't say that." Except, she had.

Finished with her meal, Nora wiped her hands on a napkin. "I bet you two get all kinds of inquiries after the segment airs tonight. I set my DVR to record the show."

"We should do that, too!" Bridget turned to Molly and waited, hands on her hips.

"What? You expect *me* to set the DVR?"

"Ah, yeah."

"I have to take this food to the bride."

"And I have to clean the kitchen."

"Fine," Molly grumbled and picked up the platter. "I'll do it."

Mindful not to drop any food in her haste, she stopped in the den and programmed the DVR—but only because her grandmother would enjoy watching the news segment when she returned from her trip.

Molly was in the middle of delivering the platter when loud male voices emanating from the foyer alerted her to the arrival of the groom and his party.

"Hurry, hurry!" The bride shooed her away.

Molly greeted the men and escorted them to the second dressing room, this one off the chapel. The groom's parents had arrived with him. The mother quickly busied herself setting out the guest book and feather pen on the table next to the bowl of birdseed packets and placing folded programs on the pews. The groom's sisters had brought champagne, and Molly directed them to the parlor where silver buckets filled with ice waited.

After cake and a toast, the wedding party and guests were traveling via chartered bus to a posh restaurant in north Scottsdale for a celebration dinner. They'd no doubt return late. Molly didn't expect to see the bride and groom again until tomorrow morning. Or even later for their carriage ride around town.

Molly was debating calling Owen when he finally strolled into the chapel. He'd swapped his vest for the Western cut sports jacket he'd worn earlier, shaved off his stubble and freshly combed his dark hair. Molly had to admit, he looked the part. The groom's sisters' giddy reaction when they saw him confirmed it.

"You ready?" she asked.

"I think so." He held up a sheet of paper. "I called Uncle Homer, and he gave me a few more tips."

"Good." She surveyed the chapel. Most of the guests had arrived and were seated. "We start in seven minutes."

"That soon?" He swallowed.

"Relax. You'll be fine. Don't forget to introduce yourself to the groom before heading to the altar." The next second, Molly's pager vibrated. "I have to go. Good luck." For one ridiculous second, she considered giving Owen a reassuring hug.

Coming to her senses, she sped off. The bride and whatever need had arisen topped Molly's list.

She didn't see Owen again until it was time for the wedding to start. Having exited the bride's dressing room only moments before the recorded wedding march began to play, she retreated to the back of the chapel near the corner.

She wasn't reassured to see Owen shifting anxiously from one foot to the other and tugging at his shirt collar. She tried to discreetly signal him without success.

Suddenly, music began playing, and the bride materialized at the entrance to a chorus of soft gasps. From then on, everyone's attention was focused on her and the besotted groom. When the music stopped and they stood side by side in front of Owen, he cleared his throat. Then, he cleared it again. When he finally spoke, his voice was dry and frog-like.

"Wa…welcome, family, friends and, um, loved ones."

Oh, no, Molly thought and clenched her fingers. Not the most impressive start.

"We're here this evening to celebrate a wonderful occasion. No, not the opening of Sweetheart Ranch. Though, that was some humdinger of an open house earlier. Sorry you missed it."

Molly cringed when no one laughed.

"Benjamin Carr and Jolyn Montgomery have invited you to witness their public commitment and declaration of love to each other." Owen stared hard at the paper he held. "Gatherings such as these are important as they mark the special milestones in our lives."

Terrific. The ceremony was sounding more like a legal proceeding than a wedding.

"Make eye contact," she murmured under her breath. "Smile."

He did neither, and listening to him was a painful experience.

"Ben and Jolyn, please join hands and look into each other's eyes." He paused. "These are the hands of your best friend. They are holding yours on your wedding day as you promise to love each other today, tomorrow and forever."

Okay, this wasn't so bad. He was reciting the "Blessing of the Hands" per the bride and groom's request. Thank goodness he was getting this part right.

Owen managed to complete the entire blessing, even smiling when he finished with, "May these hands continue to build a loving relationship that lasts a lifetime."

Molly expelled a sigh of relief. It was short-lived. Owen messed up twice during the exchange of vows and once when the unity candles were lit.

At last, he announced, "You may kiss the bride," and proclaimed the couple as Mr. and Mrs. Carr.

Molly waited until all the guests had expressed their best wishes to the glowing couple before approaching them. She was prepared to apologize for Owen's lack of polish and to explain the reason for it. Except they didn't give her a chance.

The bride pulled Molly into a fierce embrace, nearly drowning her in satin and tulle and lace. "Thank you so much. This is the best day of my life. The ceremony was wonderful. Everything I hoped for."

It was? "I'm glad," she replied automatically.

The bride was whisked away by her maid of honor before Molly could say more.

She blinked in amazement. Had that really just happened?

Knowing she should make her way to the parlor and check on progress for the reception, she cast a quick glance in Owen's direction. He flashed her a grin and lifted a shoulder as if to say, "We're home free."

Not exactly. He might be a diamond, but he was definitely still in the rough. First thing tomorrow, the two of them were practicing. Sweetheart Ranch's next guests were arriving at noon, and their wedding was scheduled for one o'clock. That left Molly and Owen very little time.

CHAPTER FOUR

OWEN HELPED CODY and Marisa onto the first pew in the chapel. He sat Willa on the floor rather than take the chance of her falling.

As it turned out, he needn't have worried for her safety. The toddler immediately collapsed onto the carpet, stuck her thumb in her mouth, pillowed her head with her other arm and stared into space. Before long, she would nod off.

Owen let her be. Neither he nor his kids had slept soundly their first night at the ranch. True to her word, Marisa objected to sharing the sofa bed with her brother and had a meltdown. Even after she gave up and accepted the inevitable, she, Cody and Willa had insisted on multiple trips to the bathroom and drinks of water and whined endlessly because they missed their mother and Oreo.

No amount of coaxing, cajoling or consoling on Owen's part had made a difference. Eventually, Willa and Marisa had cried themselves to sleep while Cody remained stubbornly awake. At a loss, Owen had finally allowed his son to crawl into the king-size bed with him where they'd both succumbed to exhaustion.

Everyone had awoken this morning tired and cranky. Owen didn't see their moods improving without a nap, which was why he let Willa sleep on the chapel floor.

"Is she okay there?" Molly asked from where she stood at the altar, her brow knitted.

"She'll be fine." Owen reached down and stroked his youngest's cheek. She would be fine, right?

Another glaring example of his below average dad skills. His ex-wife had always been the one to get up with the kids at night or tend them when they were sick. And he'd let her, seldom volunteering to take her place. It was one of his many regrets. Regrets he had the chance to remedy thanks to Jeanne.

Straightening, he said to Cody and Marisa, "All right, you two, listen up. We're playing a game."

"Yay!" Marisa's expression instantly brightened, and she bounced in her seat. "I wanna play a game."

Cody crossed his arms, considerably less enthused. "You said you had to work."

"I am working *and* we're playing a game. You get to help me." Owen removed a red paisley handkerchief from his jeans pocket and tied it around Cody's neck. The boy immediately pulled the handkerchief up over his mouth like an Old West bandit. Owen then gave Marisa a rose from last evening's wedding to hold. "We're pretending you two are guests. I'm the minister who's going to perform the service and Miss Molly is the bride."

"Can I be a bride, too?" Marisa asked.

"Next time, if you behave."

"Why does she have a mop?" Cody stared at Molly. He'd somehow deduced she was the one responsible for this girly game.

"The mop is the pretend groom," Owen said.

Over breakfast in the kitchen, he'd attempted to explain the duties of his job at Sweetheart Ranch to his kids without much success. Cody and Marisa had been very young at their aunt's wedding three years ago and didn't remember.

He'd have preferred to leave them in Nora's care for the practice. Unfortunately, she wasn't available until later, which meant the kids were currently underfoot.

No, not underfoot. Owen reminded himself that he and his kids were at Sweetheart Ranch to bond and strengthen their relationship and for him to become a better dad. Referring to them in negative terms was counterproductive.

"This game is dumb." Cody threw himself against the back of the pew.

"Would you rather be the groom and stand next to Miss Molly?"

"I'm not marrying her!" Cody pushed off the pew, prepared to make a run for it.

"Stay put, young man."

He flopped down hard enough to shake the pew.

Owen gritted his teeth, embarrassed at his oldest's rude outburst but refusing to make the situation worse by yelling.

"I don't know, son." He forced himself to speak slowly. "Might not be as bad as you think, standing next to a pretty lady."

He glanced over at Molly and found her looking at him. The moment lingered, and then her mouth curved into a small smile.

She pulled the mop closer in a mock hug and said, "Sorry. I'm already taken."

How about that? She possessed a sense of humor after all.

Owen was suddenly glad to be practicing and not because he needed to smooth out a few of his rough edges. Getting to know Molly better was proving enjoyable.

"We don't have much time," she reminded him. "We should get started."

With Willa sleeping peacefully, Owen leveled a finger at Cody and Marisa. "Be good," he warned and took his position at the altar. Facing Molly and her makeshift groom, he asked, "What ceremony did the couple request?"

"The Art of Marriage, and they're going to recite their own vows, which makes things a little easier for you." She handed him a sheet of paper on which was printed the ceremony. "This is a second wedding for both the bride and groom. Only their teenage children, parents and a few close friends are attending. They requested the ceremony have an intimate, casual feel. For you, that means infusing lots of warmth into your voice."

"Can do."

At her nod, Owen began with the same welcome speech from the previous night, including the joke about the open house.

Molly stopped him there. "Why don't we leave out the part about the open house? These people weren't here yesterday and don't care."

She was right, about that and infusing warmth. "Life is a journey," he continued.

"Wait. That's too cliché." Molly tapped a finger on her cheek. "Let's try, the journey of life is made better when traveled together. Wayne and Tasha have chosen each other to share their journey."

"You make me wish I'd brought a pen," Owen teased.

Always prepared, Molly promptly extracted a

pen from her shirt pocket and handed it to him. Owen scribbled the changes in the margin.

"You know," she said when he was nearly done. "I'm not the only person in the room. There's the groom and the guests. Look at them, too."

Busted. He had been concentrating on her. Hard to ignore those amazing green eyes which were focused directly on him.

Clearing his throat, he glanced over at his kids. By some miracle, Cody and Marisa weren't fighting. Instead, they watched him with an intensity akin to wonderment. That hadn't happened since he'd taken them to the office one Saturday when he couldn't get out of work and their mother had plans. He'd fully anticipated a trying morning filled with reminding the kids to lower their voices and stay out of trouble. Instead, they'd wound up having enormous fun.

Picking up where he'd left off, he pushed through to the end of the ceremony.

"Better," Molly announced.

"Good." He rolled the papers into a tube, assuming they were done. They weren't.

"Let's have another go from the top."

By their third run through, Cody and Marisa had grown bored and started bickering.

"He touched my rose."

"She kicked me."

"It appears the guests are growing restless," Owen said. "We can try again later."

Molly checked her watch. "Can't. Too much to do. The bride and groom's family members are staying at the ranch through Tuesday. As of this morning, we have all five available cabins rented."

"That's great."

"We're taking the entire wedding party on a hayride after the ceremony to the Poco Dinero for a barbecue dinner and line dancing. Most of the family has never been to a ranch before and they want the full cowboy experience."

"I can always practice by myself."

"Record yourself with your phone and play it back," she suggested. "Better yet, video yourself if you can."

He could do that. He had before when called on to give a speech at work functions. "Okay, you two, let's go."

Cody and Marisa immediately bolted from the pew. Owen bent and lifted Willa into his arms. She woke up only briefly, falling back sleep the moment her head found his shoulder.

She was cute like this, thumb in her mouth, wispy curls framing her face. Shame on him for leaving her and going on the road so much. He could have enjoyed countless more moments like this one.

That, too, was going to change this month at the ranch. He'd make sure of it. Nothing mattered to him more than Cody, Marisa and Willa. Even finding a new job came second. At least until after Christmas when the kids went back with their mother.

"Do you have a lot of couples like Tasha and Wayne," Owen asked, "requesting the full cowboy experience?"

"A few." Molly fell into step beside him as they left the chapel. "They want their wedding to be unique, out of the ordinary. Especially if it's a second wedding or vow renewal."

"Makes sense."

He'd do something entirely different if he ever married again. And at the moment, that was a big if. He was in no place to consider dating, much less a lifelong commitment.

"I suppose that's why Grandma and Homer eloped," Molly mused aloud. "Something out of the ordinary."

"Imagine how many weddings Uncle Homer's officiated. A tacky chapel in Reno probably appealed to him."

"I wish you hadn't said 'tacky.' Poor Grandma."

"What do you bet she doesn't care? When you're in love, you see the beauty in everything."

Molly sent him a skeptical look. "That's a rather romantic sentiment for a guy."

"I recently started marrying people for a living. Comes with the territory."

They stopped in the foyer. Cody and Marisa immediately descended on the bowl of birdseed packets.

"Hey, hands off," Owen scolded.

"Daddy, can we feed the birds?" Cody begged.

"Please," Marisa added.

He supposed they deserved a small reward for behaving reasonably well during his practice session with Molly, but it was up to her. "Do you mind?"

She bent at the waist, putting herself on eye level with the kids. "Two each. Okay?"

Ah. More softening around the edges. Nice. "You heard Miss Molly. Two each."

Jackets donned and their treasures clasped tight in their hands, Cody and Marisa dashed outside, competing to be the one to open the heavy front door. Owen and Molly followed. They stood on the veranda watching as the kids tossed handfuls of seeds onto the lawn, their loud antics scaring the birds instead of enticing them nearer.

Owen followed Molly's gaze as it wandered to the distant mountains. This time of year, at the start of winter, the greens and yellows that had previously blanketed the slopes were now a dull brown. Even so, the mountains were majestic, with Pinnacle Peak like a giant hand reaching heavenward.

"You look like you're somewhere else," he observed.

Molly shook herself. "I was, I guess."

"At your grandmother and Uncle Homer's wedding?"

She exhaled slowly. "It's hard for me to accept that she chose eloping over a wedding at Sweetheart Ranch with all her family and friends there. I keep telling myself it's her special day, she can do whatever she chooses."

"Except she chose to exclude you."

"I'm being selfish."

"No, you're not." Owen absently adjusted the blanket he'd thrown over Willa. "You love her. You want to be there. It's natural."

"I'm so glad they'll be home for Christmas."

"The holidays aren't the same without family. I'd hate to spend mine away from the kids."

"Grandma and Homer are going to renew their vows on New Year's Day and throw a big party."

"I know. Uncle Homer asked me to officiate."

"Why did I not see that coming?"

Molly laughed and, all at once, Owen glimpsed the vivacious and engaging woman hidden behind the guard she diligently maintained. Almost immediately, he began reconsidering his commitment to avoid any romantic entanglements. She was that appealing.

"Speaking of exchanging vows." She checked her watch again, and the moment vanished as quickly as it had appeared. "I have someone else's to coordinate."

"And I need to practice."

Owen called for Cody and Marisa to hurry up. They'd run out of birdseed and were climbing an antique pony cart used for a lawn ornament. No sooner had they reached the veranda steps than Nora threw open the front door.

"Molly! Hurry. We got big trouble."

"What's wrong?"

"The wireless internet's down."

Everyone rushed inside, Willa bouncing awake in Owen's arms. They all crowded around the registration desk and stared at Molly's computer with its ominous message in the center of the screen.

"Is losing the internet really such a big deal?" Owen asked, attempting to settle a now cranky Willa.

"Tasha and Wayne are planning to live stream their wedding." Molly wrung her hands. "We assured them it wouldn't be a problem."

Nora shook her head dismally. "I swear, what else could go wrong?"

Don't ask, Owen thought. He wasn't as superstitious as many of his rodeo buddies but neither did he believe in inviting trouble.

IF MOLLY THOUGHT crying would help, she'd produce racking sobs on the spot. But after twenty minutes of her asking nicely, insisting firmly, pleading her case and reading from the guarantee the internet company had given her when the equipment was installed, the representative on the other end of the line had refused to budge.

They simply couldn't get a technician out until tomorrow. Period. Sorry. Sunday was a bad day for losing internet service. They were short-handed and had a truck in the shop for repairs. Mustang Valley was outside the general service area. The excuses went on and on.

"We can have a technician there tomorrow," the man with zero compassion assured her.

A fat lot of good that did them, thought Molly.

"What time?" she asked.

"Between noon and six p.m."

She started to argue only to clamp her mouth shut. Her energy was better spent finding an alternate means of streaming today's wedding.

The representative gave her a confirmation

number and then asked, "Is there anything else I can help you with?"

He hadn't helped her much in the first place. "No, thanks."

Molly hung up just as the satisfaction survey started playing. They really didn't want her feedback.

"What are you going to do?" Owen asked.

He stood on the other side of the registration counter. His children had gone with Nora to "help" her finish prepping the cabins for their newest guests.

"I'm not sure yet."

"Do you have a mobile hotspot?"

"We keep one for backup. It's not great. Cell phone signals this far north are unreliable." She came out from behind the counter, dreading her next task. "I need to call the bride and groom, let them know they can't stream the service."

"Do you think they'll cancel?"

"Not at this late date. But they and their long-distance family members will be disappointed." She closed her eyes, wishing the throbbing in her temples would cease. "So much for the positive comments on our social media page and the TV news segment last night."

"Wait. Don't panic yet." Owen took her hand and drew her with him to the bench against the wall. "I may have a solution."

He pulled her down onto the seat beside him. She'd barely registered the sensation of his strong, warm fingers enveloping hers when he let go and pulled out his cell phone.

"There's someone I know who might be able to help," he said.

"Help how?" She stared at her hand. It didn't look any different.

"He's part owner of an IT consulting company in Phoenix and pretty savvy about this stuff."

Owen had her attention. "He can fix our internet?"

"That's what I'm hoping." Owen swiped his phone screen and searched his contacts.

"Is he a former Waverly customer?"

"We rodeoed together."

"And he co-owns an IT company?"

Owen tapped the call button and turned toward her, leaning in. "We're not all big and dumb."

"I...didn't..."

Her heart gave the same silly little leap as before. Molly bit her lip. Fortunately, his call went through, sparing her from finishing her reply.

How had she not noticed his ruggedly masculine features before and that his brown hair curled attractively at the ends? She had noticed his smile lighting up his entire face last night when she'd watched the TV news segment. And when she'd watched it a second time this morning. Nora had correctly predicted the positive response he'd have with viewers. Already today Molly had spoken to several potential clients requesting appointments.

"Yeah, Lenny. It's Owen Caufield." They exchanged a few pleasantries, and then Owen voiced the reason for his call. "I have a good friend with a serious problem. I'm hoping you can put on your superhero cape and save the day."

Good friend? Surely Owen had used the term loosely as a means of encouraging Lenny's cooperation.

"Did I say *she*?" He shot Molly an amused glance. "But you're right. My friend is a she. And to answer your second question, you'll just have to see for yourself."

Molly listened, pretending to be immune to his semiflirtatious comments and fearing she failed.

"Will something like that work?" After a long pause, Owen said, "Okay, good. The wedding's at one. Can you get here early? That'll give us time for a test run."

Still talking, he inadvertently brushed his hand across Molly's knee. She almost jerked as his palm briefly made its presence known though the fabric of her jeans. If not for the tingling sensation radiating outward from her knee, he might never have touched her.

"Thanks, man. I owe you one. Nope, that's it. I'll text you the address." Owen disconnected the call. "He's bringing a booster."

Molly sat up, quickly collecting herself. "What's that?"

"The short explanation, it's a device that strengthens a mobile signal. It'll enable your hotspot to handle streaming the wedding."

"They make such a thing?"

"Lenny says boosters aren't expensive. You might considering buying one for the future, if it works."

Owen grinned at her, his gaze roving her face and making Molly keenly aware they continued to share a very small space on the bench.

Suddenly self-conscious, she rose. "I should, um, go."

"I'd better rescue Nora from the kids." Owen also pushed to his feet. "She can't be getting much work done."

"Thank you, Owen, for saving the day."

"My pleasure."

When he didn't move, Molly tilted her head back. Way back. He was tall, she realized. Much taller than her. And he wore his height well, moving with grace and agility.

"You're proving to be more valuable than I

anticipated." She barely recognized the breathy voice as her own.

"Now if I can just get the officiating weddings part down, I'll be indispensable."

"You will. Get better at officiating," she amended. What would she do if he really did become indispensable?

"I have a good tutor. She's tough but reasonable in her expectations. Mostly."

"I apologize if I got carried away this morning at practice and when the internet went down. I want things perfect."

"You're launching a brand-new business, and you're committed to its success. Add to that, you've been hit with one problem after the other. You're understaffed, overworked, lost your regular minister and your internet service. I'd say you're entitled to get carried away." At her tentative smile, he said, "There we go," in a low voice that slowed the madly spinning wheels inside Molly's head.

Most attractive men had the opposite effect on her, causing her thoughts to race a mile a minute. She couldn't account for what made Owen different. She could account for the parade of red flags. She wasn't ready for this, and she certainly wasn't ready for a single dad of three whose life was in flux.

"I'll see you later." Molly retreated a step.

"If I'm not around when Lenny gets here, call me. You can stream me practicing the ceremony to test the equipment."

"All right." The phone on the registration counter rang. Relieved, Molly hurried to answer it. Another person had seen the TV news segment last night and wanted more information on the ranch. When she glanced up after ending the call, Owen had disappeared.

Just as well, she thought and went to the parlor where she began removing the vases of orange roses, making room for the white lilies due any moment. Molly had a standing arrangement to donate any leftover flowers to the Rio Verde Senior Living Center.

A volunteer was on their way to collect the roses. It was a shame to throw out perfectly good flowers that could brighten someone's day. Especially during the holidays when residents missed being home and with their loved ones.

Nora joined Molly in the parlor. Apparently Owen had collected his children from her. "If no one minds, I'm heading home for a while to rest these old bones."

"Before you go," Molly said, "do you want to see pictures of Grandma's wedding? She sent them earlier."

"I'd love to!"

Molly opened the file on her phone and passed

it to Nora. As the older woman studied each picture, she did something Molly had never seen before. She became weepy.

"Nora, are you okay?"

"I'm fine." She returned the phone, sniffing softly.

Molly gave her an impulsive hug. "You're sweet."

Nora harrumphed. "Did you watch the news last night? It was a dandy piece."

"I agree." Lack of airtime for Molly and Bridget aside, the reporter and camera person had done an admirable job showcasing Sweetheart Ranch and making it sound like the perfect wedding venue. "We have three appointments scheduled for later this week."

"You want me there?"

"Yes, and I think I'll ask Bridget to make some of those mini wedding cupcakes. People love them." After a moment, Molly said, "Owen came across well on TV. You were right about him."

"If you ask me, you were the one to really sell the place. You spoke from the heart, Molly, and it showed. Well done."

Two words she hadn't heard in a long time. She had to admit, it felt good.

"Thanks, Nora."

With a wave, the older woman left, a slight hobble to her step as if her bones did indeed ache.

Molly watched her go, satisfaction rushing in to fill a too-long empty place inside her. For the first time since she'd found out that her grandmother had eloped with Homer Foxworthy, Molly believed she could handle all the responsibilities thrust upon her.

Maybe for the first time in her entire professional career.

CHAPTER FIVE

OWEN SHOOK THE bride's hand and then the groom's. "Congratulations to the both of you. Best of luck."

The bride beamed. "We loved, loved, loved the ceremony."

Her new husband couldn't stop grinning. No wonder, he was riding an incredible natural high that Owen knew from personal experience was a mixture of excitement, nervousness and elation. He'd experienced the same emotions himself often. When he'd gotten married, yes. In those days, he'd been in love with Jeanne and convinced they'd conquer the many challenges facing them.

Becoming a father had also sent him soaring. And intimidated him. How was it possible to fall instantly in love with a tiny human being while simultaneously being scared witless? Truth be told, he was still frequently scared. If Cody, Marisa and Willa ever found out, he could forget all about exerting authority over them.

Most often, Owen had experienced that rush

when he was competing in the rodeo arena. Then, he'd added a goodly amount of fear to the mix. Nothing like sitting on the back of an eighteen-hundred-pound bull to get one's adrenaline flowing.

The money hadn't been bad, either. But what he'd loved and craved about the sport was the constant thrill. He sometimes missed it, though he'd been mostly joking about signing up for recreational bull riding at the Poco Dinero Bar. With three young mouths to feed, he couldn't afford to be hurt and laid up. Being unemployed, even by choice, was a heavy enough burden.

Fortunately, he had enough money set aside from his Waverly stock options that he could wait a couple months at least for the right opportunity— one with limited traveling and decent wages, that would allow him to be close to his kids and also excited him. In his opinion, slaving away at a despised or boring job was like being slowly tortured to death.

Moving on from the groom, Owen introduced himself to the various family members congregating at the back of the chapel. Taking an older, wheelchair-bound woman's hand in his, he squeezed gently.

"Mrs. Wilson, I can see where your daughter gets her good looks."

She covered her mouth with her other hand

and laughed. "And I thought I was the one with poor eyesight."

"It's an honor to meet you, ma'am."

"Can't recall ever being to a wedding with such a charming minister. Where's your church, young man? Might drop in one Sunday and hear you preach."

Owen hadn't expected this question, though, in hindsight, he should have. "I'm afraid I'm not that kind of minister. They only let me marry people. I leave the preaching to the professionals."

"A shame. You'd fill the pews."

"You're very kind."

Giving her hand another squeeze, Owen greeted the next person. From the corner of his eye, he spotted Molly. She stood near the door, discreetly surveying the room. When she caught his gaze, she nodded approvingly.

The ceremony had gone better than yesterday's. Granted, he'd tripped over his words once or twice. Okay, three times. But all in all, a marked improvement.

He was glad. Pleasing Molly had become important to him, and not because he liked her or wanted to impress her. Their relationship was entirely professional and needed to stay that way. Rather, her determination to make Sweetheart

Ranch successful was contagious and had become Owen's goal, too.

Like him, Molly had no room in her life for
dating, if she was even interested in him roman-
tically. They'd both been burned and recently.
From what Nora had told him, one of the reasons for Molly's return to Mustang Valley was to
heal her broken heart. Owen should, and would,
respect that.

Since no one had invited him to the reception,
he began edging toward the door. The newly
married couple and their guests sounded as if
they were ready for cake and a toast before em-
barking on the night's festivities.

Owen signaled Molly that he was leaving.

"Thanks, again," she mouthed, nodding at the
bride's teenage son, who held his phone up, continuing to live stream events.

Owen's friend had come through for them—
the hotspot booster worked perfectly. In return,
Owen had promised to buy his friend dinner and
a beer this coming weekend at the Poco Dinero
where they'd watch the bull riding and reminisce
about their former glory days.

"Anytime," he mouthed back to Molly. He almost added "See you later," but stopped himself.
Hadn't he moments ago reminded himself they
were coworkers and nothing more?

He was saying goodbye to the groom's parents when Marisa abruptly burst into the chapel, eyes searching frantically and her clothes disheveled. The sight of her was so unexpected, Owen didn't initially react. Not until she spotted him and started wailing.

"Daddy! Daddy! You said I could be the bride."

Not now, please, he silently begged.

As if connected by invisible strings, the wedding couple and guests backed away from Marisa, expressions of alarm and confusion on their faces. The groom's mother looked horrified.

"Hi, peanut." Owen stepped forward and reached for his daughter. Every pair of eyes in the room riveted on him, including Molly's. "Let's you and me get out of here, okay?"

His hope that Marisa would go willingly and quietly was dashed when she wriggled free from his grasp.

"I'm the bride," she shouted. "You promised."

Had he? Oh, yes. This morning. During practice. "Your turn is next."

"Nooo!"

To Owen's horror, his darling, sweet daughter whirled in a circle, lifted her hands and gave the poor *real* bride a shove. She responded by glaring down at Marisa and demanding, "Hey, what are you doing?" Several people gasped.

Before the situation could deteriorate further—if that was possible—Owen scooped a hysterical Marisa up into his arms. "I'm truly sorry," he said and made for the doorway leading from the chapel. A last glance over his shoulder caused his gut to clench. While the photographer snapped picture after picture, the teenage son followed Owen and Marisa with his phone. Molly stood watching it all, shock draining every drop of color from her face.

In his mind, he saw the video being posted online and it appearing every time someone searched Sweetheart Ranch. Not the sort of advertising the O'Malley family would appreciate.

"No, no, no!" Marisa was far from finished with her outburst. Besides crying, she flailed her arms and legs.

Owen swore he heard Molly saying, "I can't apologize enough," and, "Let me offer you a full refund," over his daughter's wails. Perhaps he should pay whatever she wound up reimbursing the couple. That would only be right.

Whisking Marisa through the parlor and into the kitchen, he reined in his temper. Doubtful the bride and groom would laugh at his daughter's tantrum—or their friends and loved ones who'd watched it via the live stream. Not like last night's couple had laughed at his flubs.

Entering the kitchen, he found Cody sitting

at the table, separating a tangerine into sections. His head snapped up when Owen and Marisa entered.

"Hi, Daddy." He stared guiltily at Marisa.

Owen was certain his son knew something and had possibly played a part in his sister crashing the wedding.

"What are you doing here?" He'd left the kids in the cabin with Nora.

"Eating." As if to prove his innocence, Cody lifted his glass of milk and took a swallow.

"Why aren't you in the cabin?"

"'Cuz we came here."

Owen sat Marisa at the table in the empty chair next to her brother. In front of her was an uneaten tangerine and untouched glass of milk. By now, she'd lost considerable steam and her sobs had diminished to mere whimpers.

"Where's Miss Nora?" Owen asked.

"The bathroom." Cody popped a tangerine section into his mouth.

"What about Miss Bridget?"

"I dunno."

Owen scrubbed his face. How in the world was he going to fix this latest disaster?

"What's wrong, Daddy?"

"Your sister…" He cast a glance at Marisa. She'd laid her cheek on the table and was twisting a lock of hair around her finger, a habit she resorted to when she was upset or afraid.

Her forlorn appearance hit him hard and sucked the fury right out of him, though not the frustration. He'd be better equipped to handle this situation if he'd been home more and not on the road.

Extending a hand, he patted her head. "She interrupted the wedding."

"Is she in trouble?"

What Owen heard his son asking was "Am I in trouble?"

"No," he said, "no one's in trouble." *Except me.*

Nora came into the kitchen, Willa toddling along beside her. "Wedding over?" she asked brightly. The next instant, her features sobered. "What's wrong?"

"Marisa intwupted the wedding," Cody answered, his mouth stuffed with tangerine pieces.

"She did what?"

Owen conveyed to Nora what had happened. "It wasn't a pretty sight." He picked up Willa and balanced her on his knee.

She immediately grabbed Marisa's tangerine. "Mine."

Marisa showed no interest in having her snack stolen.

"This is all my fault." Nora shoved at her short

gray curls. "I shouldn't have brought them to the house. I'll talk to Molly."

"No, I'll talk to her," Owen said.

"Willa needed her diaper changed. I told Cody and Marisa to stay here and be quiet, then I took her to the bathroom. I swear, we weren't gone five minutes."

Marisa must have flown out of the kitchen the instant Nora's back was turned. Owen knew how fast his kids could move, given the chance. Once, when Cody was Marisa's age, he'd pushed a chair across the kitchen floor, used it as a step stool to climb onto the counter and then hauled himself to the top of the refrigerator. Owen had left the room for a total of three minutes.

The sounds of voices carried from the parlor. Apparently the reception was underway. Owen pushed back from the table. He didn't relish the prospect of making apologies to the bride and groom but it had to be done, and the sooner the better.

"I'll be back." He gave Willa to Nora and then loomed over Cody and Marisa. "Stay put. I'm serious."

Cody nodded. Marisa just stared at him, her head still on the table. Guilt chewed a hole in Owen's gut. If he'd been with his kids and not left them with Nora, this wouldn't have happened.

"I swear to you," the older woman said, "no one will leave this room."

The bride and groom were far more gracious than necessary when Owen reiterated his apologies. That, or their happiness had dimmed the awful memory. They'd be reminded when they watched the video and possibly be mad all over again. But, for now, they told him not to worry.

When he offered to reimburse them for the cost of his services, they refused. Owen didn't insist, he was already planning on sending them tickets to a Diamondbacks game. The groom had mentioned they were huge baseball fans.

Shaking their hands one last time, Owen went in search of Molly, intending to ask her for the bride and groom's contact information. She was in the chapel and stood near the altar, her back to him. As he neared, he could hear her talking and realized she was on her phone. Deciding to return in a few minutes, he started to leave. Her words stopped him cold.

"Yes, that's right. Thursday evening. Six thirty. Uh-huh. Thanks so much for any help you can give us. We desperately need a substitute minister. No. Well, we did have one, but he's not working out."

THE SMELL OF diesel fumes filled Molly's nostrils as she stood on the veranda and watched the chartered bus leave the ranch. Its red and amber lights glowed against the backdrop of a darkening sky, growing smaller and fainter as the bus gained distance.

Relief washed over her in great, rushing waves. This day was finally over, thank goodness. The various highs and lows had left her emotionally, mentally and physically exhausted.

Her plan included readying the parlor for tomorrow's continental breakfast, rummaging through the refrigerator for a snack, taking a steaming shower that used every drop of hot water and sleeping in late the next morning. In that order.

Except, she suddenly remembered, sleeping in late wasn't an option. She had a full day ahead of her that included running errands, waiting on the internet service technician and hauling the Christmas decorations out of storage. Grandma Em wanted the entire house and outside decorated by the first week in December.

Molly had also told Nora to meet her after lunch for her first lesson in guest relations duties. And, if possible, Molly wanted to start work on the cross-promotion plan she'd proposed to the owners of Powell Ranch and the Poco Dinero before every spare second was swallowed up by the holidays.

Last, and most important, there was the matter of Owen and what to do about him. Talking with her sister earlier had prompted Molly to re-evaluate the situation but there were still several things to consider.

Rather than go inside, she leaned a shoulder against the pine column beside her, feeling every ounce of energy seep slowly from her.

This last week had taken a tremendous toll on her, between working like crazy preparing for the ranch's grand opening and their frantic scrambling after learning Grandma Em had eloped. Then there was the arrival of Owen and his children and the debacle at this afternoon's wedding when Marisa had caused a scene.

Molly did feel for the child, who was away from home and her mother for the first time and clearly having trouble adapting to her father's new role.

But the ranch couldn't afford another wedding interruption or negative publicity as a result. It was bad for business. Owen wouldn't have appreciated an out-of-control child breaking into one of his client meetings when he was working for Waverly Equine Products.

Molly had three days remaining before their next wedding to resolve the substitute minister problem. That was on top of seeing to their guests, her new client appointments and all her other work.

Expelling a weary sigh, she leaned more heavily on the pine column. Wouldn't it be nice if she had a booster, like the one Owen's friend had lent them, that could restore some of her depleted energy?

Wait. Maybe she did have a booster of sorts. Taking out her phone, she opened the file with the downloaded pictures Grandma Em had sent that morning. The next second, images filled the screen. She scrolled through them, brushing aside a tear or two. Her grandmother did look happy.

Molly next watched the short selfie video her grandmother and Homer had made at their celebration dinner. They weren't the most tech savvy people, and the video was hilarious in large part because of its mishaps.

Like the wave of a magic wand, Molly's spirits lifted. She was still exhausted and in desperate need of rest, but she felt better prepared to face the challenges that lay ahead.

Hearing the front door to the house open, she quickly put away her phone and wiped her damp eyes. Recognizing Owen's heavy boot steps crossing the veranda, she was even more determined not to be caught crying.

He sidled up beside her, instantly reminding her of their close encounter on the bench in the foyer. Only now, lines of tension bracketed his mouth and there was a hesitancy about him.

"Am I disturbing you?" he asked.

"No. I was just about to go inside."

"I have to apologize again for this afternoon. Marisa doesn't normally misbehave like that."

Molly believed him, but that didn't alter the fact the girl's behavior was unacceptable.

"Nora and I talked," she said, cutting him some slack. "She feels terrible and told me the whole thing was her fault. She left Cody and Marisa alone in the kitchen."

"They're my kids and my responsibility. Nora isn't to blame."

He didn't pass the buck. Molly was impressed.

"I offered to reimburse Wayne and Tasha the cost of the service," he said.

"I did, too. They refused." Molly hadn't cared. She'd already gone into the system and discounted the cost of their wedding service.

"Same here. So I ordered Diamondbacks tickets for them. Wayne mentioned they attend several games a year."

"You didn't have to do that, Owen. This is my problem to handle." Though it had been nice of him.

"I know someone who can get me good seats for a reasonable price."

He rested his back against the railing, crossing one boot over the other. The appealing pose he struck was enhanced by his Western jacket and the Stetson pulled low on his brow. Molly tried not to notice, but the more she tried, the more she stared.

"Another rodeo buddy?"

"What can I say? I'm likable."

He was, and Molly steeled herself. Owen had a way of affecting her unlike any other man, and she required all her wits about her for what she had to say to him.

"I like kids. Really, I do."

"Just not when they crash your weddings."

She paused, carefully forming her next words. "That can't happen again. Our customers pay good money for the services we offer. They have a right to receive those services free of preventable problems."

"Absolutely. Believe me, I understand. And it won't happen again. If necessary, I'll have Nora drive the kids to the next town over during weddings."

"Don't take this wrong," Molly said, "but can you make the necessary commitment? You have a lot on your plate. Taking care of your children. Looking for a new job. Those are important and are distracting from your duties here."

"I know you're trying to replace me. I overheard you talking on the phone after the wedding."

"Oh." She wished he hadn't heard her, but it was too late now.

"Hey, don't feel bad. I'm lucky you didn't fire me on the spot."

"I thought about it."

His grin faded. "That was a joke, right?"

"No, I really did think about it. At length."

"And why didn't you?"

She ran her hand down the smooth surface of the column. Owen wasn't the only one who was a mass of contradictions. Molly had no problem being frank and forthright with customers. In the past, she'd often been too frank and forthright, unable to find the necessary balance between honesty and tact. That inability, directly or indirectly, had cost her three jobs.

When it came to expressing her innermost feelings, however, she tended to clam up, a victim of her many insecurities. Good examples were her previous engagements. Molly hadn't expressed her concerns or her needs or asked her fiancés what they needed from her. The resulting dissatisfaction on both sides might have been avoided with a little honest communication. And compromise, something else she'd been unwilling to do.

But Owen wasn't a fiancé. He was a ranch employee, and she should be able to speak plainly with him. Yet the same insecurities she'd suffered from in her former personal relationships kept rearing their ugly heads. Why was that?

"Bridget, Grandma and I have an agreement," she finally said. "Big decisions are put to a vote."

"Your sister and grandmother voted in favor of keeping me?"

"Bridget did. I required convincing."

"And your grandmother?"

"We agreed not to tell her. Yet." Molly met his gaze. "And, honestly, I haven't been able to locate a replacement for you that we can easily afford. I won't risk having to cancel our upcoming weddings because we're short one officiant."

"So, not firing me is the lesser of two evils." He smiled.

She couldn't return it. Not yet. "Basically, yes. And to be clear, we're granting you a temporary stay. The situation must improve."

"You're something else, Molly O'Malley."

She drew back, unsure if Owen was teasing or not. "I have to do what's best for the ranch and my family. Grandma has a substantial amount of money invested." Most of which she'd set aside after selling the inn. "I would hate for her to lose it."

"Trust me, I meant that in a good way. You don't sugarcoat things and you let me know exactly where I stand. Which is, apparently, on very thin ice."

"Can I ask a personal question?"

"Fire away. Wait, wrong word."

Another time, Molly would have laughed at his joke. "Is coming to Sweetheart Ranch for a month really the best way for you and your children to reconnect? By your own admission, they're upset at being away from home and their mother. They're not sleeping well and they're cranky. You leaving them with a babysitter in order to work, albeit part-time, is only making their adjustment to change all the harder."

"That's a fair question and one I've been considering these past few hours."

"Maybe you can keep considering it over the next few days. We don't have another wedding until Thursday evening. It's a small service, and everyone's leaving right afterward for the Talking Stick Resort. In the meantime, I'll continue reaching out to my contacts for a replacement."

"That's a good plan."

"Glad you agree."

"Except I'd rather spend my time becoming a better officiator and settling my kids into our new routine so they quit acting up."

He reached for Molly's hand. While not an intimate gesture per se, it was certainly more intentional than the casual brush to her knee when they were sitting on the bench.

Molly delicately disengaged her fingers. "Owen…"

"I want this to work out. For a lot of reasons, most of them selfish, I admit it. I've neglected my personal life for years now. As a result, my marriage crumpled and my ex-wife divorced me after finding another man who paid her more attention than I did."

"That had to hurt."

"Not as much as you might think, which speaks volumes to the state of our relationship before she cheated on me. There was a reason I willingly traveled twenty out of every thirty days. I disliked being home and she disliked having me there."

"Why didn't you stop traveling after the divorce?" Molly asked.

"I couldn't. Not if I wanted to keep my job and keep receiving those hefty quarterly bonuses. I figured the next best thing to having me around was having a good provider. My kids might not see much of me, but they would lack for nothing. I realized the error of my thinking when I arrived to pick up the kids for a visit after a two-month absence. Willa shied away from me and went running to her mom's boyfriend. Cody and Marisa couldn't have cared less that I was there."

"Ouch."

"Tell me about it."

The exterior light by the front door provided enough illumination for Molly to recognize the emotions in his eyes as regret and sorrow, and she was glad she'd decided to give him a second chance. "What did you do?"

"Quit my job at Waverly the next day. No other man is going to take my place in my kids' lives. I don't care how decent he is or how well he treats them. I'm their father. Which is why this month at Sweetheart Ranch is so important to me. I'll do whatever is required to make it work out."

"Don't take this wrong, but you could have bonded with your children at home and had more time with them, in fact."

"You're right. But Uncle Homer asked me to cover for him. He's been good to me and my family in the past, Helping us though some rough times. I felt like I owed him."

Molly's resistance waned, and she found herself warming to Owen. Again.

What might have happened to her former engagements if she'd been as determined as him to make right what had gone wrong? Bridget had once accused Molly of being more in love with the idea of getting married than in love with the man she was marrying.

"I just hope I'm not too late," Owen said. "I have a history of ignoring the people close to me."

"Your kids adore you. I can see it even if you can't."

"We just need to work on their separation anxiety. One incident of Marisa bursting in at an inappropriate time is all I can take."

"I know how she feels," Molly admitted. "I went through a similar bout after my dad died, and I drove my mom nuts."

"How old were you?"

"Much older than Marisa. Twelve. According to the school counselor, some form of separation anxiety is fairly common for children who've lost a parent. I suppose long absences aren't that different from a death."

"How'd you get so smart?"

"I'm not sure I am. If I was, I wouldn't have a string of broken engagements and former jobs to my credit."

"Life's a constant learning curve."

Molly snapped her mouth shut. She hadn't intended to reveal so much about herself. The broken engagements he already knew about. But not the rest.

"It's getting late," she said in an effort to cover her embarrassment, "and I have a big day tomorrow."

He opened the door and waited for her to enter first. As she went in search of her sister, Molly had the sneaking suspicion Owen's temporary stay would soon become permanent.

CHAPTER SIX

MOLLY DROVE HER SUV behind the ranch house and along the dirt road to the horse stable, passing the cabins as she did. Tasha and Wayne's teenage children had gone with them on their carriage ride through town that morning. Molly didn't think she'd want anyone else along if she were on a romantic carriage ride with her new husband, but to each their own.

At the morning's continental breakfast, Wayne and Tasha's family had discussed how to spend their afternoon. The adults voted for shopping at the specialty stores in Fountain Hills. The teenagers had pleaded to be dropped off at the laser tag arena.

Wherever they wound up, they'd promised to return in time for the evening campfire. It would be the first one at Sweetheart Ranch with actual guests.

Then again, if the wood delivery didn't arrive soon, Molly would be making excuses to their guests rather than assembling the ingredients for s'mores. The delivery had been scheduled for the previous week, but the guy had called and said he'd be delayed. At the time, Molly had thought having no firewood would be their worst catastrophe. Little had she known.

With luck, the remainder of Tasha and Wayne's stay would go well, canceling out any residual negativity from Marisa's interruption. So far, Molly hadn't seen the video Tasha's son had taken appearing anywhere online, but that could still happen.

Because she needed to be available all afternoon for the internet repair technician, and get a start on the Christmas decorations, she'd opted to run her errands in the morning. After a stop at the feed store for grain and hoof ointment, she'd made a trip to her favorite antiques shop, where she purchased a silver frame for Grandma Em and Homer. She'd noticed it on a previous trip and thought it would make a lovely wedding gift.

Parking in front of the stables, Molly hopped out of the SUV and opened the rear door. She was instantly engulfed by the fragrant, earthy aroma of grain. A memory surfaced—her as a child digging her hands into the barrels and lifting handfuls of grain to her nose.

Grandma Em was usually the one to feed and tend the horses on their part-time wrangler's days off. In her absence, Molly and Bridget were sharing the task. Neither of them minded. Their grandparents had always kept a horse or two, and the sisters had spent their summers riding whenever they weren't working at the inn in town.

What Molly did mind was lugging fifty-pound sacks from the vehicle to the stables. One, she could handle. Two were manageable. Ten would exhaust her.

She headed for the stables where a handcart leaned against the wall. At the entrance, the sound of now familiar voices drew her to a halt. Owen's children were here, and they wouldn't be alone.

Molly automatically finger-combed her hair before giving herself a silent reprimand. What did it matter how she looked? She wasn't trying to impress him.

Inside the stables, she found Owen brushing Amos, though only his boots and the bottom halves of his legs were visible beneath the big gelding's belly. The older of the two draft horses was tethered to a pole in front of the stalls. Cody and Marisa sat double on his back with Marisa in front. She was bent over and burying her face in the horse's long blond mane while Cody squirmed and twisted and flung his feet in every direction.

Amos paid them no attention whatsoever. Draft horses were notoriously gentle and these two Haflinger brothers were especially so, making them ideally suited for the O'Malleys' purposes.

Cody spotted her first. "Hi, Miss Molly. We're riding."

"I see that." They weren't actually going anywhere, but that didn't seem to spoil their fun. Molly couldn't help smiling. "Where's Willa?"

Owen stepped out from behind Amos and flashed her a grin, the one that did funny little things to her insides. "Right here."

He turned and presented his back. Willa sat in a contraption that was part backpack and part baby seat, her legs dangling. She cranked her head sideways in order to see Molly.

"Want down," she demanded.

"No can do, squirt." He addressed Molly. "She was getting into some things best left alone."

"Like horse manure?"

Owen grimaced. "I came close to hosing her down. This torture device is our compromise. I almost told her mother not to pack it. Now, I'm glad she did."

Like last evening on the veranda, there was no rancor or disdain in his voice when he mentioned his ex-wife. That was good. Children of parents who were at odds often suffered, and from what Owen had told Molly about his past, he and his ex-wife could easily have been at odds.

"I'm sure I look pretty ridiculous," he said and bent to brush Amos's front legs."

Willa giggled at being tipped forward.

"Not too ridiculous." Secretly, Molly found him much more endearing and attractive than ridiculous.

When he straightened, Willa extended her arm toward her siblings. "Want down, Daddy."

"What she really wants is to sit with Cody and Marisa." Owen patted Amos's thick, muscled neck. "I may put her up there for a minute or two when we're done. You think Amos will be okay with that?"

"It wouldn't be his first time," Molly said. "Nora's had her grandchildren on both horses. Willa should be fine for a minute as long as you don't let go of her."

"I figured as much."

"Where's Big Jim, by the way?"

"His wife's sick with the flu. She called right when he was bringing Wayne and Tasha back from their carriage ride. Apparently, she was feeling dizzy and took a tumble in the laundry room. I told him to go on home and that I'd unharness and brush the horses."

Alarm coursed through Molly. "Is she all right?"

"He said not to worry and that he'll call you later."

"Okay." She'd worry anyway. A tumble sounded serious. Glancing at the harness rack, she noted the various pieces were correctly hung on the right hooks. "Let me guess. You know how to harness horses."

Owen shrugged. "The basics."

"From your rodeo days?"

He laughed, a rich, appealing sound. "My grandfather used to compete in pulling contests at state and county fairs. He took me along when I was young and let me help."

She'd heard of pulling contests and seen pictures. "Did he win?"

"Had the best teams in Fort Scott, Kansas."

"Is that where you're from?"

"Originally. I moved to Arizona because the kids' mother is from here."

And his children were the reason he stayed.

"Do you miss your family?"

"I visit them two or three times a year. One of the few perks of traveling for work. I saw them more often when I was rodeoing. The folks would come and watch me compete."

Supportive parents. He was fortunate. Molly had known that joy up until her father died.

Owen returned the brush to its hook beside the shelf. "They're coming for a visit next February. They haven't seen Willa since she was born."

"That'll be nice."

"I was hoping to bring them here to Sweetheart Ranch. I know my mom would love to see the place."

"Absolutely."

"She's checked out your website."

"Really?"

"She suggested to Dad they rent a cabin for the weekend."

"We'd be delighted to have them." Molly realized with a start that she looked forward to meeting Owen's parents, who were no doubt charming given they'd raised such a charming son. Going to the far wall where the handcart was stowed, she said, "I'd better unload the grain."

"I'll do it."

"You have the children to watch." She steered the handcart ahead of her and toward the door.

Owen wasn't easily dissuaded. Before the first wheel bounced over the threshold, he'd lifted first Marisa and then Cody off Amos and deposited them on the ground, ignoring their objections.

"Why?" Cody complained.

"We're helping Miss Molly."

"Why?" he repeated.

"That's the nice thing to do. Help people who need it."

Even with Willa strapped to his back and his two oldest trying their best to get in the way, Owen unloaded the ten bags of grain and wheeled them into the stables in half the time it would've taken Molly.

Without her asking, he ripped open the last bag and dumped the contents into the grain barrel, filling it to the top.

"Thanks, Owen," she said when he'd secured the lid and the remaining bags were stowed neatly in the corner.

"Any excuse to be around horses again. I'd be happy to help with feeding Amos and Moses and cleaning the stalls until your grandmother and Homer return."

"That's not part of your job description."

"I don't mind. It'd give me and the kids something else to keep us busy and out of trouble. I'm starting to run low on ideas."

She could use a hand, and he was more than qualified. "If you're sure."

"Anything else you need, just give a holler."

"I don't want to interfere with your job hunting or dad duties."

"You're not."

He began unbuckling the toddler carrier and easing his arms through the straps. Next, he carefully lowered the device and Willa to the ground. Once the toddler was free, he settled her on Amos's back. Rather than squealing with delight, she burst into tears.

"Down, down. Want down."

Owen obliged her, chuckling in bewilderment. "That didn't last long."

"Amos is tall," Molly said. "And she's awfully little. I'm sure she just got scared."

"Are these guys as good to ride as they are at pulling a carriage?" He patted Amos on the rump.

"Depends on what you're looking for." Molly untied Amos and returned him to his stall next to his brother. "Haflingers are big and sturdy but not built for speed."

He let Willa go, and she scampered over to join her siblings who were attempting to scale the twin stacks of grain bags. They weren't excited to have her horn in on their game and demanded she "Get down!"

"Cody and Marisa." Owen sent them a stern look. "What did we talk about earlier?"

"Not leaving our toys on the floor?" Cody offered.

"No, sharing. Now let your little sister play with you."

Marisa pouted. Cody reluctantly moved aside.

Mission accomplished, Molly thought. "Good job, Dad."

"I'm trying."

"And making headway from what I can see."

"I've got a long way to go." He locked Amos's stall. "Mind if I take one of these guys for a spin sometime? Been a few months since I've been on the back of a horse."

"Not at all. I've ridden them on the easier trails up the mountain, and they do well enough." Molly checked Moses's stall door. "I wouldn't feel comfortable with you taking the children, though. The horses are too big, and I'd worry about them falling. Our neighbor Powell Ranch has kid-friendly ponies to rent. And faster horses if you want more of a challenge."

"Less challenging is my style these days. I've had my fill of adrenaline rushes."

"And here I thought you were considering bull riding one weekend at the Poco Dinero."

"Considering is a far cry from attempting. And I've been out of the game a long time now."

Molly imagined Owen on the back of a wildly bucking bull and thought that would be something worth seeing.

"Any chance you'd come with me?"

She blinked in surprise. "To watch the bull riding?"

He grinned. "I like that idea. But I was talking about Amos and Moses. Though, if you're free for—"

"I… No…I can't." She was spared having to

say more by the low rumble of an approaching truck.

"I bet that's the guy delivering our firewood." She hesitated at the door, her hand resting on the jamb. "Thanks again for taking care of the horses."

"No problem."

Jumping into her SUV, she executed a U-turn and beeped her horn, waving at the driver to follow when she had his attention. As she led him to the north side of the clubhouse, she was thinking not of the firewood but of going on a trail ride or watching the bull riding with one very handsome cowboy at her side.

AFTER INSTRUCTING THE delivery guy where to stack the half cord of firewood, Molly went inside the house. It was just before noon, time to begin waiting on the internet service technician who probably wouldn't arrive until closer to six.

No matter, Molly had plenty of tasks to accomplish, including a training session with Nora on guest relations. The ranch's next wedding, on Thursday, would be held outside on the veranda. The bride was a former army officer who'd suffered third-degree burns on over 50 percent of her body in a bomb explosion. Now, two years later, she was walking down the aisle.

Molly was determined that everything be perfect, right down to the tiniest detail. To that end, she started on the Christmas decorations, first stringing lights along the veranda railing and then tying big red ribbons on the columns. She was almost done with hanging a sprig of mistletoe in the foyer when she heard the wood delivery truck leaving.

Annoyed that the driver hadn't checked in with her first, she set aside the pruning shears, brushed off the front of her pants and trotted down the steps. She'd no sooner rounded the house than she spotted the stacked wood, thirty feet from where it should be and out in the open rather than tucked beneath the shelter of the eave.

"What the…!"

She immediately dialed the delivery guy's number. Naturally, he didn't pick up. Why hadn't she stayed and watched him? This was her fault, which irritated Molly all the more.

Huffing, she stared at the stacked wood, willing it to magically transport itself to the right location.

"Something wrong?"

She whirled at the sound of Owen's voice. He'd developed this irritating habit of sneaking up on her.

"The guy left the wood in the wrong place. It's supposed to be stacked against the building and out of the elements. I called but he won't answer his phone."

"I'll move it for you."

She eyed him dubiously. "That's a lot of work. You just unharnessed the horses and carried in ten sacks of grain."

"I don't mind. Really."

"It's all right." She huffed again. "I'll take care of it. Somehow."

"Come on. Let me help."

She wavered. "What about the kids?"

"Tracee is watching them. I called her earlier."

She noticed he held his truck keys. "You obviously have plans or you wouldn't have hired her to babysit."

"I was hoping to get a jump on some Christmas shopping before the rush. Other than the kids and Uncle Homer, all my gift recipients live in another state. Then I saw you standing here looking mad."

"Don't let me keep you."

"I can go another day. Or shop online and have the packages shipped like the rest of the world."

"I refuse to let you pay for a babysitter while you're restacking firewood for me. Let me at least reimburse you what she charges."

"No way."

"Owen." Molly planted her hands on her hips.

This was too reminiscent of their conversation in the stables. Her in a fix and him offering to help.

"Tell you what. I'll trade you."

"Trade me?" she asked suspiciously.

"The kids want to come to the campfire tonight."

"Of course they can come. You don't have to restack the firework for that."

"*And* some of Bridget's homemade macaroni and cheese. The kids love it." He grinned. "Okay, I confess. I love it, too."

Macaroni and cheese would require that Molly involve her sister, which definitely wasn't her preference. On the other hand, if Owen didn't move the firewood, that left it up to Molly. She either battled the delivery guy to come back and fix his mistake or she moved the firewood herself.

"Quit being stubborn," he said.

"You're doing so much already."

"I like earning my keep."

Only because she wanted Thursday's wedding to be perfect, right down to the grounds being in tip-top shape, she relented. "You have a deal."

His grin widened as if he'd just won the lottery.

She showed him exactly where she wanted the firewood stacked and then started for the house. But not before getting one last look at him over her shoulder. He'd removed his jacket and rolled up his shirtsleeves, revealing his muscular, tanned forearms. When he waved at her, she quickly pivoted, pretending not to have seen him.

Her cheeks were still burning when she entered the kitchen, slamming the back door a little too forcefully. Bridget was sitting at the table with her feet propped on an adjoining chair. She'd been staring at her electronic tablet until Molly entered.

"Easy there," Bridget cautioned. "That door's breakable."

Molly ripped off her sweatshirt and made straight for the refrigerator and a cold soda. While there, she began lifting lids and peering beneath plastic wrap for something to eat. She should finish trimming the roses but had decided on a lunch break instead.

"What's wrong?" Bridget asked when Molly surfaced with a bowl of chicken salad.

"Nothing."

"Liar."

"The delivery guy stacked the firewood in the wrong place." She wasn't about to admit to her sister that she was embarrassed because Owen had caught her checking him out.

"Won't he come back and move it?"

"Owen's doing that now."

"Is he?" Bridget laid down the tablet. She kept her recipes stored on it and was always researching new ones in her spare time. "That was nice of him."

"We made a deal."

Bridget's eyes lit with interest. "What kind of deal? Please tell me it involves sharing a romantic candlelight dinner in a cozy corner booth."

"What? No! Don't be ridiculous."

Possibly trail riding or watching the bull riding, if she said yes. Which she wouldn't.

"I'm not being ridiculous. Trust me. I've seen you looking at him."

How could Molly deny the accusation when only moments ago she'd been ogling Owen's forearms?

"I don't know what gave you that idea." She opened the vegetable bin and selected a beefsteak tomato purchased from the nearby farmer's market.

"He looks at you, too."

"Nonsense. He's just being friendly and accommodating. That's part of his job." Which reminded her of the deal. "He agreed to move the firewood in exchange for some of your macaroni and cheese. His kids apparently love it."

"I can do that." Bridget stood and stretched. "Then maybe I could take it over to his cabin. See if he looks at me the same way he does you."

Molly ignored the annoying twinge in her tummy, which couldn't possibly be jealousy, and began slicing the tomato. "Suit yourself."

"You don't mind?"

"Why would I?"

"Okay. Good, then. Macaroni and cheese it is."

Bridget disappeared into the pantry and returned with a bag of elbow pasta. By then, Molly had carried her plate of chicken salad and tomato to the table.

"Oh, my, would you look at that." Bridget stopped in her tracks and peered out the window over the sink.

"What?" Molly feigned indifference.

"Owen. He took off his shirt."

Her sister was teasing her. Molly was convinced of it and remained glued to her chair. The weather was warmer today but not that warm.

"Don't you want to see?" Bridget asked, her tone cajoling.

"You're just saying that so I'll jump up and run to the window. Then you can have a good laugh at my expense." To her chagrin, Molly had fallen for he sister's ploy before when they were teenagers and, yes, even more recently than that.

"I'm not joking." Bridget released a long, lazy sigh.

When her sister still didn't move, Molly finally went over to join her, certain she was going to be sorry. She was.

"Gotcha!" Bridget elbowed her in the ribs. "You're so gullible."

Molly ignored her. She knew she should go back to eating her lunch. Instead, she continued to stare.

Owen had located the wheelbarrow and was loading it with wood. When the wheelbarrow was full, he pushed it to the stack he'd started up against the building. There, he unloaded the logs, five or six at a time.

After two more loads, Molly straightened and turned.

"Welcome back," Bridget said from the counter. "You were gone a long time."

"Don't be ridiculous."

"I thought you'd fallen into a coma induced by the sight of his broad shoulders."

Molly glanced around. Either her sister had managed to heat a pot of water to boiling in three seconds and shred an entire block of cheddar cheese or she'd been staring at Owen a humiliating length of time.

"I'm sure he'd ask you out if you dropped a hint."

"I don't want to go out with him." Molly sat at the table and attacked her lunch.

"Why not? You're both single."

"Let's start with Cody, Marisa and Willa."

"You're a kid person. What's the problem?"

"I'm not ready for an instant family. That's a lot to take on and, in case you forgot, we have a brand-new business to run. Grandma's depending on us. More so now that she's married. She'll want to spend time with Homer."

"Lucky her."

"Plus, Owen's made it very clear his priority for being here is to reconnect with his children and look for a new job. I don't want to interfere with that."

"What about after he's reconnected with them and found a job?"

"Who's to say when that'll happen?"

"You're being intentionally difficult."

"I am not!"

"Oh, yeah?" Bridget selected a colander hanging from the overhead rack and set it in the sink. "Why don't you ask your two former fiancés?"

The dig hurt, and Molly glanced away.

"I'm sorry." Bridget's tone was contrite. "That wasn't nice. I forget sometimes how hurt you were over that last breakup. You handled it so well."

No, what Molly had done was throw herself into work and ignore the pain until it lessened.

"I'm envious of you," Bridget said.

"And my two broken engagements?"

"Of the fact Owen's attracted to you and not me. And how awesome you're doing filling in for Grandma. You've really stepped up in a big way."

"Thanks." Two compliments in a row from her sister. Molly wasn't sure what to think.

Bridget dropped into the seat across from Molly. "Nora said our website hits have tripled this week and that we have fifty-something new likes on our social media page."

"That has nothing to do with me being awesome."

"Hard work deserves to be rewarded." Bridget wriggled her eyebrows. "Go out and have some fun, will you? Good-looking man in residence… one of us should take advantage."

Molly changed tactics, trying to discourage her sister. "If you like Owen so much, why don't you drop a hint, as you said, and go out with him? He's more your type than mine anyway."

Bridget shrugged. "I tried that already."

Molly almost choked on her chicken salad. "You did?"

"Yes. He's super attractive, and I'm not made of stone. Naturally I flirted."

"What, um…" Molly couldn't bring herself to ask.

"What was his response? He didn't have one.

Zero. I might as well have been flirting with a statue."

"Somehow I doubt that." Men were unable to resist her sister when she set her sights on them.

"He didn't respond because you're the one he's smitten with."

Molly stabbed a piece of tomato. "If that's true, he's wasting his time because the feeling isn't reciprocated."

Bridget broke into laughter. "I'd believe you if not for all the nose prints on the window."

Molly ignored her sister, only to sneak a peek at the window the moment Bridget's back was turned.

CHAPTER SEVEN

"I WANNA LIGHT the fire, too." Cody crept forward, inch by inch.

"No, son. Stay by the chairs like I told you."

To Owen's increasing frustration, his three young hooligans had developed a dangerous fascination with the campfire. Marisa and Willa didn't fully understand the concept, having no previous experience with fire. Cody was old enough to remember a week they'd spent at a lodge in the Christopher Creek area where there had also been a campfire.

Jeanne had been eight months pregnant with Willa, and Marisa barely walking. His ex-wife had insisted on one last vacation before the birth of their third child, claiming the getaway would do their marriage good.

Sadly, she'd been wrong. Their relationship had deteriorated beyond what a single weeklong vacation could repair. He was glad all Cody remembered from that tension-filled trip was the communal fire they'd sat at each evening and not the almost constant arguing between his parents.

"Don't come any closer." Owen held his free hand up in a stop-right-there gesture when Cody continued to inch forward. "Fire isn't a toy to be played with."

"I won't play," Cody said.

Yeah, right. The boy's entire life was one big playground.

"Can I call Mommy?" Marisa asked for the third time in the last hour. She and Willa were squished together in one of the lawn chairs circling the fire pit.

"You just talked to her before dinner."

"I forgot to tell her about feeding the horses."

Owen had held Marisa while she dumped scoops of grain into each horse's feed trough. "You can call her tomorrow, peanut."

"That's too long."

Satisfied the kindling had caught, Owen stood and backed away from the fire pit. For whatever reason, his kids were more homesick today than usual. And here he'd been feeling optimistic about them adjusting to life at Sweetheart Ranch. Maybe the relapse was related to Jeanne telling the kids she and her boyfriend were leaving on Thursday for a ski trip.

Marisa had gotten confused and immediately jumped to the wrong conclusion, that her mother wasn't returning until after Christmas. That morphed into Santa not visiting. Eventually, Owen and Jeanne had calmed her down but Marisa continued to be upset.

Owen had begun to suspect that his kids' insecurities of late had as much to do with Jeanne's growing relationship with her boyfriend as being temporarily uprooted and left in his sole care. She and her boyfriend were discussing "the next step," though Jeanne hadn't told the kids. Still, they were clearly sensing a shift in the dynamics at home and possibly responding.

Which led Owen to ponder how the kids would react if, and when, he found someone new. Naturally, an image of Molly instantly came to him.

His attraction to her was increasing day by day. She was a complicated woman which, in his mind, made her all the more interesting. She kept his attention when a less complicated woman would have bored him silly. Challenging, yes. She could test a man's patience. But Owen liked challenges and seldom shied from them. Especially when they were as pretty as Molly O'Malley.

In the next instant, common sense reared its head, warning him that diving in before either of them was ready would practically guarantee disaster. Owen listened, but it was getting harder and harder.

He slipped the long-reach lighter he'd been

using into his coat pocket. He wasn't about to let it fall into the hands of his kids or any of the younger guests like Wayne and Tasha's teenagers.

"I wanna sit with Daddy," Marisa announced the moment he lowered himself into one of the lawn chairs. Then she shoved her little sister out of the way.

Poor Willa fell onto the cold ground and instantly started crying.

Owen bent and lifted her onto his lap. "I have two knees," he said, silencing Marisa's objection. "One for each of you."

She crawled into his lap beside her sister. He kept an eye on both Cody and the fire, ensuring a safe distance remained between them at all times. The low circular block wall surrounding the fire pit was no deterrent to a rambunctious five-year-old.

Snaps and pops punctuated the air as greedy flames consumed the kindling and engulfed the logs. When a small spray of sparks erupted into the air, the girls gasped with delight.

Owen allowed Cody to retrieve a log from the stack he'd brought over and deposit it a few feet from the campfire. Molly hadn't asked Owen to take charge of the fire, he'd volunteered. And, like before, he'd had to convince Molly to let him. She resisted being beholden to anyone. Him in particular.

A wedge of golden light appeared on the veranda as the door to the ranch house opened. Molly stepped out, a tray balanced in her hands, and walked the hundred or so feet across the front yard to the fire pit. Owen couldn't look away—she was a lovely sight.

"The fire looks good," she said, placing the tray on the folding table Owen had set up earlier. Like his kids, she was bundled up against the chilly night air. Puffy coat, knit cap, scarf and mittens. Lipstick. Yes, he noticed.

"Can I help?" He started to rise, causing the girls to squeal.

"Thanks. I've got this, and you have your hands full."

More like he had his lap full.

"Whatcha making?" Cody stared inquisitively but didn't venture from behind Owen's chair where he'd been instructed to stay.

"S'mores," Molly said, sending him a smile. "For the guests. They'll be here any second."

The debacle yesterday had made the kids hesitant around Molly. Owen's fault, he'd chastised them soundly. But progress had been made this morning at the stables. That, or his kids had short memories.

Owen was relieved to see Molly wasn't holding a grudge against Marisa. Or him. Then again, had Tasha and Wayne been less understanding, Owen might have been packing his bags this morning rather than helping with the horses.

"I like s'mores," Cody told Molly, hope in his voice.

"Want to help?"

"Can I, Daddy?"

Owen sent Molly a look that silently asked, "Are you sure?" At her nod, he said, "Go ahead, son, but listen to what Miss Molly tells you."

Cody rushed to the table and began grabbing things. "What are these?"

"Cody!" Owen started to rise.

"Marshmallow roasting sticks." Molly plucked the long, sharp metal objects from Cody's hands, much to Cody's disappointment. "You can't have them without your father's permission."

Owen sat back down, expelling a long breath.

"Can I have a marshmallow?" Cody asked.

"Not until everyone gets here." Molly handed him the bag. "But you can open this for me if you want."

Owen expected most of the marshmallows to end up on the ground. When Cody successfully executed the small task, Owen relaxed.

Molly surveyed the table. Apparently satisfied, she announced, "I'll be right back. I need to get the hot chocolate."

Cody ran to Owen and grabbed the chair arm. "Can I go, too, Daddy?"

"I…don't…"

"It's all right," Molly said. "He can carry the paper cups for me."

Cody let out a whoop.

Owen watched their retreating backs and smiled to himself. One small step for Cody and Molly in the right direction, thanks to the power of s'mores and hot chocolate.

Marisa and Willa slumped against him, their stares fixed on the flickering flames. The fire was, indeed, hypnotic, and Owen allowed himself to relax. Before long, Molly and Cody returned. With everything ready to go, she made a final inspection of the area and nodded with satisfaction when she was done.

"Have a seat." Owen reached over and patted the armrest on the lawn chair beside him.

To his delight, she accepted the offer. "Tasha, Wayne and their family should be here any minute."

Their conversation roused the girls who sat up.

"I wanna call Mommy," Marisa complained again.

"Mommy," Willa seconded around the thumb she was sucking.

"They talked to her before dinner," Owen explained to Molly.

"I didn't tell her about feeding the horses." Marisa's voice rose by degrees until it verged on a whine.

"Missing your mom is hard," Molly said compassionately. "They're young, and it's their first time away from her."

Owen had been ready to be annoyed at his kids for attempting to manipulate him with their whining. Molly changed his mind completely.

"Thank you," he said.

"For what?"

She turned those vivid green eyes on him, the color heightened by the firelight. If not for Marisa tugging on his coat collar, he'd have stared at Molly indefinitely.

"Reminding me of what's important. My kids." He removed his phone and dialed Jeanne's number. The moment she answered, he passed the phone to Marisa. "It's Mommy."

A squeal of delight followed and then Marisa launched into a rapid-fire story about the horses, much of it hard to understand. Owen set both girls on the ground in front of him, his eardrums unable to tolerate the strain. By now, Cody had found a stick and was carving shapes in the dirt behind them.

"You've done so much today," Molly said hesitantly, "I hate to ask another favor."

"What is it?"

"Any chance you can help with stringing the Christmas lights before the wedding on Thursday? I was able to get the ones along the veranda railing. I can't reach the eave and have trouble with the staple gun."

Owen envisioned Molly on a ladder, wielding a staple gun. He very much wanted to be part of that picture. "Just let me know when."

"I still need to buy a Christmas tree for the foyer."

"We'll take my truck."

"I wasn't hinting for help, Owen."

"I know you weren't."

"Thanks." She sent him a smile that warmed him more than the campfire. "Grandma insists on making Sweetheart Ranch's first holiday special." Molly laughed. "Who am I kidding? Grandma loves the holidays and always decorates like crazy. The whole family does. It's a tradition."

"My family's more laid back," Owen said. "'Course, since the kids were born, Christmas has centered on them."

"It can't be easy, after your divorce."

"Jeanne and I have tried to make things as normal as possible. Though, this year we'll be celebrating here. In the early morning anyway. She's picking the kids up after breakfast. Not sure how we're going to explain Santa making two stops."

"I think the children will like it here," Molly said softly, her gaze falling on the girls "The ranch will be beautiful. All lit up on the outside and with a big tree in the foyer. And there's several holiday events in town. Craft fairs and the Holly Daze Festival."

"Thanks again." Owen rested his hand on Molly's arm. "You have a knack for saying the right words at the right time."

She stared at him as if seeing him with new eyes. "I don't think anyone's ever told me that before."

"Maybe they didn't get to know you well enough."

"Maybe I didn't let them."

"If you're referring to your former fiancés, they obviously didn't know a good thing when they had it."

"They weren't to blame. I rushed the relationships. I thought I was ready. That being married guaranteed a happy life. I was wrong about that and wrong to rush them. My broken heart was my fault. Both times."

"Is your heart still broken?"

"Only a little," she admitted. "Coming to

Mustang Valley and working for Grandma was the best decision I could have made. I love helping couples realize their dream weddings and honeymoons. It's very satisfying."

Owen shouldn't be relieved that Molly was well on the road to recovery. He wasn't in a position to start dating, and until he found a job, he wouldn't consider himself a decent prospect for any woman.

Yet, he was relieved to learn Molly's heart was mostly healed. She deserved that happy life she wanted.

"I wonder what's keeping Wayne and Tasha?" She glanced over her shoulder, ending her moment with Owen.

"They just got married. Who wants company on their honeymoon?"

"I figured their family would be here at least. They'd sounded excited on the carriage ride this morning."

"Nothing like brisk air and being outdoors to tire a person out." Owen had suffered an energy lull after unharnessing the horses and had practically snoozed through lunch.

"I brought enough s'mores ingredients for an army." Molly looked back at the house. "Nora and Bridget said they'd stop by, too."

Cody jumped up and grabbed the back of

Owen's chair, pulling hard enough to rock him. "I want s'mores."

"You can have one."

"When?"

"When everyone else gets here."

Sulking, he resumed carving in the dirt, stabbing it with his stick rather than drawing shapes.

"Jeanne and her boyfriend are going away on a ski trip," Owen said. "It's upset the kids. She hasn't done this before."

"What about you? Are you upset?"

"Naw." He shook his head.

"You did mention not wanting another man in your children's lives."

"I don't want a man taking my place in their lives. Realistically, I can't prevent one from occupying a place in Jeanne's. Nor would I, as long as he treats her well. Not because I'm jealous," he quickly clarified. "For the kids' sakes. A happy Jeanne is a happy mom. A happy mom makes for a happy Cody, Marisa and Willa."

"I have to quit asking personal questions that are none of my business." Molly looked chagrined.

"I don't mind. I'm an open book. For the most part."

"I envy you." She shifted in her chair. "I'm not good at expressing my feelings."

"You can trust me, Molly. I won't hurt you."

She gaped at him, her eyes wide. "It's not that."

"My mistake. Sometimes people don't talk about themselves because they're afraid of being hurt."

She didn't respond, which in itself was an answer. Molly feared another heartbreak, and Owen would be wise to treat her emotions tenderly.

"Hello," Cody called out.

Wayne, Tasha and their family were strolling down the walkway toward the campfire. Molly jumped from her chair to welcome them and reorganize the already organized table. Tasha complained about doing nothing but eating the past few days when Molly offered s'mores.

An hour was apparently enough to satisfy everyone's campfire fix. Between the hot chocolate and s'mores, Owen doubted he'd be able to get Cody and Marisa to sleep. They were riding a sugar high amplified by the excitement of playing with older kids. Willa, conversely, had nodded off in one of the lawn chairs.

"I'll put out the fire," Owen said when he, Molly and Nora were the only adults left. The flames had long died down, leaving a pile of glowing embers.

"Let me get these three out of your hair." Nora reached for Willa and lifted the limp child.

"I hate to impose."

"No bother. I'll have them bathed and in their pajamas by the time you get back." She beckoned to Cody and Marisa. "Come on, you two."

"She's not taking no for an answer," Molly observed after they'd gone.

"Guilt." Owen knotted the ties on a plastic trash bag. "She still feels bad about losing track of Marisa yesterday. I told her it's fine, but you know Nora."

"She's been extra helpful with me, too."

He looked in the direction of the house. "Will that garden hose reach or should I fill buckets with water to douse the fire?"

"It'll reach."

She had her tray loaded and ready to carry inside when he returned dragging the hose. Adjusting the setting on the spray nozzle, Owen squeezed the handle and expelled a fine mist.

The embers sizzled before extinguishing. Smoke and ash particles rose in a dense cloud, scattering in the breeze.

Molly coughed and waved her hand in front of her face.

Owen was instantly contrite. "Sorry. I should have warned you."

Squinting, she held out a shovel. "I figured you might need this."

"Thanks." He dropped the hose and stirred the

ashes. A second and third dousing with water produced no smoke or ash particles. "I say we're in good shape," he pronounced.

"Let me help you."

She carried the shovel to the side of the house while he rolled up the hose and hung it on the rack.

"Good night, Owen." She started to leave.

He reached for her. "Wait."

"What?"

Placing his hands on her shoulders, he tilted her toward the porch light. "You have some soot on your face."

"Do I?" She dabbed at her cheeks, smearing rather than removing the soot.

"Here. Let me."

He removed a kerchief from his coat pocket and gently wiped her face. While pretending to scrutinize his work, he studied her eyes, which never veered from his.

Molly might have trouble expressing her innermost feelings, but they were clearly telegraphed in the tiny nuances of her expression. What Owen saw made his heart bounce wildly inside his chest. She didn't entirely object to his touch. Even enjoyed it.

He took a leap, not caring about the consequences. "I'm going to kiss you, Molly."

"You are?" she breathed.

"Unless you object."

He waited for her to say she did. When one moment stretched into two, he dipped his head and brushed his lips slowly across hers. The sparks he knew were there waiting to erupt did in a flurry, snapping and popping like the campfire had earlier.

Owen pulled her closer into his embrace, savoring the sweet taste and soft, satiny texture of her mouth. She resisted for a fraction longer before slowly melting against him. He tasted her again. Then a third time. Her hands clutched the fabric of his coat, not in need but invitation. Owen wanted to shout. Instead, he circled her waist with his arms.

For something that should be completely wrong, everything about their kiss was wonderfully right and incredibly perfect. They fit and moved together as if by design. Owen tried to tell her without words how special she and this moment were to him. Her response let him know she understood and reciprocated his feelings.

For the moment. Nothing lasted, unfortunately. At the first tug from Molly, he stopped and rested his forehead against hers. He wasn't yet willing to break all contact. Nor, was she.

"We probably shouldn't have done that."

"No," he agreed. "But I'm glad we did."

"It can't happen again, Owen. You're here for

your children. Distracting you would hardly be fair to them."

She was right, unfortunately.

"It was the smudges on your cheeks. I lost control."

"I think we both lost control." She extracted herself then, reluctantly.

He, in turn, reluctantly released her. "What if things were different, Molly? What then?"

"But they aren't different, and there's no sense tearing ourselves up over a situation we can't change."

She was the first to walk away. Owen had no excuse to stay. He did anyway, until she was inside and safely away from him.

He hadn't been lying when he'd told her he was glad they'd kissed. It was something he'd remember for a long, long time. Perhaps the rest of his life.

SEVERAL DAYS HAD passed without incident. Owen hesitated about patting himself on the back; it was too soon to assume he had everything under control. Kids were kids and unpredictable by definition.

Aw, what the heck. He deserved some kudos and let himself feel good. Things were definitely on the upswing. He and Nora had developed a better system for supervising his rambunctious offspring. And while he wasn't going down in history as the best wedding officiant ever, he was steadily improving. Like the old saying went, practice made perfect. He now boasted two more weddings under his belt. Tonight's service would be his fifth to date.

The bride and groom, a really cute couple in their seventies—they'd dropped by yesterday morning to consult with Molly on some last-minute arrangements—had requested a traditional service with the basic do-you-take vows. Owen was feeling confident enough that he'd only practiced once in front of the mirror before determining he was ready.

"What can I do to help?" he asked, striding into the parlor.

Molly paused and gave him a casual, yet thorough, hat-to-boot inspection. Nothing about it indicated they'd shared a brief yet electrifying kiss the other night after the campfire.

"You look nice."

"Glad you approve." He'd swapped his usual sports jacket for a deep green Western shirt and his leather vest. Molly had requested the wardrobe change. The couple were wearing Christmas colors for their wedding and wanted Owen to match them for the photographs, which would be taken with the Christmas lights and decorated tree in the background.

This was his and Molly's first real conversation since their kiss. Owen wasn't sure if she'd been avoiding him because she regretted what had happened or was afraid the two of them might accidentally repeat their mistake and fall into each other's arms.

"Would you mind helping me take the leaf out of the table?" she asked. "The sliders can sometimes stick."

"Furniture rearranging. My specialty."

She looked pretty, as always. One of Owen's favorite parts of officiating weddings was seeing Molly in a dress as opposed to her jeans. The burgundy-and-gold outfit she wore today looked conservative and professional, like all her other wedding coordinator clothes. Molly would never detract attention from the bride. It nonetheless hinted at her lovely figure when she walked and showed off enough of her gorgeous legs to keep his gaze riveted.

"One, two, three," she said.

They each pulled on their end of the antique table. It was stiff at first and then gave. A little like Molly when Owen had kissed her.

He needed to stop thinking about her and the other night. It wasn't easy when she stood next to him smelling like a bouquet of fresh flowers.

When he took the leaf from her, their fingers brushed, resulting in a small jolt of awareness.

Owen quickly manufactured an excuse to distance himself before all the arguments against them getting involved stopped making sense.

"Where do you want this?" he asked.

"The hall storage closet."

"Incoming!" Bridget called, entering the parlor shortly after Owen returned. She carried a glass vase filled with red tulips in each hand.

He almost groaned with relief, grateful for the distraction. He'd been completely absorbed with staring at the generous expanse of Molly's legs that was revealed as she reached high to smooth and rearrange the drapes.

Molly lowered her arms and faced her sister. "Aren't those pretty."

She didn't appear at all stressed by Owen's presence or unable to tear her gaze away from him. So much for mutual attraction.

"I think the bride will like them. They're close in color to her dress." Bridget set the vases on the lace-covered buffet.

Only then did Owen notice the water containing the flowers was a pale pink. That was different.

Bridget caught him looking and said, "It's food dye."

A clever trick. "I like it."

With more than an hour before the service, they were right on schedule. The bride and groom and their attendants would be arriving soon. Owen wouldn't see much of Molly after that.

"Do we have enough ice?" she asked Bridget.

"The chest is full and ready for the champagne bottles."

"And the music?"

"That's your department."

"Right." She rubbed her forehead in concentration. "The bride and groom requested 'It's Your Love' by Tim McGraw. I'd better make sure I have the right song downloaded." She spun and headed for the chapel.

"Bridget, you in here?" Nora poked her head around the corner.

"Yeah, what's up?"

She didn't come into the room. Owen knew why. Cody, Marisa and Willa were in the kitchen, waiting for Nora to take them on a playdate with her grandkids. It was the latest move in their plan to prevent trouble. Nora was probably making a human shield of herself lest someone attempt to push by and enter the forbidden zone.

"Just wanted to tell you," Nora said, "the bride and groom phoned. They requested eggs Benedict for breakfast tomorrow and to deliver it by eight as their carriage ride is scheduled for ten."

"Gotcha." Bridget started across the room toward Nora. "I wonder if I have enough unsalted butter." When she met up with Nora at the door-way, she stopped. "Hey, you three, what are you doing here?"

Uh-oh. Owen's kids must be right behind Nora, not in the kitchen. This could be trouble.

"Can I see the flowers?" he heard Marisa ask.

"Maybe later," Nora said. "After we get home."

And the bride and groom were long gone.

"Please?"

"One quick look won't hurt." Bridget took hold of Marisa's hand and drew her into the parlor.

Owen tried to stop them. "I don't think this is a good idea."

"She'll behave." Bridget smiled winningly down at Marisa. "Won't you, sweetie?"

Marisa nodded, her small face aglow.

"I promised Molly not to let the kids near any weddings or receptions."

"Don't worry, Owen. I'll handle my sister."

"Marisa can wait," he insisted, intent on avoid-ing a tug-of-war with Bridget over his daughter but equally determined to stand his ground.

At that instant, Molly swept into the room, only to come to a halt. "Oh. The children are here." She looked at Owen, brows raised in ques-tion.

"We're leaving right now."

"Marisa wanted to see the flowers," Bridget said and put an arm on the little girl's shoulder, drawing her closer to the buffet.

Whether from hearing her name, or sensing she was somewhere she shouldn't be, or startled by Bridget's touch, Marisa jumped back—right into the buffet. The impact was forceful enough to topple the flower vases. Bridget gasped and lunged, catching the closest one. The second one slipped through her fingers.

For a moment, time stood still. Then, the vase landed on its side and dumped half its contents before rolling off the buffet. Hitting the floor, it shattered into a dozen pieces. In the time it took to blink, pale red water saturated the entire lace runner.

"No!" Molly hurled herself at the buffet.

Marisa let out a cry and ran from Bridget. Owen went after her, but Nora grabbed the girl as she tried to squeeze past. By then, Marisa was nearly hysterical.

Owen reached the doorway. "Cody, go to the kitchen. Now." He tried to pick up Marisa, but she dodged his grasp. "I'm not mad at you, peanut."

No, he was furious with himself. He should have removed Marisa from the room when he had the chance.

"I'll take her," Nora said, her voice contrite. She probably blamed herself, too.

"*I* will. You help clean up."

Bridget had already made a run to the hall closet for towels. Nora went after her. Owen grabbed Willa. Tucking her under his arm, he went after Marisa. He knew he should participate in the cleanup, but better he got the kids as far away as possible before something else went wrong.

He didn't admit a few minutes apart might do both him and Molly good before they faced each other. Not that Owen would concoct an excuse. It was simply that he subscribed to cooler heads prevailing, a lesson he'd learned young from his father.

Finding Marisa on the floor behind the kitchen table, crouching low to make herself small, he set Willa down.

"Come on out, peanut. Don't be afraid."

"I'm s-s-sorry." Tears clogged Marisa's voice and filled her eyes.

"It was an accident. No one's mad at you."

"I wanna go home."

"You will. Just not today. But you can call your mom if you want."

That did the trick, and Marisa emerged. He sat at the table with her in his lap. Cody had been put in charge of watching Willa and for once he complied. In the background, they could hear Molly, Bridget and Nora scrambling to restore order to the parlor. Bridget whizzed past them on her way to the laundry, the lace runner wadded into a ball.

When Nora entered the kitchen a few minutes later, Marisa's tears had dried and she was considerably calmer. Owen was calmer, too. Marginally.

"I told her she could call her mom," he said when the older woman corralled the kids to take them to their playdate with her grandchildren. "Can she use your phone?"

"Of course." Nora had Jeanne's number programed in her phone for emergencies. "We'll be back by eight."

"Bye, guys." Owen kissed the girls and pulled Cody against him before ruffling his hair. "Be good."

They hadn't quite made it out the back door when Molly entered the kitchen, her features unreadable. "Wait a minute," she called.

Owen assumed she wanted to speak to Nora. Perhaps chastise her for bringing the kids into the house so soon before a wedding started. He was wrong. Molly approached Marisa instead. When she got there, she went down on her knees.

"Don't be upset, okay? Promise me. I'm not angry at you. It was an accident."

Marisa nodded solemnly.

"Okay." Molly reached up and patted Marisa's hair. Awkwardly at first, then with more confidence.

Marisa continued to stare at the floor. Owen, however, couldn't take his eyes off Molly. She had every right to be furious. Only here she was being kind.

Unless she was saving her anger for him. There was that distinct possibility.

"I want you to have fun with Miss Nora's grandchildren." Molly stood. "You can come by tomorrow if you want to see the flowers."

Nora shuffled the kids through the door. Owen got up from the table and waited for Molly to go first.

"The runner was a wedding gift to Grandma Em from her cousin. Her first wedding. To my grandfather."

"I'll replace it."

"Things like that can't be replaced."

"All right, then. I can have our stuff packed and be out of the cabin by tonight."

"Owen." She sighed. "I didn't tell you about the runner because I want you to leave. Bridget's the one who brought Marisa over to see the flowers. And believe you me, she and I are going to have a talk."

"I don't want to be the cause of friction between you two."

"You're not. I love her to pieces, but we fight. The O'Malley temper, I suppose." She squared her shoulders. "I told you about the runner because, like everything at Sweetheart Ranch, it's important to me. And to my family."

"I understand."

"I get that I can be demanding at times, and I suppose a little stern."

"Not always." He was thinking of how she'd been with Marisa a few minutes ago.

"Grandma is counting on me to cover for her while she's gone. That's a lot of responsibility. I can't slack off for even a minute."

"You don't have to explain yourself."

"I'm not. I'm just clarifying things in my head. Reestablishing my priorities. And speaking of priorities…" She left without finishing her thought.

She didn't need to. Owen filled in the blanks. She'd been reminding him in a roundabout way the many reasons they needed to maintain a strictly platonic relationship.

Bridget returned from the laundry room on the heels of Molly's exit. "Is the coast clear?"

"For the moment," Owen said.

"Don't worry. Her bark is worse than her bite."

"She went easy on me. More than I deserved."

Bridget gave him a knowing smile. "That's because she likes you, and she's worried about liking you too much. She has this notion that romance doesn't mix well with work."

"It doesn't always. My job was terrible for my marriage."

"Yeah, well, being dumped twice and then her last three jobs not working out did a real number on Molly. She's determined to prove herself no matter what."

Three jobs? That could excuse a large amount of overzealousness.

"The ranch's success is her main focus," Bridget went on. "Which it should be. Certainly while Grandma's gone. And, let's be honest, you've got a lot on your plate, too. I'm all for the two of you dating but now maybe isn't the best time."

"Who says I'm interested in dating?"

"You don't have to say it. I see the way you look at her and hear how your voice gets all soft and sugary when you talk to her. What I'd give to have a man talk to me like that."

Sugary? Was he that obvious? Apparently so.

"She looks at you, too," Bridget continued.

Owen recalled her words from a few minutes earlier about Molly liking him too much. "I don't think there's anything to worry about after today."

"Whether there is or isn't, my main concern is Molly. I don't want to see her hurt again. Not this soon." Bridget wiped her hands together. "If you'll excuse me, I have wine buckets to fill with ice."

Owen made his way to the chapel on the other side of the house, wishing Molly's sister wasn't so right about everything.

CHAPTER EIGHT

MOLLY STOOD AT the registration counter, reviewing her schedule for the next several months and making follow-up phone calls. February was traditionally a busy month for weddings, and it would be no different at Sweetheart Ranch. Also, apparently, would Christmas Eve and New Year's Eve. They had twenty-three ceremonies booked between now and Valentine's Day and potentially several more based on upcoming appointments.

Most of those weddings had been booked by Grandma Em before she eloped with Homer, but a few tentative couples had called Molly to confirm after seeing the TV news segment or visiting the open house.

She had had appointments this week with four brand-new couples. Hopefully, she'd close those sales on her own and without her grandmother's help. If she didn't hear back from them by tomorrow, she'd follow up with phone calls.

For someone determined to prove herself, Molly wasn't making much progress. Then again, excelling at sales wasn't her superpower. Unlike her grandmother. Or Owen. Everyone seemed to love him, even if he stumbled over the occasional word or his daughter caused a scene.

If she could only swallow the huge chunk of pride lodged in her throat, she'd ask for his help. Molly wasn't quite ready for that.

Three more weeks to go and then life would return to normal—normal being Grandma Em back home, and Molly no longer filling in as wedding coordinator. It would also mean Owen and his children being gone.

She should be glad. After their kiss—their amazing kiss that had left her far too eager for more and contemplating what-ifs rather than better-nots—they'd both benefit from some distance.

But a part of her liked him being around. He'd picked up a fair amount of slack and was handy.

Yeah, right, the other part of her argued. *You enjoy seeing him every day.*

A small notification box suddenly appeared in the lower right corner of her computer screen. Molly read the message and bit her lip. Then, she read it again.

Tasha had left a review on the ranch's social media page. It wasn't bad. Neither was it good. She'd written, Despite several problems, our stay wound up to be everything we'd hoped for. Whatever else was there flew past Molly. She saw only "several problems."

"Hi, Molly. You have a minute?"

Startled by the crusty male voice, she glanced up to see Big Jim approaching the registration desk and immediately wondered why he was here. It was nine thirty, and he was due to take their latest wedding couple on a carriage ride at ten. He should be harnessing the horses. Plus, he rarely used the front entrance.

"What's up?" Composing herself, she rolled back her chair and stood.

"I hate to spring this on you at the last minute, but I'm turning in my notice. Today is going to have to be my last day."

"Big Jim, no!" The mediocre review from Tasha was instantly forgotten.

"It's my wife. I wound up taking her to the emergency room last night."

"My God. Is she all right?"

"For now, yes." He momentarily struggled. "She had a cardiac episode. The doctor at the hospital recommended she see a specialist and have some tests done. Seems the virus we thought she had wasn't a virus at all but fluid around her heart. I won't lie, she's scared."

Concern filled Molly. "I understand, Jim. But I hate to see you go."

"Me, too. The thing is, I need a month or

more. Too long for me to leave you and your sister hanging. Better I just resign. That way, you can replace me, and I'll be free to look after my wife. I'm past retiring age as it is."

"I won't accept your resignation. We'll consider it a leave of absence. I'm sure we can find a replacement for you." She'd call Powell Ranch next door. They might have someone qualified looking for part-time work.

"Thank you." Big Jim shifted from one foot to the other. "I think Owen can handle the carriage rides. He already takes care of Amos and Moses on my days off."

"Something the matter with Amos and Moses?" Bridget asked, rounding the corner into the foyer.

"Big Jim needs some time off," Molly said and explained about his wife.

Bridget placed her hand on the older man's shoulder. "Please give her our best. And don't you worry about a thing."

"I appreciate your understanding more than you know." He lifted his hat in a farewell gesture. "I'd best get going. The bride and groom will be wanting their ride."

Molly and Bridget stared after him, exchanging concerned glances. Big Jim and his wife were two of their favorite people.

"I know you're reluctant to give Owen any

additional responsibility." Bridget faced Molly. "But what choice do we have other than letting him take over the carriage rides?"

"We should call Grandma."

"We don't need to bother her with this."

"She's the owner of the ranch and in charge of personnel," Molly said firmly. "She should be informed."

"Says the person who just gave Big Jim a leave of absence without consulting Grandma."

"Not the same thing." Molly tapped some papers into a neat stack.

"Owen's already here. He's experienced and available and we both know Grandma will say yes."

"We shouldn't assume. Owen's children will need watching while he gives the rides, and Grandma needs to approve the added babysitting expense. And who knows if Nora's free. She only agreed to work part-time."

"Point made."

Molly lifted the desk phone receiver, pausing before dialing. "We got a mediocre review this morning on our social media page. From Tasha, the bride Owen's daughter pushed."

"How mediocre?"

"A five, on a scale of one to ten."

"You're not planning on telling that to Grandma."

"It could affect her decision about Owen," Molly countered.

"Don't you utter one peep. We are not ruining Grandma's honeymoon. And anyway, the situation with his kids is taken care of."

Molly punched in their grandmother's number.

"Put her on speaker."

She huffed but did as her sister requested. A moment later, Grandma Em's trilling voice filled the foyer.

"Hello!"

"Hi, Grandma. It's Molly and Bridget."

"The two of you. How nice. We're just getting ready for a big brunch with Olive and her husband."

Olive. She must be referring to Homer's daughter.

"We can talk to you later, Grandma," Bridget said.

"No, no. I have a few minutes until we leave for the restaurant. What's going on?"

Molly gave her grandmother the lowdown, starting with Big Jim needing time off because of his wife's health issues and ending with Owen potentially taking over. "Though, we haven't asked him yet."

"What are you waiting for? Get to asking."

"We still have to confirm with Nora. She may not be available to babysit."

"If she's not free, see if her granddaughter Tracee is. Those carriage rides are our signature amenity. We can't cancel them."

"There's another problem." At Bridget's jab to her side, Molly rephrased what she'd been about to say. "Owen's children can be a handful."

"Most small children are." Grandma Em's tone didn't convey any concern.

"They…interfered with one of our weddings."

"It's no big deal," Bridget insisted. "Molly did a fantastic job smoothing things over. The bride and groom were delighted with the ceremony and they loved Owen. He has a real down-home way of delivering the services."

"I knew I was right in placing my trust in you two," Grandma Em said.

Nothing else could have silenced Molly better.

"I get that young children aren't always easy to have in the house, but Owen gave up a month of his life to cover for Homer. We owe him."

"And we one-hundred-percent agree with you," Bridget said.

Molly shut up. People were making noise in the background, and her grandmother was becoming distracted.

"Have fun at your brunch," Bridget said. "Don't give us a second thought."

Grandma wasn't quite finished. "Molly, have you booked any weddings?"

"I had four appointments this week," she answered, wishing she had better news to report. "They're supposed to let us know by tomorrow. And we've been getting at least ten phone calls every day since the open house from people asking for information." If only she could turn more of those inquiries into appointments.

"You've been busy," Grandma Em said.

"I also came up with a cross-promotion campaign—"

"Can't wait to hear all about it." She spoke to someone there. Probably Homer. "I've got to run, sweeties. Talk to you soon. And Owen will be fine. Everything will be fine. You'll see."

Her optimism was that of someone thrilled with life who wanted everyone else to be thrilled along with them. Molly kept her voice bright and cheery when saying goodbye.

"You want to talk to Owen or should I?" Bridget asked before Molly had hung up.

"About taking over for Big Jim? I will."

Molly wound her way through the house and out the kitchen door, her destination Owen's cabin. She gave the other cabins no more than a cursory glance, unconcerned about the occupants. Nora was seeing to all their needs, and

Molly had to admit their grandmother's best friend did have a knack for the job.

At the door to his cabin, Molly squared her shoulders and knocked. When he didn't immediately answer, she knocked again. The door finally swung wide, and she was greeted by Cody.

"Hello there." She smiled fondly at him. "How are you?"

"We're playing hide-and-seek," he announced.

"What fun!"

The next instant, Owen appeared behind his son and placed a restraining hand on him. "What did I tell you about not opening the door to strangers?"

Cody twisted sideways to peer up at his dad. "Miss Molly isn't a stranger."

"But we didn't know that until you opened the door. You're supposed to wait for me."

"You were hiding."

Molly tried really hard not to find the exchange amusing, but they were awfully cute.

"Am I interrupting?" she asked.

"No. Come on in."

Molly stepped inside. At the same time, she noticed Marisa's head peeking out from behind the chair. Just as quick, the little girl ducked down. Molly went along, pretending not to see her.

"Where's Willa?"

"Under a blanket in her crib." Owen tipped his head toward the bedroom. "I can't believe she hasn't started crying yet."

Cody pulled on Owen's arm. "Come on, Daddy. You're supposed to be hiding."

"In a minute, son."

"I won't keep you." Molly met Owen's inquisitive gaze. "Big Jim's taking a leave of absence. His wife had a cardiac episode and needs some tests done."

"I'm sorry to hear that. Is she all right?"

Molly conveyed the details. "We were, um, hoping you could fill in for him with the carriage rides."

"I was going to offer."

"Thanks." She turned toward the door. "We have four weddings this week. Thursday, Friday and two on Saturday. The carriage rides are the following mornings."

Owen nodded thoughtfully. "I'd better plan on at least one practice run before then. Possibly two."

"Good idea." The doorknob was almost within reach.

"When are you free?"

"Free?" She paused.

"I'm going to need help. A navigator and someone to supervise the kids."

"Can't Nora watch them?"

"She's busy. Helping with a Christmas pageant at church. Her granddaughters are playing angels."

"Right." Molly had forgotten.

"Guess that leaves you."

She didn't really like his smile. It was much too satisfied.

The problem was, she had little choice. Bridget would be cooking. "What about tomorrow morning? My afternoon is fully booked."

"Nine o'clock?"

"See you then."

Molly chose that moment to leave, her emotions at odds as they often were around Owen. If his cute antics with his children weren't enough to dent her armor, he'd agreed to replace Big Jim without the slightest hesitation.

It was enough to make her look forward to tomorrow. Almost.

OWEN STUDIED THE CARRIAGE. His first solo attempt at harnessing Amos and Moses had gone without a hitch, no pun intended, and he mentally patted himself on the back. Muscle memory had kicked in, and the myriad straps, reins, bands, tugs, buckles and chains magically fell into their proper place. Grandpa would be proud.

Amos bobbed his head as if in approval. Moses

pawed the ground, his way of telling Owen to quit dawdling already and get a move on.

Owen's gaze traveled from the carriage to the kids, who'd been instructed not to cross an invisible line during the harnessing process. They were currently investigating a hole at the base of a Palo Verde tree. He hoped the hole wasn't home to anything poisonous, like a rattlesnake or a scorpion.

"Stay away from that tree," he hollered, wishing he didn't always feel the need to raise his voice with his kids.

"We're digging for buried bones," Cody said.

Owen really needed to pay more attention to what they watched on TV. "Hurry up. Time's a wastin'."

While they dawdled, Owen's mind returned to the original problem he'd been contemplating—how to manage the trip from the stables to the ranch house. Cody, Marisa and Willa couldn't be trusted on their own in the back of the carriage, even for such a short distance. One of them was bound to fall out. Letting them ride up front with him wasn't an option, either. Carriages didn't come with seat belts, and he needed both hands to drive the horses.

He should have told Molly to meet him here when they'd agreed to this adventure. Okay, when he'd *coerced* her. She was probably expecting him to drive the carriage to the house and pick her up there, like he would the bride and groom.

Calling her was the obvious solution, and he reached into his coat pocket for his phone.

"Daddy, can I be the princess?" Marisa hollered. They'd moved from the tree and were now bunched together at the invisible line waiting on him.

"Sure. What kind of princess?" Since becoming a full-time dad to his kids, he'd learned a lot about animated princesses.

"Cinderella. She has a carriage."

Owen imagined Marisa being annoyed at Molly for sitting in the carriage with her and there being another shoving incident. He couldn't live that down a second time.

"Okay, but you have to let someone else be the princess if they want a turn." They'd been working on sharing this past week with moderate success.

"I'm first," Marisa insisted. "It's my game."

Another lesson. Whoever came up with the game got to be first. He thought Molly would go along with that.

As if his thoughts had conjured her, she appeared from the clubhouse courtyard, opening the gate and then closing it behind her. Owen's hand moved in slow motion, returning the phone to his pocket. He missed the opening, too intent on watching her stroll toward them to pay attention.

Her demeanor was unhurried. Because she dreaded the carriage ride with him or was relaxing for once?

Either way, he enjoyed the leisurely swing of her arms and the enticing sway of her hips. She wore a straw hat, an old college sweatshirt and a fanny pack around her waist. Did people still own those? She was probably thinking ahead— there was a good chance she'd be called on to wrangle his rowdy bunch.

"Hi," he said when she neared. "I was just about to call you."

"I saw you getting ready and figured you could use a hand."

"Saw me?"

There wasn't a clear view of the stables from the ranch house. He pictured her stealing a peek at him from behind the clubhouse and grinned. In response, she averted her gaze and readjusted her hat.

Was she recalling their kiss from the other night? He certainly had. Every few minutes. He need only close his eyes and concentrate to taste again the delightful flavor of her lips or feel her going soft in his arms.

She'd been adamant about their not being a

repeat performance. Owen would respect her wishes, hard as it was for him. But if she gave him the slightest indication she'd changed her mind, he was all in.

"What I want to know," he asked, "is when did harnessing two horses become easier than managing three kids?"

"No offence, but Amos and Moses might be better trained."

A joke? He got his answer when her lovely mouth tipped up into a smile. Owen was captivated. No, he was smitten. It had been a while, he realized.

"Did you have a chance to eat breakfast?" She rummaged through her fanny pack and withdrew a pair of sunglasses. "There are plenty of leftover croissants in the kitchen."

Owen had to admit croissants sounded a whole lot better than what he and the kids had eaten. "Tempting, but we had toaster pastries."

"Yum."

Another joke? She was in rare form this morning.

"Yeah. Tell me about it." He turned toward the kids. "Hurry up, you three. The train's loading."

"You said we were riding in the carriage," Marisa complained, scuffing her feet as she walked.

Cody ran ahead. "I want to go on a train!"

"It's a saying." Owen grabbed his son before he spooked the horses. "Where's Willa?"

"I'll get her." Molly fetched his youngest and lifted her onto a hip.

Willa instantly reached for Molly's hat and tugged on the brim. "Pretty!"

The hat, no, Owen thought, but Molly, yes.

"Did you put sunscreen on the children?" she asked, scrutinizing Willa's face.

"No. Should I? It's winter. And chilly."

"The sun's out, and they have sensitive skin." Molly removed a tube from her fanny pack. Owen was curious what else she had stashed in there. "They can use mine."

Their mother had packed sunscreen; Owen recalled seeing the bottle. But he hadn't considered using it. How else was he failing as a father? And why did Molly, who had no children, remember it? Were women naturally born with a parenting instinct that men lacked?

She applied sunscreen to Willa first, smearing a liberal amount on the little girl's face and then her hands. When instructed, Cody and Marisa lined up for their turn, each of them squirming and grimacing. Molly wasn't deterred, and Owen was impressed. She clearly had a knack with kids.

"Let me get in first and turn the carriage

around," he said. "Get the horses heading in the right direction."

Amos and Moses behaved like champs, executing the half turn with proficiency equal to Owen's grandfather's team. He reminded himself that he really should take the pair out on the trails for a leisurely ride *and* invite Molly. Strictly to exercise the horses.

Uh-huh.

With a loud "Whoa," he reined the team to a stop. Though they jerked on their bits, they stood in place while Molly loaded the kids into the carriage and climbed in after them.

"I'm the princess," Marisa announced.

"Then you sit here." Molly patted the seat across from her that faced backward.

Cody wasn't happy to be stuck with the girls. "Can I ride with you, Daddy?"

"In a little while. If you behave." Owen thought about how nice it would be to have Molly seated beside him. Perhaps another day.

With Cody on Molly's right, Willa in her lap and Marisa waving in her best princess imitation to an imaginary crowd, Owen jiggled the reins and clucked to the horses. The next instant, they were off.

He didn't have to work too hard. Amos and Moses knew their job. Even before he had a chance to turn them in the right direction, they headed for the ranch house, their hooves executing a lively clip-clop as they trotted briskly on the dirt road.

The front door to the house opened, and Bridget emerged. "Looking mighty good," she hollered and waved.

"You want to come along?" Molly asked.

"I wouldn't dream of intruding."

Did her sister suspect Owen and Molly had kissed? Owen recalled Bridget's warning about Molly carrying a heavy load. She may not approve.

"Be back soon." He clucked again to the horses, and off they went. The next moment, they passed through the ranch's main gate.

"We can drive on the road," Molly said from behind him. "Vehicles are required to yield to horses."

Owen nodded. He'd learned a lot about Mustang Valley in the last week and a half. The town was in some ways straight out of the Old West. Horses and riders on the streets were a regular occurrence. Many buildings, including the Cowboy Up Café, boasted hitching rails along the sides that were actively used. In the center of town was a park with a designated horse path and public riding arena. A twenty-miles-per-hour speed limit was strictly enforced throughout town, including in residential areas.

Owen liked the ambiance of the town and had from the first moment he'd arrived. Here was a place he could see himself settling down and raising his kids. Though a little farther away from Jeanne's place than he wanted, the distance was doable. Especially if he found a job somewhere between Jeanne's and Mustang Valley.

Living in the same town as Molly would be a perk, too. He glanced over his shoulder and was glad to see his brood behaving.

Molly noticed. "How's it going?"

"Good. These boys are pros."

Amos and Moses had expended their excess energy in the first few minutes by moving at a brisk trot. They'd since slowed their pace to a comfortable walk. Ears pricked forward, heads down and tails swishing, they plodded along, requiring very little guidance from Owen.

"Turn left on Saguaro Lane. It's the first road past the gas station and will lead us to the park. We can go through town but with passengers it's better to avoid as much traffic as possible."

"Will do."

"Let's circle the park on the horse path and then make a bigger circle around town. There's a really nice view of the mountains on one side and the valley on the other. The trip should last about an hour, give or take. I can draw you a map if you want for the next time."

"I think I've got it."

"Daddy, can I ride with you now?" Cody asked.

"Not yet. When we get to the park."

At the intersection of Main and Saguaro, Owen pulled the horses to a stop and waited for a pickup truck to pass. The driver honked a neighborly hello, prompting the kids and Molly to wave.

By now, Willa was cuddled adorably against Molly. Even Cody participated in the chatter and Molly's game of pointing out different things of interest like the snowman family at the entrance to the park and the giant candy canes stuck in the ground near the playground. The whole town seemed to be getting into the holiday spirit. Several houses and yards were already decorated and Christmas music played from outdoor speakers.

As the ride continued, Owen became increasingly intrigued by this different version of Molly. Apparently, the secret to freeing her easygoing side was getting her away from Sweetheart Ranch.

"What are you looking at?" she asked.

He swallowed a groan. Busted again. "Nothing."

"Tell me."

"A very beautiful lady," he finally admitted.

She dismissed him with a head shake.

Except Owen wasn't put off that easily. Molly had far more layers than she allowed people to see. Interesting, fascinating layers. These quick little glimpses only made him that much more curious to discover the next one.

The rest of the carriage ride went smoothly. Owen couldn't recall when all three kids had behaved for a full hour. As they were leaving the park, however, Cody grew restless. Stopping for a moment and letting him sit up front with Owen nipped that problem in the bud. Shortly after that, Willa fell asleep, and Marisa was close to joining her.

"Stop in front of the cabin," Molly instructed. "I'll get Willa and Marisa settled while you un-harness. Cody can stay with you."

"Good idea." He'd have probably left the girls to nap on the carriage seats.

Guests from cabin three stepped out onto their porch to have a look as the carriage passed. They'd be checking out by Wednesday morning along with several others, in time for the next round of weddings.

At his cabin, Molly climbed down first, Willa clinging to her neck. Marisa followed. Halfway up the walkway, she reached for Molly's hand, and Owen allowed himself a moment's pleasure.

Without his sisters to distract him, Cody was

a help rather than a hindrance. Old enough and big enough to carry some of the equipment, he happily assisted Owen with the unharnessing. He briefly wondered if his son would take after him and make rodeo his career or be the world's next superhero, Cody's latest obsession. Marisa had her heart set on becoming a princess. Owen saw her as a future rodeo queen. Little Willa was too young for choosing a future career, but Owen was sure whatever she did, she'd be the one in charge.

Inside the cabin, Molly sat on the couch with Marisa's head in her lap and the TV on low. She placed a finger to her lips and said in a whisper, "She's asleep. Willa's in the crib."

After settling Cody on the floor in front of the TV, a juice box in his hand, Owen walked Molly outside.

"Thanks for your help today," he said. "Couldn't have managed without you."

"Just returning the favor."

He reached up and brushed a loose hair from her face, marveling at the strawberry blond color. All the feelings he'd been having about her during the drive merged together, and he lowered his head.

"Didn't we agree kissing was a bad idea?"

Owen didn't trust himself to stop, but he somehow did. "I've been reconsidering."

Her eyes searched his. The next instant, allure replaced resistance. "I don't generally go around kissing employees."

"Make an exception."

"Just this once." Her breath hitched.

He gently covered her lips with his. She tasted as sweet as he remembered and felt just as soft. When she leaned into him, Owen wrapped his arms around her and let the rest of the world disappear until only the two of them remained.

She could do that to him, take him to a place where nothing mattered but her and him. Where problems and obstacles didn't exist. Where a future was possible.

He murmured her name, the letters etching on the surface of his heart. He almost asked her then to stay with him, like this, forever.

Too soon, unfortunately, reality returned, and Molly ended the kiss. He reluctantly released her, keeping hold of her hand.

"You confuse me, Owen Caufield," she said.

"How so?"

"Sometimes, you make me so mad I could scream. Other times, you…"

"Tell me more about the *other* times."

"I think I could like you."

"And here I was convinced you already did."

"No matter how much we may want it, there's a lot to overcome."

"Let's focus on the positive," he said.

"I wish it were that easy." She stepped away from him, taking her hands with her. "Are your children ready for another woman in their lives?"

"They do all right with Jeanne's boyfriend."

"Do they or is that what she tells you?"

Owen thought a moment. How did his kids feel? He should probably ask them when the right moment arose.

"To be honest," Molly continued, "I'm not entirely sure I'm ready to be part of their lives. Don't get me wrong, the children are great. They're also a lot of responsibility. You have joint custody, and if things were to become serious between us, well, I'd have to share some of that responsibility. I do want children. Someday when I'm ready. What if I'm not there yet? What if I disappoint them? Disappoint you? What if I fail?"

"I hadn't considered that," Owen admitted.

"I think we should. I certainly should."

She hadn't mentioned his lack of employment. She didn't have to, it weighed plenty heavy on Owen. At the moment, he didn't have much to offer her. That needed to change before they went any further.

"Fair enough, Molly O'Malley." His mimicking her use of his full name earned him a smile that, for him, pushed all doubts momentarily aside. "But be warned, I'm not giving up yet."

Starting today, he'd ratchet up his job hunting and call that head hunter a friend had told him about.

"I'd better run," Molly said. "Tidy up before my afternoon appointment. One of the couples I met with before is coming back."

Owen remained on the cabin porch as she walked to the clubhouse. Her protests weren't without merit. But Owen was hoping to help her see that the obstacles facing them weren't insurmountable when both people were determined.

Opening the cabin door, he was met with pandemonium. During the five minutes he and Molly had stood outside, Willa had awakened and was wailing from her crib in the bedroom. Marisa had Cody in a choke hold on the floor and was attempting to pry one of her pony toys from his clutches.

"What's going on here?" Owen demanded, again in a too-loud voice.

Cody and Marisa broke apart. "I wanna go home," they cried simultaneously and loud enough to drown out Willa.

So much for Owen thinking the rest of their stay at Sweetheart Ranch would be smooth sailing.

CHAPTER NINE

FROM WHAT OWEN was able to piece together—translating sobbing kid-speak required an expert—Cody had jumped on the couch, disturbing Marisa. Her cries, in turn, had wakened Willa. After that, pandemonium had erupted.

"I want Mommy," Marisa whined.

Willa added a whimper for good measure.

"When are we going home?" Cody asked, kicking at a spot on the carpet.

Owen understood they missed their mother. Busy with the ski trip, Jeanne had been calling less often and conversations with the kids were significantly shorter in duration. They'd responded to their mother's lack of availability by acting out. Spending time with Molly this morning may have filled the void by a small amount but had also made the kids miss their mother all the more.

Time to take control. Owen made a snap decision. He was mostly free for the rest of the day, other than feeding the horses and cleaning their stalls before dinner. A trip to town seemed in order. He'd noticed both a public library and a playground in the park during the carriage ride. With luck, he could tire them out and chase a few job leads on his laptop while they slept.

A quick lunch of peanut butter and jelly sandwiches and bananas helped settle the kids. By then, they were ready to go.

Evidently the kids had never been in a bank before. When Owen stopped there first to arrange a transfer of funds, they gawked in amazement as if entering a magical city. The effect was heightened by a twelve-foot Christmas tree in the lobby. Best of all, the teller gave them mini candy canes.

Because Owen didn't live in Mustang Valley, the librarian told him he couldn't check out any books. But then he mentioned working temporarily at Sweetheart Ranch, and she called Molly who allowed him to check out books and movies on her card. Owen thought that probably wouldn't happen in a big city.

Choosing just ten books and movies was a time-consuming process. Marisa didn't want Willa to have any picture books, those were for babies. Cody was less interested in reading and more interested in the DVD collection. He dawdled over choosing a book when Owen insisted he pick at least one or they weren't getting any movies.

"How about we stop at the feed store?" he announced as they left the library, carting their books and DVDs. He didn't really need anything, he just liked feed stores. They were reminders of both his former rodeo career and his years at Waverly Equine Products.

"Can we sit on the big plastic horse?" Cody asked.

"We'll see."

The sign warning Do Not Sit on the Horse elicited a round of moans. It was a poor substitute, but Owen convinced the kids to stand in front of the horse for pictures. This one wore an evergreen wreath around its neck and red bow on its tail. Through the front window framed with lights Owen could see a decorated Christmas tree. The ornaments were all horses or related to horses, like mini red barns and sleighs with runners.

"Who wants to help me send this picture to Grandma?" he asked.

"Me, me," they all cried.

Owen sent three pictures to his mother, letting each kid press the send button.

Inside the store, he was welcomed by smells and sights and sounds as familiar to him as his favorite pair of jeans. The rich, pungent aroma of leather goods and oils. Saddles and bridles for sale—the former sitting on stands and the latter hanging from racks. The customers' and proprietor's small talk about the weather or the latest local happenings.

Owen let his gaze wander. Unlike many similar establishments, this store sold considerably more than livestock and pet products. The entire left side of the store held Western apparel and accessories while every piece of horse equipment imaginable was displayed on the other side. Owen felt right at home.

"Look, kittens!" Marisa gasped with delight and charged ahead.

Kittens?

"I want to see the kittens." Cody took off after her, Willa bringing up the rear.

Owen caught up to them just as all three kids were reaching into a box on the floor where five mewing balls of fluff frolicked. Beside the box sat a girl of about twelve. Immediately pegging Owen as the one in charge, she directed her sales pitch to him.

"Do you want a kitten, mister? They're only ten dollars each. Two for fifteen."

What a deal.

The girl handed a kitten to Marisa. Owen gave her credit. Placing the item in the customer's hands was half the battle in sales.

"Can we have one?" Marisa begged. "Please,

Daddy." She was practically crushing the poor little thing.

"I don't know. They look young."

"Eight weeks old," the girl informed them. "Already weaned and litter box trained."

"What's weaned?" Cody asked.

"I'll tell you later," Owen mumbled. *Much later.*

Cody then issued his standard we'll-be-good promise.

"You'd have to ask your mother," Owen said. She'd be the one keeping the kitten when the kids left Sweetheart Ranch on Christmas morning.

Marisa pouted. "She's busy."

Was that the excuse Jeanne had given the kids for being less available? Owen wasn't complaining. She deserved a break. She'd been the primary caregiver for the last several years. Her unavailability was also prompting the kids to rely more on him, which was his goal in coming to Mustang Valley.

"I don't think Miss Molly will let us keep a kitten," he said, trying a different approach. "Remember what she told you? No pets at the ranch other than service animals."

"It can be a service animal," Cody insisted.

"Good try, son."

"We'll feed it and pet it and comb it," Marisa

chimed in. She held an orange-striped kitten that adorably batted the string on her jacket hood.

"You could give us the kitten for Christmas," Cody suggested.

"We won't fight anymore, Daddy." Marisa's sweet expression could melt polar ice caps.

He was intent on resisting only to reconsider. Perhaps he could turn this into another "teaching moment." His parents had given him a puppy when he was Cody's age on the condition he took care of it. Later, at twelve, he'd been given his first horse with the same condition and been required to earn money during the summer doing odd jobs to help pay for the horse's expenses.

"Kittens are a lot of work," he said. "And they cost money for food and a litter box and veterinarian exams." His mom owned two cats, and he was amazed at how much she spent on them. "Are you willing to help pay?"

Cody dug in his pants pocket and extracted some coins. "I have sixty-three cents."

"Kittens cost more than that."

Owen was met with three blank stares. In Willa's defense, she had no concept of money.

"Most people earn money by doing work. Like when I go to the office. If you do the chores I give you, then I'll pay you for them. But you have to use the money to buy food and other things for the kitten."

The blank stares didn't waver. Even the young girl selling the kittens watched unblinkingly.

"You get the kitten in exchange for doing chores. Understand?"

"We get a kitten!" Cody hollered.

"Shake on it." Owen held out his hands. "That's how adults make a deal."

Cody and Marisa took turns shaking his hand. Willa wanted a hug.

Elated, the young girl pointed to the counter. "There's food and litter and boxes for sale over there."

Owen removed a ten-dollar bill from his wallet. "You have to agree on which one."

"One kitten for each of us!" Marisa exclaimed.

"Just one. You'll share, and there will be absolutely no fighting. Otherwise, I'm bringing the kitten back." He wasn't sure he could carry through with the threat, but it sounded good.

The kids jumped up to wrap their arms around him. Owen felt ten feet tall. He was convinced he could talk Molly into letting him keep the kitten for the duration of his stay, once he explained his reasoning to her. She supported his goal to be a better father, and instilling responsibility in kids was what a father did.

While the kids played with the kittens and argued over which one they should pick, Owen perused the store. He recalled being here during his earlier years at Waverly, before he'd moved up the ranks. Not much had changed since then.

Inspired, he used the opportunity to pick out a few Christmas gifts for Santa to deliver Christmas morning while the kids were preoccupied. A pair of boots for Cody. Toy horses for Marisa and a stuffed pony for Willa.

He hurried to the counter. The kids had narrowed down their kitten selection, giving him little time to pay for his purchases before they noticed.

"Afternoon." The older man behind the counter offered Owen a hearty grin. "Looks like you found everything."

"And then some. Can we get these bagged up quickly before I'm found out." As the man scanned and slipped the purchases into a plastic bag, Owen said, "Appears I'm also going to need kitten chow, litter and a box."

"My neighbor's daughter." The man shook his head sympathetically. "She's under strict instructions by her mother to find homes for the kittens before the end of the week. All the money she earns will go toward having the mama cat spayed."

Owen laughed. "I had a similar chat with my three just now."

The portly proprietor paused and studied Owen intently. "Say, aren't you that new minister at Sweetheart Ranch? I stopped by the open house but don't think we had a chance to meet."

"Online minister, and guilty as charged."

"Name's Fred." The man extended his hand, and Owen shook it. "Glad to make your acquaintance."

"Owen Caufield. I used to work for Waverly Equine Products. I'm pretty sure I've been here before. Years ago."

Fred wagged a finger at him. "I thought you looked familiar at the open house, but I just assumed I'd seen you around town. Well, fancy that!" He shook Owen's hand again.

"You have a nice store here. Well laid out. A wide variety of products. Good location."

Fred exhaled slowly. "Gonna miss Mustang Valley, that's for sure."

"You leaving?"

"I'm selling the place." He pointed to a sign in the window Owen hadn't noticed. "If I can find a buyer."

"Retiring?"

"Yeah." He released another slow breath. "My wife's been begging me to move to Minnesota."

"Minnesota? That's a long way from Arizona."

"We're originally from there and still have family in the Saint Paul area. She's always wanted to go home eventually. Seems a fair trade-off—we've been living in the desert these past thirty-eight years. My choice."

"Take a warm coat," Owen advised.

"Gonna be a change for sure," Fred agreed. "Our worst winter day here is like spring in Saint Paul."

With their transaction complete, Owen fetched the kids, along with their new acquisition. He tried not to worry about what Molly would say. Or Jeanne, who may not relish the prospect of a second pet.

Worst-case scenario, Owen would keep the kitten. Cats weren't as much trouble as dogs. Plus, his mom would be a wealth of information.

Marisa took the lead for once, and Cody obliged her. She campaigned for the orange kitten and promptly named it Pinkie Pie after one of the *My Little Pony* movie characters.

"She's so cute, Daddy."

"Are you sure the kitten is a girl?" Owen asked.

Marisa glared at him as if he'd suggested the unthinkable. Since a trip to the vet was in the near future, he figured they'd confirm Pinkie Pie's gender then.

He'd just gotten all three kids loaded in the backseat of his truck when he heard his name being called. Turning, he spotted a man coming toward him and broke into a grin.

"Arnie! What the heck are you doing here?"

They clasped hands and slapped each other on the shoulder. "I'm making a sales call," Arnie told him. "Mustang Valley is my territory. But I could ask the same thing. What are *you* doing here? I heard you quit Waverly."

"I did." Owen brought his friend up to date.

He and Arnie went way back and had been professional associates rather than competitors. Arnie worked for Craft-Right Portable Horse Stalls. The two men had crossed paths often through the years.

"You know," Arnie said when Owen finished, "I'm leaving Craft-Right at the end of January."

"No fooling! You've been with them a long time."

"I'm taking a few years off. Doing the Mister Mom thing. My wife just got promoted to junior partner at her law firm, and the hours are insane. Mine, too, and we hate leaving the boys with a sitter all day, every day."

Since Arnie appeared pleased, Owen congratulated him. "Good for you."

"Craft-Right's looking to hire my replacement. I'm sure Old Man Hickman would love to talk to you. You should give him a call."

"Appreciate the suggestion, but I don't want to be on the road that much."

"The way I heard it," Arnie said, "they're

changing the job to more office based and less traveling."

"How much less?"

"Two days a week max."

Though not the largest company out there, Craft-Right Portable Horse Stalls had a good reputation and manufactured a superior product. And two days a week traveling was doable.

"Would I be stepping on anyone's toes?"

"If you're asking, are they promoting from within, the answer is no."

The job was starting to sound interesting, even if it wasn't exactly what Owen wanted. "I'll call him. Thanks."

Willa had fallen asleep in her car seat, but Cody and Marisa were eager to get back to the cabin and play with their new "toy."

Owen hitched his thumb at the truck. "These three have had their fill. I'd best hit the road."

"And I'm late for my appointment with Fred. I hope for the sake of my replacement whoever he sells this store to is as easy to work with as him."

"Nice seeing you, Arnie."

The kitten meowed the entire ride home, making a racket too loud to come from such a tiny creature. At the cabin, Owen carried Willa inside and lay her down in her crib. Careful not to wake her, he removed her jacket. After helping him with the litter box and food dish, Marisa and Cody watched the kitten's every move until it collapsed from exhaustion in a corner of the couch.

Marisa fell asleep, too, curled up next to the kitten, while Cody watched one of the movies from the library.

Sitting at the small dining table, Owen pulled out his phone. Happy to find he still had Craft-Right's phone number in his contacts, he placed a call.

Arnie had been right, Monty Hickman was glad to hear from Owen. He came right out and mentioned the job opening without Owen having to casually work it into the conversation.

By the time he disconnected, Owen was feeling pretty darn good. His kids were content, and he had an interview lined up for a week from tomorrow.

MOLLY CARRIED ON an internal conversation with herself during the walk to Owen's cabin. She could call him, there was no reason to disturb him and the kids. They were likely busy, given she'd hardly seen hide nor hair of them since the carriage ride yesterday morning.

Instead, she was delivering the message in person. Why?

To see him, whispered the small voice inside her.

No, she countered. She'd opted for a face to face because…because… Oh, heck, just because.

At the cabin door, she hesitated, slightly embarrassed when the guests in the next-door cabin suddenly emerged and headed toward their car. She smiled and waved as if seeking out Owen was no big deal. After all, she was acting ranch manager and he an employee. Naturally they spoke.

Lifting her hand, she rapped loudly. When Owen didn't immediately answer, she looked for his truck. Yes, it was parked in its usual place. He and the kids weren't at the clubhouse playing Ping-Pong—she'd have seen them on the way here. It was possible they'd taken a short hike on the nearby trails or gone next door to Powell Ranch.

She rapped a second time and leaned her ear toward the door. No, not her imagination. Noises were coming from inside the cabin. Muffled voices and footsteps and a door closing. Another game of hide and seek?

Feeling stupid, she turned and started to leave. He obviously didn't want to talk to her. And he'd know it was her if he bothered to look through the peephole. Just when her foot reached the edge of the stoop the door abruptly opened.

"Hi. Sorry about that." Owen glanced behind

him. "Had a little situation with the kids to handle first."

She swung around, took one look at him and stopped. "It must have been some situation."

Owen appeared mildly flustered, something out of the ordinary for him.

"Are you okay?" she asked.

"Yeah. Fine. What's up?" He stood in the middle of the open door as if to prevent her from entering.

"I wanted to tell you about a change in our schedule this week. We have a last-minute wedding tomorrow evening at seven."

"Okay."

"Did you make other plans?"

"Nope."

What was with the short answers?

"I spoke to Nora already," Molly said. "She'll watch the kids. And the couple will be emailing their vows later today."

"Got it."

"They're friends with the Herrerras." When he didn't react, she explained, "The army vet with burn scars, you remember her? In this case, the groom is shipping out two days after Christmas. He and the bride want to get married before he does. They'd like something more intimate and personal than the courthouse downtown. I said we can accommodate them."

Owen nodded. "Sounds good. That it?"

Molly tried to peer around him. Clearly, he didn't want her here. But why?

"Where are the children?" She swore he moved slightly to block her view.

"In the bedroom. Playing."

"Hmm." Molly strained to hear. Voices and footsteps continued emanating from farther inside the cabin but nothing out of the ordinary for three youngsters. "We're having a quick runthrough at four today. Just us, the couple won't be here. Is that going to be a problem?"

"Not at all."

"If it is, you can bring the kids to the house. Bridget's experimenting with a new pumpkin bread recipe. She'll keep an eye on them until Nora arrives."

"We'll see."

More abrupt responses. "Owen, did I say or do something yesterday to upset you? Because if I did, we can talk about it."

"No. Absolutely not."

"You seem distracted."

"There is something I want to discuss with you, now that you mention it."

At a loud noise from the bedroom, Owen momentarily froze. When nothing came of it, he returned his attention to Molly.

"Is it about work?" she prompted, admittedly curious.

"Kind of."

"Did you find a job?" What if he was giving his notice and leaving the ranch in a bind? That might explain his distraction.

"No. Though I have an interview next Tuesday with Craft-Right Portable Horse Stalls."

"Congratulations!"

"I ran into a buddy of mine outside of the feed store yesterday. He told me about the job opening. I called the president of the company. He remembered me. Luckily, favorably."

"I'm glad for you."

"The pay isn't quite what I'm used to. On the other hand, the location is great. Plenty close to the kids. And there's potential to advance."

"Well, good luck, though I'm sure you'll breeze through the interview."

"Craft-Right's office isn't too far from Mustang Valley." He grinned, and for the first time since opening the door, he looked like his usual self. "We can see each other."

"Um…"

"Could be a chance for us to test the waters."

"Maybe. Let's see. We have Grandma and Homer's vow renewal and party on January first. And February will be crazy busy, what with Valentine's Day. We have three weddings scheduled already that day and I expect more. Not sure I can squeeze in dating."

"You're stalling."

"I'm listening to reason." And to her head. "I came to Mustang Valley to get my life together—which was a mess after losing another job and my fiancé walking out three days before our wedding—and to help my grandmother with her new and demanding business. You came here to bond with your children, become a better, more attentive father and to find a job. Dating isn't conducive to any of those things."

"If I'm employed, that's one less obstacle. And your grandmother will be home in two-and-a-half weeks. You'll have help. Another obstacle gone."

"I don't disagree, but there are still other things to consider."

Shouting erupted from behind the closed bedroom door, and Owen muttered, "I should check on the kids."

Yes, Molly concurred, he should. "I'll see you later at the run-through."

Before she could say goodbye, the bedroom door exploded open, issuing an ear-splitting bang as it hit the wall. Unable to help herself, Molly cringed. The next second, Owen's three children spilled into the living room, arms and legs flying.

"Daddy, Daddy," Marisa hollered, "Pinkie Pie is stuck."

"She climbed the curtain," Cody added as they came to a stop behind Owen. "All the way to the top."

Willa plopped to the floor, thumb in her mouth, eyes forlorn.

"She's going to die," Marisa wailed.

"I'll be right there," Owen said firmly. "Now get back to the room and shut the door."

Molly didn't move. Something wasn't right, and who the heck was Pinkie Pie?

Marisa and Cody returned to the bedroom, their feet dragging. Willa disobeyed Owen completely and toddled toward him, wrapping her arms around his legs.

"Daddy, Daddy! Kitty hurt."

Kitty? Molly drew back. "Owen, who is Pinkie Pie? Or should I ask what?"

"Pinkie Pie is a kitten," he answered slowly. "An early Christmas present for the kids. That's what I was going to talk to you about."

"I don't understand."

"We stopped at the feed store yesterday and a girl was selling the kittens. The kids went nuts over them, and I saw a good opportunity to teach them about responsibility. They're going to earn food and supplies for the kitten by performing chores."

Molly stood there, dumbstruck. "Pets aren't allowed at the ranch."

"We won't let her outside. She can stay in the cabin, and if there's any damage I'll pay for it."

"That's not the problem. You should have spoken to me first."

"I honestly didn't think you'd mind."

Was he actually surprised at her reaction? "I don't mind the kitten. What I do mind and very much is that you took advantage of our relationship and my fondness for your children."

"It wasn't like that."

"Then you took advantage of your job here and the fact that we can't operate without a wedding officiator. Or maybe it was my grandmother's relationship with your uncle. Choose whichever one you like, Owen."

He actually appeared confused and then grim. "If you want, I can take the kitten back."

"Right. And make me the bad guy. Your children will hate me. That's hardly fair when you're the one in the wrong."

"Can we please discuss this?"

His complete lack of consideration for her feelings and for her position at the ranch hurt. Whatever he argued to the contrary, it remained he had broken the rules and disrespected her. Disrespected her entire family.

The next second, Cody and Marisa came barreling out of the bedroom.

"Pinkie Pie climbed down from the curtains," Cody said in a rush, "but then she ran under the bed."

"Help us get her, Daddy," Marisa begged.

"What do you want me to do, Molly?" Owen asked. "How can I make this right?"

"I'm not sure yet. I'll let you know tomorrow."

Her anger at him was justified, she told herself on the return walk to the house. Owen could have handled the situation much better. Instead, he'd leaped without looking first and justified his actions based on good intentions.

Was what had happened a preview of their potential relationship? If so, better she found out before they went any further.

CHAPTER TEN

OWEN STOOD TO the side and watched the exchange between Molly and Bridget and the newlyweds and their two witnesses.

"Best wishes and good luck to you."

"Thank you for your service. We're honored to have hosted your wedding."

"We can't tell you how wonderful it was."

The small wedding had gone smoothly. Owen had stuck to a mostly traditional ceremony with the couple reciting their own vows.

With the groom in uniform and the bride wearing flowers in her hair, the service had been sweet and heartfelt and very moving. Everyone there knew the groom would be shipping out soon for his overseas tour. The couple talked excitedly about him returning in the spring for leave, with no one mentioning the possibility that he might not return in one piece or at all.

They were spending the night in a cabin, a gift from the groom's out-of-state parents. From talking to the couple after the ceremony, Owen had gathered they didn't have a lot of money, and the honeymoon stay was a real treat for them.

Molly and Bridget must have decided the same thing for Bridget had provided her specialty wedding cupcakes at no charge and Molly had arranged for champagne and fresh strawberries to be delivered to the cabin.

Not much, Owen mused. Cupcakes, champagne and strawberries. But the gestures would likely be treasured memories that lasted the couple's lifetime. Hopefully, a *long* lifetime.

Molly and her sister clearly belonged in the wedding business, because their hearts were truly in the right place. Their grandmother must have known that when she'd put them in charge while she was gone.

As Owen watched, Molly escorted the couple from the parlor to the foyer where she took several more pictures of them kissing beneath the mistletoe. She'd taken pictures throughout the ceremony—the couple couldn't afford a photographer. Though it was chilly outside, she continued to stand on the veranda chatting with them.

"Good heavens, she must be freezing!" Bridget appeared beside Owen.

"Maybe I should bring her a coat." He'd rather put his arms around her.

"Not a good idea." Bridget wore a bemused expression.

"I'm guessing you heard."

"About your stowaway? Yes, indeed." She tsked, though with a hint of mirth that made him think she wasn't mad about the kitten. "Owen, Owen, Owen. What are we going to do with you?"

"I blew it. I get that."

"Have you always been such a rule breaker?"

"Not exactly. More like a risk taker." Another trait that had helped propel him to the top of his rodeo and sales careers. "With a spontaneous streak."

"Yeah, Molly's the polar opposite of spontaneous."

"So I'm discovering."

"She wasn't always like that," Bridget said. "Dad dying when we were young affected her. Affected all of us, Mom included. Just look at her and Doug. A marriage not made in heaven because Mom dreads being alone."

"Tragedy changes people."

"Molly became a stickler for rules. They make her feel in control and give her a sense of security. Something she didn't feel after Dad died."

They stood adjacent to the reception counter in a shadowy corner of the foyer. Owen had chosen the spot because he didn't want Molly to see him staring at her.

"If I could go back in time," he said, "I'd have…"

"Not taken the kitten?" Bridget prompted.

"Called Molly first. Or waited to get the kids a kitten until after leaving Sweetheart Ranch."

A thought occurred to him. Was he trying to compete with Jeanne? Was that why he'd agreed to get the kitten? Owen didn't like thinking the answer might be yes.

"I told Molly I'd see if the girl who sold us Pinkie Pie could take her back."

"I doubt that'll be necessary," Bridget said. "Molly understands why you got the kitten, even if she won't admit it. She'll probably allow you to keep it, but let her be the one to tell you. Don't ask or start with the hard-core sales pitch."

"Do I do that?"

"Sometimes. It's your nature. This is one of those times you need to curb it."

Owen had believed he could convince Molly. That had been presumptuous of him. Heck, it had been selfish of him.

He really did wish he could go back in time to the previous day. He wouldn't call Molly. He'd have told his children no and dealt with the crying and the whining and the pouting. Being a parent meant having to take the path of more resistance.

"I'm off to clean the parlor," Bridget announced before slipping away. "Tell Molly there's very little mess, and she doesn't have to help me."

He waited in the corner, not moving. Molly remained on the veranda, waving goodbye until the witnesses were heading down the driveway and the newlyweds had left for their cabin. By the time she came inside, she was clutching her middle and shivering from head to toe.

Reaching for the switch, she shut off the overhead light. The only remaining illumination in the foyer came from the Christmas tree. The one he'd gone with her to purchase back when they weren't at odds. When he hadn't let her down and disappointed her.

"Molly. Do you have a minute?"

She hesitated, seeming to compose herself. "I thought you'd left already."

"Any chance we can have that talk?"

She nodded.

"I owe you an apology. You were right. I took advantage of you and my job here. I wish I could tell you that's not like me, except it is. I'm used to being in charge. At work and in my personal life. That can be an asset in the right circumstances and a detriment in the wrong ones. Yesterday was a mistake."

"You can keep the kitten," Molly said without emotion.

"That's much more than I deserve."

"I'm not saying yes for you. I won't break the children's hearts."

He definitely had that coming.

"I do have a condition," she said.

"Absolutely."

"You give me space and no more talk about dating. I don't want to keep being confused by you."

What other choice did Owen have but to agree? "Still friends?" He flashed a smile only to immediately sober lest he be accused of employing his sales pitch tactics again.

"*Only* friends," Molly said.

What else did he expect? He'd brought this on himself and would have to accept the consequences. Didn't mean he wouldn't move mountains to try and change things.

OWEN WALKED OUT of the president's office at the Craft-Right Portable Horse Stalls production plant. He'd felt mostly good about the meeting, though his mind hadn't always been on it. Molly kept invading his thoughts.

She wasn't holding a grudge about the kitten. Rather, she acted as if all was fine between them. Business as usual and nothing but business. Owen had made sure the kids thanked her for letting them keep Pinkie Pie, and she'd graciously accepted their thanks.

For Owen's part, he'd given her the space she requested. Not easy for him, it had been a long and difficult eight days. Apparently, a lot easier for her. Molly had appeared mostly unaffected. That, or she hid it well.

She was the first woman he'd been interested in since his divorce, and he'd gone and blown it.

In the lobby, he ran into his friend Arnie.

"How goes it, pal?" He gave Owen's hand an exuberant shake. "Have the interview yet?"

"Just came from meeting with Monty." The man had invited Owen to call him by his first name.

"And? What's the good word?"

"He has two more people he wants me to meet. The head of manufacturing and the chief financial officer."

"All right! I don't know of anyone else who's made it that far."

"Monty said the official start date isn't until after the first of the year."

That would give Owen two to three weeks to work with Arnie before he left in January. *If* Owen got the job. He wasn't the only candidate being considered.

Not pinning all his hopes on Craft-Right, he'd continued job hunting despite it being the holidays. His severance package from Waverly would run out in the next couple of months, and he didn't want to touch his 401(k) account if possible. Unfortunately, a lot of businesses were slowing down this time of year.

"I'm sure you'll get the job," Arnie stated. "They'd be foolish not to hire you."

"Monty gave me a full tour of the plant. It's quite a place."

"I realize I'm prejudiced, but Craft-Right is a top-notch outfit. They treat their employees well."

"Glad to hear that."

Owen did like the company and had been impressed with the operation. He was a little disappointed with the salary offered, though Monty had assured him once Owen proved his worth, he'd be fairly compensated with bonuses. The benefits were also good, and Monty had reiterated that Owen would spend no more than two days a week on the road.

He should be thrilled. Pleased at the very least. If he got the job, he'd be able to provide for his kids and have one big dating obstacle removed. Then there was the matter of his pride, which had been taking a beating of late. Owen wasn't the kind of person who liked being out of work.

Only he wasn't thrilled or even pleased about

the potential job with Craft-Right and couldn't put his finger on why.

"When are you coming back for the follow-up meeting?" Arnie asked.

"On Friday. At ten thirty."

"Great! I'll be in town then. What do you say we grab some lunch afterward? There's a bistro down the road with the best salads and brioche you've ever tasted."

Owen almost burst into laughter. A bistro with salads and brioche? When had his cowboy buddies stopped frequenting steak houses and burger joints for lunch?

They chatted another minute or two about their Christmas plans. Owen mentioned his uncle's and Emily's vow renewal ceremony on New Year's Day. Owen was leaving the ranch on Christmas but would return New Year's Day to officiate.

By then, Arnie was late for a staff meeting. Owen headed outside to his truck, wishing once again he could be more excited about the job. It really was his best opportunity to date.

During the drive, he thought about the holidays. During one of the few times he and Molly had talked this past week, she'd mentioned there being weddings scheduled every day between Christmas Eve and New Year's Eve. Obviously several of her meetings with prospective clients had resulted in bookings. But only four weddings were scheduled between now and Christmas Eve.

It was going to be a long, slow lull. He guessed most people were busy with holiday shopping or cooking or preparing for out-of-town guests.

His parents certainly were. His mother baked no less than a hundred loaves of various breads to give as gifts. His father, a tinkerer by nature, built handcrafted wooden toys for his grandkids and to donate to charities.

They'd asked Owen to visit for the holidays. Sadly, he'd turned them down, committed at the ranch through Christmas day and the vow renewal ceremony on New Year's Day. But he'd promised to send plenty of videos and assured his parents they'd have a fantastic time when they visited in February.

Mustang Valley was less than twenty miles from Craft-Right. Owen drove through town on his way to the ranch. As he passed now familiar sights and landmarks, it occurred to him again how much he liked it here.

Even more this past week. Mustang Valley had gone through a transformation. Holiday decorations adorned every storefront window, including the gas station and tire shop. The park in the center of town had become a wonderland of lights and music as preparations for the annual Holly Daze Festival progressed. Silver and gold bells attached to red ribbons hung from street signs.

The goings-on reminded him a little of his hometown, and a wave of nostalgia for Christmases past washed over him. He remembered going out into the mountains near his grandparents' home and battling blizzards to cut down a tree, then hauling it home where the whole family participated in decorating it with construction paper ornaments.

It rarely snowed in this part of Arizona, perhaps once every twenty or thirty years. And then, the flakes melted the instant they touched the ground. During particularly cold winters, snow often gathered on the tops of the nearby McDowell Mountains and remained for weeks. That was as close to snow in the desert as one could get.

Tourists were arriving daily in droves, loving the fair weather and small town holiday ambiance. The local café had a special breakfast menu for the season that included eggnog pancakes and gingerbread waffles. Owen had taken the kids there yesterday morning, skipping breakfast at the ranch house.

Not that he'd been getting many invitations to dine with Molly or her sister, and he wasn't expecting any.

On impulse, Owen stopped at the bookstore and novelty shop that catered to out-of-towners. He still needed to buy a few more presents for the kids, and the store boasted a small toy section. Parking in the crowded lot, he gave Nora a call and let her know he'd be late. Not a problem, the older woman reported, as only two couples were presently staying at the ranch.

Owen quickly finished his shopping, adding gifts for the kids to give to Molly, Bridget and Nora.

Tossing his bags onto the truck's passenger seat, Owen suddenly remembered he needed more kitten food and drove to the feed store. Pinkie Pie could eat twice her weight in kibble at every meal.

Yes, his time would be better spent composing an email to Monty at Craft-Right, thanking him for the interview, confirming their Friday meeting and reiterating why he'd be a good fit for the job. Then again, if he emailed Monty too soon, he might appear desperate. Overeager at the least.

Fred called out a friendly hello when Owen entered the store. "Hey, how goes it?"

"Can't complain."

The portly store owner wore a Santa hat. All he required was a fluffy white beard to fully play the part. "Looking for something special?"

"More kitten chow and litter."

Fred chuckled. "How's the little scamp doing?"

"Fine. Growing like a weed and getting into everything. The trash bin, the lower cupboards, you name it. She's especially fond of climbing the curtains and hiding behind the sofa. I'm going to have to fork over a lot of cash for repairs. But she has the kids wrapped around her tiny paw and is using the litter box regularly, so I can't complain too much."

"If you're interested, I hear there's one left. The runt."

Owen groaned. "No, thanks. I'm not entirely sure what I'm going to do with the first one once I leave Sweetheart Ranch."

"How soon's that?" Fred walked out from behind the counter and led Owen to the aisle containing pet food and supplies.

"My uncle Homer and his blushing bride will be home on the twenty-third. My kids are leaving Christmas morning, their mom is picking them up. I'll either go home that day or the next."

"We're going to miss you, Owen."

"I'm going to miss this place, too."

Fred pointed to a shelf. "Right here are the brands I carry. Let me know if you need anything else."

At the counter, Owen looked around the store

while Fred ran his debit card. He noticed the for-sale sign in the window, partially hidden behind a strand of lights.

"Any luck finding a buyer for this place?"

"Naw." Fred gave his head a dismal shake and passed Owen the keypad device to enter his PIN number. "The real estate market slows this time of year."

"I suppose so."

"Good news, business in the store is booming. This is the first it's been empty since I opened this morning. Gotta love the Holly Daze Festival. Tourists figure Mustang Valley is the next best thing to spending Christmas at home." He presented Owen the sales slip. "By the way, how's the job hunting going?"

"Just came from an interview with Craft-Right Portable Horse Stalls."

"You getting Arnie's job? He mentioned he was leaving. Nice guy."

"I haven't been hired yet. I'm going back Friday for a second meeting."

Fred rested his forearms on the counter. "Don't take this wrong, but you don't sound too enthused."

"It's a good job. A reputable company. I like their business model. There's potential for advancement."

"Just not what you're looking for."

"Would you think I'm completely crazy if I said I'd like to see what else is out there?"

"Not at all. A person needs to love what they're doing." Fred absently adjusted his Santa Claus hat. "That's why I've owned my own business these many years. I understand self-employment isn't for people who need a regular paycheck and company-paid benefits. But I've made a decent living. Enough to comfortably retire. And I'm my own boss."

"There's a lot to be said for that." But with three young kids, benefits were an important part of any job Owen took. Especially health insurance. Right now, he was paying through the nose.

"You need a bag?" Fred pointed to the kibble and litter.

"I'm good." Owen picked up his purchases.

"If I don't see you before, have a merry Christmas."

"You, too." He was about to leave when he spied a stack of brochures on the end of the counter. A picture of Sweetheart Ranch jumped out at him. "What are these?" He set down the bag of kitten chow and picked up a brochure.

"Molly asked if I'd put those out for her. Some kind of joint promotion between her place, the Poco Dinero Bar and Grill and Powell Ranch. I hear she's got them all over town."

A memory surfaced of her mentioning something either during or after the open house. Owen hadn't been aware she'd gone so far as to design a brochure and have it printed. That was what he got for royally screwing up and creating friction between them.

"I'm almost out, thanks to the tourists." Fred greeted a pair of customers who strolled through the door, returning to his conversation with Owen only after asking if he could help them with anything. They were just browsing. "I imagine you'll have a steep rise in business. Well, the ranch, not you," Fred corrected himself. "Seeing as you won't be here much longer."

No Owen wouldn't. He'd miss experiencing the fruits of Molly's labor. The thought made him a tad melancholy.

On the outskirts of town, he drove past a sign advertising the Holly Daze Festival. It was starting tomorrow, and he made a spur-of-the-moment decision to take his kids. They'd been doing reasonably well this past week, behaving more than misbehaving, taking care of Pinkie Pie and performing the chores he'd assigned them. Some with assistance from Owen.

Mostly, he could use an outing to lift his lagging spirits. He was disliking the idea of leaving Molly and Mustang Valley more and more. When he returned to the ranch, he went straight to the house rather than his cabin. Leaving his purchases in the truck, he went inside to search for Molly. He'd use the brochure as an excuse. He was fed up with their cordial but impersonal conversations. Past time to kiss and make up.

At least, the make-up part. Kissing was out.

He didn't have to go far to find her. Recognizing her voice as one of those whooping and hollering from the kitchen, he quickened his pace.

Molly and Bridget were standing in the center of the room, grabbing each other by the shoulders and jumping up and down. Their matching smiles stretched from ear to ear.

"You two look happy," Owen said.

Molly spun to face him, for once this week her expression completely unguarded. He let himself relish every drop of the radiance she showered on him.

"I just got a call from *Southwest Bride Magazine*. Someone on their staff saw the TV news segment from the day of the open house. Their head columnist and a photographer will be here a week from today. They want to include Sweetheart Ranch in their Valentine's Day feature on the top ten most unique wedding venues in the state! Top ten," she repeated.

"Congratulations!" Owen grinned. "Well deserved."

Intense emotion must have caused Molly to suffer a memory lapse, for she hurled herself at Owen and hugged him fiercely. Lucky for him she didn't come to her senses until the kitchen door opened a full thirty seconds later.

CHAPTER ELEVEN

"DADDY, DADDY!" CODY led the pack, charging into the kitchen. Right behind him came Marisa, Willa and Nora. "You're home."

Molly flung herself away from Owen as if he'd caught fire. Bad enough she'd forgotten herself and hugged him. Worse, his children had seen them. And Nora. And Bridget.

She wasn't the impulsive type and hated to imagine what Owen thought of her. Heat from his solidly built body still lingered, leaving her feeling flushed and mildly disoriented.

"Hey, you three." He bent and opened his arms.

Like well-trained puppies, his children bounded toward him, eagerly accepting his hugs and kisses. Willa latched on to his leg as if he'd been gone for days and not a few hours.

"Did you get the job?" Cody asked.

"Not yet." Owen smiled at his son. "I have another meeting on Friday."

"Am I correct in assuming the interview went well?" Nora began peeling outerwear off the children. After adding Owen's coat, she hung the entire collection on the knotty-pine coatrack by the door.

Molly decided Nora must have dressed the children today for they wore matching holiday sweatshirts. Or was Owen responsible? He had been working hard on being a more attentive father. Molly wasn't blind and had noticed his efforts.

He answered Nora with a smile that, to Molly, seemed forced. "It did. Pretty well."

"We should celebrate." Bridget clapped her hands, and Willa mimicked her.

"Let's wait. I'd rather not jinx anything."

"They'd be crazy not to hire you," Nora said and winked at Molly. "I'd say a second interview deserves a hug."

"I…no…the hug was for…" Molly pulled herself together. "*Southwest Bride Magazine* called. They're going to interview us and take pictures." She explained about the ranch being featured in the February edition.

"One of the top ten wedding venues in the state." Nora's placed a hand to her chest. "That's fantastic. Have you told your grandmother yet?"

"We just found out. Right before Owen…" Right before Molly had made a complete fool of herself. "I'll call her now."

"Even more reason to celebrate." Bridget addressed the children. "What shall we have?"

"S'mores!" Cody hollered.

"Cupcakes," Marisa added.

Willa made an unintelligible sound that might have been *spaghetti*.

Molly stepped to the side and dialed her grandmother, who didn't answer. She and Homer were probably out of range or doing something fun and had turned off their phones.

After leaving a detailed message, ending with "Call me back as soon as you can," Molly returned to the group.

Owen sent her a welcoming smile.

"Good luck with the second interview," she said, genuinely pleased for him.

"Thanks."

"How about cookies and milk?" Bridget asked. Receiving a chorus of yeses, she removed a large cookie tin from the counter. "I made these yesterday." She opened the lid to reveal sugar cookies in the shapes of wreaths, snowmen and Christmas trees, and decorated with glitter and icing. The children went into an instant frenzy.

"I want one!"

"Me, too."

"I'll get the milk." Nora opened the refrigerator door.

Owen sat the children at the table, reminding them to be polite and not grab. Bridget placed the tin of cookies in the center of the table and plopped down beside Willa. That left two empty chairs, one next to Owen.

Molly circled the table and slid into the chair across from him, glad for the breathing room. What she hadn't counted on was feeling his gaze on her and connecting with it each time she looked up. Was there no escaping him?

"I got a call from the mayor's office today," Bridget said. "They asked if we'd like a bigger space for the Holly Daze Festival. There was a cancellation."

Darn it. With everything going on lately, her tiff with Owen included, the annual town event had slipped Molly's mind.

"What do you think?" she asked her sister.

"That if we don't get to work today on our display, we won't be able to fill the space already assigned to us. The festival starts on Friday."

That soon! Molly cringed. "Any ideas? There are plenty of the new brochures left."

"I saw them at the feed store," Owen interjected. He'd eaten two cookies and was eyeing a third. "You did a good job. Fred's given most of his away."

"Thanks." She wished his praise didn't ignite a soft glow inside her.

Bridget frowned. "I'm not going to sit at a table for hours on end just to hand out brochures."

"What about a giveaway people enter to win?"

Luckily, the children were occupied with their afternoon snack and being relatively quiet, allowing the adults to converse.

"We could hold a raffle for a free Valentine's Day wedding," Nora suggested. "Just the basic ceremony. None of the extras."

Molly considered that. "We already have multiple weddings booked that day and I'm sure we'll get more requests. I'd rather leave the day open for paying clients."

It was a popular day for weddings as well as proposals, Molly had learned. They'd agreed they could accommodate as many as six ceremonies if they adhered to a strict schedule. Their closest competitor, a Victorian house in Gilbert, had ten weddings scheduled.

"A Valentine's Day Eve ceremony? Or a romantic couples weekend?" Nora snapped her fingers. "I know, a discount on any of our services or the cabins." Her executive assistant experience was showing.

"Maybe." Molly liked the idea of raffling off discount tickets best. "Let's look at costs and dates after we're done here. We could easily print up our own entry tickets."

Nora popped a snowman's head into her mouth. "Don't forget to include a line for email addresses."

Molly had already thought of that.

The ideas continued to flow for the next ten minutes, many of them good. Owen suggested they take the carriage and horses to the festival and tie them to a stake behind the table. Everyone agreed that was sure to draw people. Bridget offered to bring some of her holiday treats. She had a new recipe to try.

"I also think Owen should come decked out in his wedding officiator clothes." Nora patted his arm. "People will love meeting you."

"I agree!" Bridget exclaimed. "You're so handsome and charming, we'll have the most popular table there."

Looking chagrined, Owen reached for the third cookie. "I can't stay all day. Not with having to watch these guys. But I'll be there both Friday and Saturday evenings and on Sunday afternoon. As long as I can bring them with me and have some free time each day to take in the festival."

"That'll work." Bridget beamed.

"If we're done, let me help with the dishes." Owen stood and began collecting empty milk glasses. "Willa's ready for her nap."

The toddler was falling asleep in her chair.

"You go on," Bridget insisted. "There's hardly any mess."

"Daddy." Marisa tugged on his sleeve. "I'm bored. Can we play Twister?"

"After Willa wakes up."

Molly waited for Owen to say something to her about the hug, only he didn't. Grabbing their coats and jackets, he wrangled his kids into them with Nora's help and then started to leave by way of the parlor, Willa in his arms and holding Marisa by the hand. Cody tried to run ahead but Owen called him back.

"Say goodbye, everyone."

His two oldest dutifully did as told. Willa looked over Owen's shoulder and waved.

Molly stalled for a minute, checking her phone. There was no return call from Grandma Em and no pressing emails.

"If you're just going to stand there," Bridget said, motioning to the sink, "grab a washrag and wipe down the table."

Molly moved but not toward the sink. "I'll be right back."

"Where are you going!"

"Be right back," she repeated and hurried through the parlor to the foyer and out the front door. Owen was loading his children into his truck. "Owen," she called. "Wait up."

He peered over his shoulder. "Did I forget something?"

"I wanted to explain." She slowed to a stop a few feet from the truck, not wishing to be overheard.

"About what?" He issued a warning to his children to stay and then joined Molly.

Her courage promptly abandoned her. She cleared her throat to buy time. Owen waited, humor lighting his eyes. Did he find her discomfort amusing?

"The hug in the kitchen," she forced herself to say. "I, um, don't want you to get the wrong idea. It meant nothing. I was excited about the magazine article is all."

"I know."

"Ah, okay. I wanted to make sure."

"No worries."

Seriously? Had he not felt the same sizzling electricity as her when they were entwined like a pair of cuddle bugs?

He looked at her quizzically. "Is that it?"

"Yes. No."

"Which is it?"

Why had she come outside? Dumb decision on her part. "Thank you for not making more of the hug than it was."

"I said I'd give you space, Molly."

And he had. He'd been a perfect gentleman

all this week, which inexplicably annoyed her, as did this conversation.

The next instant, his lips were perilously close to hers, catching her off guard. "FYI, if this job with Craft-Right works out, all agreements are null and void."

Molly stilled, and a small tingle blossomed in her heart. She locked her knees before they buckled.

I'm mad at him, she thought. *Mad and hurt.*

Except she wasn't. Not anymore.

"See you later," Owen murmured in a voice like honey.

If she stayed a moment longer, she wouldn't be responsible for her actions. Pivoting, she hurried into the house. Bridget and Nora were waiting for her in the kitchen, and the two of them immediately confronted Molly.

"What's going on with you and Owen?" Bridget demanded.

"Nothing."

Both Bridget and Nora laughed. "You are such a liar," Bridget accused. "We saw you through the parlor window."

"You were spying on me?"

"I thought he was going to kiss you," Nora remarked.

"I thought *she* was going to kiss *him*," Bridget countered. "You should have seen them hugging. I came this close to dousing them with cold water."

"You're both being ridiculous." Molly then attempted to throw them off by bringing up the Holly Daze Festival.

She had no intention of letting anyone know she'd already kissed Owen. Twice. Especially Bridget, who'd never let Molly live it down.

MOLLY SAT AT the table, rubbing her gloved hands together. Though not freezing cold, it was a chilly December evening in Mustang Valley. A full moon and strikingly clear sky made it a perfect night to kick off the Holly Daze Festival. Locals had come in droves, along with visitors from as far away as Casa Grande to the southeast and Surprise to the northwest.

By alternating shifts, Molly and Bridget would be able to man their table at the festival for the full three days. Not, however, without help from Nora, her granddaughter Tracee and—Molly bit down on her lip—Owen.

They still weren't speaking all that much. Molly's doing entirely, her post-hug awkward feelings continuing to linger. Plus, they were busy. Besides preparing for the festival, a last-minute wedding had been booked for Sunday evening at seven. Like the previous week, this one would be simple and small and not a lot of work. The festival closed at five that day; Molly and Bridget would be scrambling to pack up and return to the ranch in time to greet the couple.

Molly had booked a second wedding on New Year's Eve. Adding to their workload, Grandma Em called earlier with several requests for her and Homer's vow renewal ceremony New Year's Day. Molly barely had a free minute to breathe.

Thankfully, Nora and Tracee had volunteered to assist at the festival all day Saturday, allowing Molly and Bridget to take breaks. The teenager was cute and friendly and would be great at passing out brochures and raffle entry tickets. That left Molly, Bridget and Owen alone tonight.

The park in the center of town had been transformed. The long expanse of green stretching between the riding trails, playground and the community center was covered with three-sided tents, open tables, food trucks, a ten-foot-tall inflatable snowman with a mechanical waving arm and cordoned-off displays, including an interactive Santa's workshop.

One of the more popular attractions was the petting zoo. Confined inside the temporary fencing were a trio of disinterested sheep, a family of rambunctious goats that tried to make meals of buttons and shoelaces, a potbellied pig determined to hide in the corner, and two of the cutest miniature horses on the planet.

Molly wondered if the petting zoo proprietor would be willing to walk the tiny equines over to where Amos and Moses were standing quietly beside Sweetheart Ranch's table. The four of them, on opposite ends of the size spectrum, would make an adorable picture the ranch could use in their advertisements.

The horses didn't mind standing for several hours or being petted by hundreds of strangers. People climbing in and out of the carriage and taking endless pictures earned no more than an ear flicker.

The Haflingers and their miniature cousins weren't alone at the festival. Several locals had ridden their horses to the park rather than driving vehicles, causing quite a stir with the out-of-towners.

Molly had been fielding questions and dropping entry tickets in the fishbowl since the festival gates had opened ninety minutes ago. She and Bridget had arrived an hour earlier than that to set up.

Owen, too. He'd driven the carriage from the ranch to the park, about a two-mile trip. The children had come with him, and Tracee went along to supervise. She'd disappeared to meet up with friends the moment they'd arrived at the park.

Together, Molly and Bridget had delivered everything else needed for their display to the park. It was a big job, and her back and legs were paying the price.

"Where's Owen?" Bridget asked. She sat beside Molly at the table, holiday bread samples on a tray in front of her. At the last minute, she'd painted a poster board sign which they'd hung from the table.

"He took the children to the petting zoo and to eat at one of the food vendors." Molly kept a keen eye on the horses, ready to jump up whenever someone neared.

"Lucky them. I'm starving." Bridget lifted her nose and filled her lungs. "Don't you just love the smell of kettle corn and cinnamon buns?"

Molly did. And the calories went straight to her hips. "Go ahead and take off when Owen comes back." They needed a minimum of two people, one at the table and one to watch the horses.

"You think he's okay?" Bridget asked, her brows scrunched together.

"Owen? Sure. Why?"

"He's been acting differently these past few days. Did you two fight again?"

"No. We're getting along fine."

Their conversation was put on hold as a large group meandered over. Bridget passed out bread samples while Molly chatted up the raffle prizes.

"I wonder how his second interview with Craft-Right went," Bridget said when the group left. "Wasn't it today?"

"He didn't say a word to me." In hindsight, Molly should have inquired. With everything going on, she'd forgotten to wish him luck and check in with him after the interview.

"How did he look afterward? Happy or disappointed?"

"I was gone when he came home. I mean got back."

Owen's home was in north Phoenix, and he'd be returning there when he left the ranch.

A heavy weight suddenly formed inside Molly's chest and pressed against her heart. She was convinced it had nothing to do with Owen leaving in the near future and that she'd miss him. Must be her tummy complaining about missing dinner.

"I'm crossing my fingers for him." Bridget straightened the tray of samples in preparation of a young family breaking free from the flowing stream of humanity and coming toward them.

After patiently listening to Molly's pitch and filling out the entry ticket for the raffle, the mom asked Molly if she'd mind taking a picture of them with the horses.

"Please?" She smiled hopefully.

"Happy to." Molly accepted the woman's phone and directed the shot.

The family left and others took their place. Molly had just finished assisting a charming older couple down from the carriage when a low-flying missile collided with the back of her sore legs. Emitting out a loud "Oomph," she pitched forward, managing to catch herself on the carriage door a split second before she face planted on the ground.

The missile, human apparently, had grown arms and now had a hold of Molly's knees. She looked down to see a Rudolph the Red-Nosed Reindeer cap and pink jacket.

Willa.

Owen rounded the carriage and grabbed her arm. "You okay?"

"Yeah." She straightened.

"Willa took off running the second she saw you. I couldn't stop her."

"Hey, little one." She tugged on Rudolph's red nose. Willa hadn't yet released her.

Neither had Owen. His hand remained firmly in place. Through the layers of her sweater and coat, she could feel the pressure of his strong fingers, and her body reacted by humming softly. She may not want to like his touch but she did.

Willa finally let go and raised her arms to

Molly in the universal pick-me-up gesture. "Mawee."

It was the first time Willa had used Molly's name, and the weight in her chest grew a little heavier. Owen wasn't the only one she'd miss. She'd miss his children, too, when they left on Christmas morning. Maybe she should buy them gifts.

Swinging Willa high in the air, Molly propped her on a hip. The movement dislodged Owen's hand, and he let it fall to his side. Cold air rushed to fill the spot where he'd held her.

"Are you having fun at the festival?" Molly asked the toddler.

Willa babbled a lengthy answer. Molly had no idea what she was saying but Willa pointed in the direction of the Christmas tree in the center of the park and the petting zoo.

Holding her, Molly was reminded of the day they'd ridden in the carriage through town and Willa had sat in her lap. That had been nice. This was, too.

Cody came over. "Daddy gave us ten dollars each to spend. Then he made us give two dollars to the charity." He said "charity" as if trying it out for the first time. "For kids who Santa doesn't visit."

"The holiday toy drive," Owen said.

Marisa looked ready to cry. "What if Santa can't find us here?"

"You could write him a letter," Molly suggested. "I'm sure your dad will help."

"If he doesn't come," Cody announced, "then we get toys from the charity."

Owen tugged on his son's ear. "So much for showing them the value of giving back."

Molly thought he'd done a wonderful job.

"I'm starving," Bridget proclaimed and stood up from the table. Marisa and Cody were there, having coaxed her out of yet another piece of holiday bread. "Molly, do you and Owen mind holding down the fort for a while? I absolutely have to eat."

A short while after she left, Nora came by with her daughter and several of her younger grandchildren. She gave Molly a curious look but made no comment about her holding Willa, who abruptly wanted down to play with the other children.

"Owen, why don't I take your three with us?" Nora offered.

"You sure?"

In response, Nora asked, "Who wants to jump in the bouncy house?"

Two minutes later, Molly and Owen were left alone.

He stood next to the horses and introduced

himself as Sweetheart Ranch's resident wedding officiator. As always, his naturally charming personality paid off. The number of entry tickets in the fishbowl nearly doubled while the stack of brochures shrank at record speed. One couple actually scheduled an appointment with Molly for early January. That was after Owen mentioned the ranch being featured in an upcoming issue of *Southwest Bride Magazine*—something Molly mentally kicked herself for not thinking of.

With his Stetson hat and rugged good looks, people flocked to him like flies to molasses. Molly appreciated his assistance. She was also glad she hadn't put her foot down and fired him after the kitten incident. Sometimes, depending on circumstances, it was okay to bend the rules for the greater good. That was another lesson she'd learned since coming to Mustang Valley.

Bridget returned and squeezed into her seat at the table. "Yikes, I leave for a few minutes and business is booming."

"No kidding." Molly rubbed her temple.

"Headache?"

"A small one." That was growing by the minute. "I should have asked you to bring me back some food."

"What happened while I was gone?"

Molly informed Bridget of the excellent progress they'd made in her absence while Owen bedazzled a trio of college-aged women who didn't hide the fact they were smitten with him. They each made a point of touching his arm or shoulder when he helped them down from the carriage and cozying up next to him afterward.

"I don't know why he's wasting his efforts on those three," Molly muttered under her breath. "They won't be booking a wedding."

"You jealous?" Bridget asked.

Molly rolled her eyes.

"I have an idea," Bridget said to Owen when the young women were finally on their way. "Why don't you and Molly check out the festival? She has a hangry headache—part hungry and part angry."

"I'm not hangry." All right, just a little. "And anyway, you can't handle the table *and* the horses by yourself."

"Big Jim will help me."

Molly glanced in the direction her sister indicated. Their former part-time employee and his wife strolled toward them, smiles on their faces.

As Bridget predicted, Big Jim was glad to lend a hand. His wife needed a short rest anyway and sat at the table with Bridget. She reported she was feeling better, but her energy level hadn't yet returned to normal.

"It's settled." Bridget shooed Molly and Owen away.

Molly didn't object. She really was hungry, and her headache throbbed.

"This way," Owen said and captured her hand.

Seeing Bridget's self-satisfied grin, Molly realized too late her sister was playing matchmaker.

CHAPTER TWELVE

THEY STOPPED IN front of the row of food vendor trucks.

"Chicken on a stick, street tacos, barbecue brisket or fry bread?" Owen asked. "You have your pick."

"Give me a second to decide." Molly scanned the various menus posted in large print.

To their left was a dining area with plastic folding tables and chairs. Placed among the tables and chairs were tall stainless steel propane heaters, each one emitting streams of warm air. Molly wasn't sure which she was more desperate for, sustenance or relief from the cold.

Funny, she'd been less aware of the temperature drop while Owen was holding her hand. He'd let go the moment they approached the food trucks.

As if reading her mind, he leaned closer to her until their shoulders bumped. "I hear the barbecue is good."

"It is."

"You've had it before?"

"Often. I-Hart-Catering is owned by Frankie Hart. She used to work at the Cowboy Up Café and quit a while back to start her own catering company."

"Another successful small business owner. You O'Malleys are in good company."

"You say that like you haven't abandoned the idea of owning your own business."

"I haven't. It's just not in the cards for me right now. Hopefully, when the kids are older. Like through college."

"How'd your meeting with Craft-Right go? I should have asked you earlier."

"Okay."

She heard hesitation in his voice. "Only okay?"

"Let's talk over dinner."

The way he said *dinner* sounded like they were on a date. Molly reminded herself they were merely eating together.

"I recommend the brisket." The sweet, spicy aroma of Frankie's secret sauce had Molly's mouth watering.

"You've convinced me."

"Didn't you eat earlier with your children?"

"I wasn't in the mood for corn dogs."

He stayed glued to her side while they moved forward in line. Occasionally, his fingers would not-quite-accidentally brush her arm or he'd lower his mouth to her ear in order to be heard above the noise. Each small contact or warm breath caressing her skin made her pulse quicken.

She told herself she wasn't like those silly college girls fawning over him. Yet with every passing moment, she resembled them more and more, laughing at his remarks and basking in his attention.

By the time they reached the truck's order window, Molly had forgotten all about her *hangry* headache.

"Hi, Molly!" From behind the glass window, Frankie bent slightly to address her. She wore a white apron over her Christmas sweater, the belt double-wrapped and tied in front. "How goes it?"

"Excellent. There's a good crowd tonight, and we've had a lot of people stop at our table." She didn't add that Owen's presence was responsible. "What about you?"

"We'll sell out soon at this rate."

"Do you have enough brisket left for two orders?"

"Absolutely." At the mention of two, Frankie tilted her head to better see who had accompanied Molly. "Is this the new wedding guy?"

"Temporary wedding guy. Until Homer and Grandma return."

"I heard they eloped. Who'd have guessed? Dad's belonged to Homer's church for years and had no idea."

"Neither did any of us."

"Give your grandmother my best when you talk to her next. Are they having a party when they get home?"

"I will. And, yes, they are. Look for an invitation."

"I'd love to supply some of the food. As a wedding gift, of course. Free of charge."

"That's very generous of you. I'll pass it on."

"Now, introduce me to *your friend*." Frankie emphasized the last two words in a way that suggested Owen was a lot more than a friend to Molly.

"Owen Caufield." He tugged on the brim of his cowboy hat. "A pleasure to meet you, ma'am."

"Call me Frankie. And I'm pleased to meet you, too." Her glance darted questioningly between Molly and Owen.

Molly shook her head.

"Right." Frankie's grin said she didn't believe Molly.

She wasn't alone. Molly didn't believe herself, either.

"Two orders of brisket with all the fixings," Frankie called out to her helpers.

Owen insisted on paying, though Molly tried to contribute her half. She and Owen bid Frankie goodbye and moved to the pickup window at the other end of the truck. While Owen waited for their food, Molly grabbed napkins, plastic forks and straws.

Their order was delivered quickly, arriving in paper boats. At the first whiff, Molly's stomach nearly climbed up her throat. She couldn't wait and snuck a quick bite on their walk to a table. Owen found two empty seats near the center of the dining area and right beside a heater.

"Hey, check that out." Owen nodded toward a large screen at the far end of the food court.

"It's the kiss cam."

Molly recalled the gimmick from last year. A camera operator strolled the festival grounds taking videos of couples kissing, which then appeared on the big screen.

"Someone at the petting zoo mentioned there was a proposal last year."

"Yeah." Molly swallowed a forkful of brisket, thinking she'd died and gone to heaven. "Grandma was here and told us all about it."

"If that happens again, maybe the ranch could offer the couple a discount."

She stopped eating to look at him. "Do you always have such good ideas?"

"What I do for a living." He shoveled a generous bite into his mouth. "Oh, wow. This is good."

"Best in the valley."

Owen grabbed a napkin. "Frankie seems nice."

"She is. Her younger sister and Bridget are friends." Molly took a sip of her soda. She'd eaten enough that her hunger was marginally sated. "They hung out together a lot during the summers when we stayed with Grandma and Grandpa."

"That must have been nice for you, already knowing people when you moved here."

"It was. Though I haven't had much time for socializing. Turns out running a wedding ranch is time consuming."

"Things won't be letting up, either. The magazine article is bound to generate business."

"I hope. One can never predict. We might bomb despite our best efforts." Molly sampled her coleslaw. "I really wish Grandma was here for the interview. She's the owner and founder of the ranch. Seems a shame not to include her."

"Any chance the magazine can delay the interview?"

"Not a prayer. I'm told their production schedule is set in stone."

"How did you all decide on a Western-themed wedding venue anyway?" Owen asked.

"It was Grandma's idea. She hosted several weddings in the past for friends and family. Word got out and she began getting requests."

"Let me guess. Being a smart business woman, she recognized a need and the idea for Sweetheart Ranch was born."

"Pretty much. Six months into the renovations, she asked Bridget and me to join her."

"And as they say, the rest is history."

Molly took a sip of her soda. "What happened at your meeting with Craft-Right? Did they offer you the job?"

Owen wiped barbecue sauce from his face and hands. "Not exactly, but they probably will. If the board agrees, they'll present me with a formal offer on Monday."

"I'm happy for you."

"Let's not get ahead of ourselves. The board still needs to vote."

Molly studied him. "Why am I sensing hesitancy?"

He shrugged. "The starting salary is lower than I'd hoped for, but they do offer decent benefits and pay quarterly bonuses."

"Money isn't everything. There's job satisfaction." Molly was happier at Sweetheart Ranch than any of her former jobs. She loved being part of a business from the ground up and having a vested interest in the business's success.

"True," Owen admitted. "Job satisfaction is important. I like the way Craft-Right runs their operation, and their product is first-rate. Best on the market. The location is all right, too."

"Is it the traveling?"

"I was assured no more than two days a week on the road."

"I'm not hearing any negatives."

Owen pushed his empty paper boat away. "You want my honest answer?"

She nodded. "Yes."

"This would be a good job for me. Other than a lower salary, it meets all my requirements. In addition, the hours are reasonable, leaving me plenty of time for the kids. Most importantly, I'd be employed. That matters to me for a lot of reasons, pride among them. I don't like being out of work. It goes against my nature. There's also the matter of us."

"Us?" she asked hesitantly.

"I wouldn't ask you to get involved when I have nothing to offer."

"Please don't factor me or us into your decision. You have to do what's best for you and your children and only you and your children."

"You're right. And what's best for them and me is that I'm employed."

"I hear a but."

"I like sales and I'm good at it. I'm also weary

of the grind." He offered her a weak smile. "That's the first time I've admitted it. To myself or anyone."

Molly sympathized with him. She'd felt much like he did about her last job. But he was right in that he did need to work.

"Maybe you could take the job at Craft-Right and keep looking elsewhere. You might discover you like it there."

"Maybe." Using the side of his hand, he brushed crumbs off the table. "Can we change the subject? I don't want to ruin our date."

"Not a date," she reminded him, yet her heart kicked into higher gear at the mention of the word.

"It could be."

"Not yet. We still have our goals. Mine is to Sweetheart Ranch. Yours is to improve your relationship with your children. Those have to come first."

"I suppose you're right."

"Just look at all the progress you've made, Owen. I can see it."

"Thanks to you and your willingness to bend." His voice took on a husky quality. "For a while, I thought I'd lost them."

Molly was touched. "I'm glad."

"And you. You're doing an incredible job."

"I really love what I do and want to be the best

at it. For Grandma's sake as well as my own. Someday, when she's ready to retire, my dream is to run Sweetheart Ranch with Bridget." She sat up straight. "Not have my head in the clouds over some guy."

"Some guy being me?" The glint reappeared in Owen's eyes.

"Yes," she confessed. "Some guy being you."

"People hold down jobs and have romantic relationships all the time."

"It hasn't worked well for me in the past. I quit my last job because my boss was about to fire me. I *was* fired from the job before that. If Grandma Em hadn't called and asked me to come to Mustang Valley, who knows what I would have done."

"People bounce around from job to job early in their careers."

"Fired, Owen. I was fired. And Grandma saved me. I owe her. At the very least, I owe her my complete attention while Sweetheart Ranch is launching."

"What would she say if she knew about us?"

There was no "us," though Molly didn't correct him. "She'd give me an evening off and say go for it. But Grandma just eloped. She'd like to see everyone in love and happy like her."

He reached across the table for her hand and folded it inside his. "I like you, Molly. I'm pretty sure you like me, too. Can't we at least explore the possibilities? Once I have a job," he added.

The sincerity of his words, combined with the hope in his voice and his strong fingers curling around hers, was difficult—no, impossible—to resist.

"What are you doing Christmas night?" she asked, surprising herself.

"Um, I don't know. I haven't thought about it. Packing to leave the ranch, I guess."

She suddenly didn't want him to be alone on that most special of days. "Come have dinner with us. That is, if you don't mind sitting through a very long and possibly boring-for-you present opening session."

"Nothing I'd like better."

They shared a smile and a look that went on and on.

"How about a kiss for the kiss cam?" A young man pointed a video camera directly at them.

"We're not a couple—"

Her protest died when Owen leaned in and covered her mouth with his.

"How can we possibly finish in time?" Molly was very aware her voice had risen a full octave. "We must have been crazy to agree to this."

"Relax." Bridget refastened a bow to the back

of the last pew. "We'll manage. Just like we always do."

"I don't know how." Molly furiously rubbed a soft cloth over a silver candlestick, attempting to remove a barely visible speck of tarnish. "We shouldn't have spent all weekend at the festival. It would have been better to get ready for the magazine interview tomorrow instead. They're going to be here at one." As if her sister didn't already know that.

"Are you kidding! Five new appointments this week alone and a wedding in March. All from the festival."

"One wedding." The speck of tarnish defied Molly's efforts. "Three full days, a ton of hard work, and that's all we have to show for it."

"Quit being a Debbie Downer. You know most promotion efforts don't have instant results. We passed out five hundred flyers, at least, and collected almost as many email addresses."

Molly's goal was to send out a monthly newsletter, a project she'd tackle once they survived the holidays, the vow renewal ceremony and this blasted interview.

"You're just worried because Grandma's coming home soon," Bridget said, "and you wanted to show her a filled appointment calendar."

Not wrong. They'd been talking to Grandma Em with increasing regularity these last few days as the end of her and Homer's trip neared. They were due to arrive on Wednesday, Thursday at the latest. Grandma seemed to have returned to Earth after spending weeks on cloud nine. Suddenly, she was all business again and voicing concerns about vacancies and the number of package deals sold.

That was good and not so good. Last evening, Molly had burned the midnight oil updating the financial records. While they'd taken in decent revenues since their grand opening, the ranch continued to operate in the red. Grandma Em had assured Molly businesses often lost money during their first years of operation, and Sweetheart Ranch had been open less than a month.

Molly longed to be the exception to the rule, to prove Grandma Em had been right in hiring her.

"I'm leaving shortly to do some shopping." Molly moved to the next candlestick.

Bridget was picking dead leaves from the poinsettias and turning the pots so that the plants' best sides were showing. "Where are you going?"

"The nursery, for wreaths to hang on the gate."

"We have wreaths."

"Some of the needles are turning brown."

"Stop obsessing. It's fine."

"What are you baking for them?" "Them"

being the magazine's columnist and photographer.

"Pumpkin squares and strawberry-and-cream truffles in case one of them is gluten intolerant."

"Do you think we should offer them a carriage ride?"

Molly was undecided. Then again, she'd been attempting to put Owen and all things associated with him from her mind since Friday night at the festival and their very public kiss.

How she could have completely forgotten they were seated among a hundred people and being filmed was beyond her. Yet, she *had* forgotten from the moment their mouths connected. He alone could do that to her.

"Definitely," Bridget said. "They may not want to go, but we should certainly have the horses harnessed and ready. For pictures if nothing else. We're the only wedding venue in the state to offer on-site carriage and hayrides, which is probably the reason we're in *Southwest Bride*'s top ten."

Darn her sister for making perfect sense. "I'll tell Owen."

"I'm glad you two are back to talking. Though, from what I saw, you're doing a whole lot more than that."

Molly's head snapped up. "What?"

"Your kiss at the Holly Daze Festival. It was scrumptious."

When no one had mentioned Molly's moment of weakness, she'd hoped—stupidly, apparently—that she and Owen had escaped her family's notice.

"No big deal," she lied.

"You should have told me. I practically spit out my breakfast when I checked the town's social media page."

Molly dropped the candlestick. "Social media page?"

"The town posted all the kiss cam videos from the entire weekend. Yours and Owen's is there. In fact, you're in third place."

"Third place?" She dreaded asking.

"The town is having a contest. Viewers can vote on their favorite couple. The winner'll be announced at noon on Christmas Eve. They win a dinner for two at the Poco Dinero. You really should go online and look."

Molly grabbed her phone and with fumbling fingers found the page. Her stomach sank as her and Owen's kiss cam video appeared, third from the top. Just how many people had watched it? According to the counter: 1897. Had Owen?

Well, he'd probably think it was funny, considering he hadn't hesitated planting one on her the moment the guy pointed the camera at them.

"Oh, brother." Molly closed the phone's app and shut her eyes.

"You didn't vote." Bridget had watched over Molly's shoulder.

"And I'm not going to."

Bridget resumed plucking brown poinsettia leaves. "I don't understand the problem. He'll be leaving us shortly. When he does, there'll be no conflict of interest and nothing stopping you two from dating."

Molly recalled her and Owen's most recent kiss. Like the others, the sensation of his lips on hers had lingered. If she concentrated, she could feel his skilled mouth coaxing a reaction from her. He hadn't needed to exert much effort, Molly had participated fully.

"That's not the only reason I'm reluctant. He's not in a good place for dating. We talked the other night."

"When you weren't kissing?"

"Be serious. His kids come first. What if he decides shortly into dating that he can't commit or that family responsibilities are too demanding?" Or what if he realized she simply wasn't the one? That had happened to Molly before.

"Just watch the video." Bridget's voice softened. "Owen likes you. Anyone can see it."

"We're busy. I can barely carve out time to eat and sleep."

"Why don't you just admit it? You're afraid of being dumped."

Her sister's observation struck a nerve. Was Molly manufacturing excuses not to date Owen because she was afraid of failing at yet another relationship? She was certainly afraid of failing at yet another job.

Molly detested self-examination. In her experience, the process was painful rather than enlightening.

As it turned out, she was spared. Owen chose that moment to breeze into the chapel, bringing the outdoors with him as well as memories of their searing kiss.

"There you are." He strode toward Molly, taking off his cowboy hat and coat and dropping them onto a pew. The cold weather had painted a ruddy glow on his cheeks. "I was looking for you."

"I bet," Bridget murmured under her breath but loud enough for Molly to hear.

"I have some questions about Friday evening's wedding," he said.

Business. Molly hid her enormous relief. There was still a chance he hadn't seen the video of their kiss. "Fire away."

"Am I reading this right?" He unfolded a piece of paper Molly recognized as the notes she'd left for him earlier. "The Millers want to sing their vows?"

"They're both musicians and wrote the song."

"Okay. Should I stand to the side? Will they be playing instruments or is the music recorded?"

"Recorded. And they'll be holding hands in front of you. A lot like a regular wedding."

He had several more questions, and Molly appreciated him being conscientious about his job. She probably should have talked to him in person rather than leave notes, except then she'd be alone with him. Not that she expected him to kiss her again without warning.

"Have you heard back from Craft-Right yet?" Bridget asked when Owen and Molly were done.

"They emailed me an offer this morning. I'm reviewing it."

He didn't act very excited. "Not what you were expecting?" Molly asked.

"They made some changes from what we originally discussed. I'm going to counter after I've checked with a few friends whose opinions I trust."

So, he was countering. That must mean he was considering taking the job. Hopefully for the right reasons.

"Darn." Bridget made a sad face. "And here I was planning on you sticking around. Me and everyone else." She cast a pointed glance at Molly.

Molly attempted to derail her sister. "Good luck with whatever you decide."

"I'm free if you need a hand," Owen said. "When Nora picked up the kids for a playdate, she told me you two are working round the clock getting this place in shape for the interview tomorrow."

"Funny you should mention it." Bridget smiled sweetly. "Molly is about ready to have a meltdown."

"I am not."

"What can I do?" Owen seemed oblivious to the subtle dynamics between Molly and her sister.

"Just have the carriage ready in case they want a ride."

"I've been cleaning the stables and carriage house and polishing the harnesses. I'm planning on grooming the horses this afternoon."

"What if we had the campfire set to light?" Molly asked. "That might make a nice picture."

"Consider it done."

"And several of the Christmas lights on the veranda are out. Can you replace them?"

Molly rattled off a few more items. Owen, good sport that he was, jotted them down on the paper with the wedding notes.

"How are we ever going to survive without you when you leave?" Bridget asked. "I'm becoming convinced the ranch needs a man around the place on a full-time basis."

"I'll come back anytime you ask."

Bridget held up her phone, the display facing Owen. "Have you seen this? Yours and Molly's kiss cam video is posted on the town's social media page. You were in third place, now you're in second!"

Molly groaned in frustration. Why couldn't her sister keep her big mouth shut?

CHAPTER THIRTEEN

"Now, I want you both on your best behavior." Owen stared back at the two pairs of dark brown eyes watching him intently. "The ladies from the magazine are going to be here any second, and we need to make a good impression. Molly is counting on us."

Amos snorted. Moses turned his big head away as if he couldn't be bothered.

The horses were tied to the hitching post outside the stables. Every hair on their hide gleamed from a thorough brushing. Their polished hooves shone, their manes were braided with red and green ribbons, and their combed blond tails nearly reached the ground, thanks to Tracee.

Molly had no idea, and he hoped she approved. Owen had paid the teenager out of his own pocket. Yes, he was trying to score points with Molly. She'd appeared distraught yesterday when her sister showed Owen the kiss cam video.

He, on the other hand, was anything but distraught. He'd liked the video plenty and had downloaded it to his phone. He'd also cast his vote. If he and Molly won the dinner-for-two first-place prize, he'd use the opportunity to tell her how he really felt about her.

With luck, he'd have a job by then. Craft-Right had yet to respond to his counteroffer in which Owen had asked for more creative freedom and more decision making authority. Something he thought might make the job more appealing to him.

After the kiss last Friday evening, he was ready to move ahead with Molly. He'd achieved his goal with the kids. Landing a good job was all that remained.

He finished attaching an old leather strap with six jingle bells to Amos's bridle. He'd come across the strap and bells yesterday while cleaning the carriage house and thought, should the columnist and photographer want a carriage ride, jingling bells chiming in rhythm to the clip-clop of horse hooves would be a nice touch.

Hearing the bells now, Owen turned to see what had caused the horses to raise their heads. Three people approached at a brisk pace. Molly, a woman Owen took to be the photographer because of the camera bag slung over her shoulder and a third woman Owen pegged as the columnist by default. The columnist and photographer appeared delighted. Molly's smile was strained.

His heart went out to her. She so badly wanted this interview to go well, and he was determined to do his part.

"Hello!" the columnist called out as they neared and waved. "You must be the wedding officiator slash ranch hand. I've heard a lot about you."

Owen tipped his cowboy hat. "Welcome to the stables."

Both women proceeded to praise the ranch. Molly had taken them on a walking tour of the entire grounds, with the stables being their last stop.

"This place is a treasure. Very picturesque. Including these two." The photographer removed her camera from the bag and immediately started snapping pictures of the horses from different angles.

"What kind are they?" the columnist asked. She'd already removed her voice recorder from her purse and activated it. "They're so beautiful. And those ribbons and bells. Straight from the front of a Christmas card."

"Haflingers. A type of draft horse. Would you ladies like a ride?"

"Yes! Love one. After the interview?"

"Absolutely." Escorting them to the carriage house, Owen went on to explain a little about the rides and show them the wagon.

"Hayrides are usually requested by couples with large families and who want the full cowboy experience," Molly contributed.

"Sounds fun!"

Owen liked the columnist and photographer. They were both on the younger side, in their early or midthirties, and clearly enjoyed their jobs.

"There are places where you can rent horse-drawn carriages for your wedding," Molly said. "At the moment, we're the only wedding venue in Arizona including it as a standard part of our package deals. And our cabins are unlike any others, making for a very special honeymoon."

"So, tell us," the columnist said to Owen, "what do you like best about marrying people, and how did you come to be a wedding officiator?"

"I'm just filling in for my uncle Homer. He's the regular minister here at Sweetheart Ranch. He and Molly's grandmother recently eloped. They'll be home in a day or two."

"We heard!" The columnist exchanged glances with Molly, her eyes dancing. "How romantic and perfect for the owner of a wedding ranch."

"As far as getting ordained online, my buddy asked me to officiate at his wedding earlier this year." Owen shrugged. "Luckily, I was available to cover for Uncle Homer while he and Emily went on their trip."

"Because of Owen," Molly said, "Sweetheart Ranch was able to open on schedule."

Had she just thanked him?

"I *adore* this story. Owner and minister of wedding venue elope." The columnist spoke as if reciting a headline. "We'll have to come back for a follow-up after they return. Or at least call them."

"Hey, I have a thought." The photographer nudged the columnist. "You mentioned romantic shots on the drive here. Why don't we have Molly and Owen pose for us?"

"Oh…" Molly instantly shook her head. "I don't think—"

"That's a wonderful idea," the columnist agreed. "We don't have to show your faces in the pictures. In fact, that would be better. Readers will be able to imagine themselves in the setting. Of course, we do want shots of you and Owen and your sister, Bridget, going about your normal duties at the ranch. Like you behind the registration counter and Owen driving the carriage. But we can use the pair of you for shots in a cabin and the chapel and…"

"Don't forget the veranda." The photographer returned from snapping a picture of the stables.

"That pine railing and porch swing will make a lovely background."

"Wouldn't a real couple be better?" Molly asked, her tone tentative.

"You two are a real couple."

"No, we're not!"

The columnist appeared confused. "I watched your kiss video on the town's social media page."

Owen knew enough to keep quiet. Molly wouldn't appreciate him commenting.

"The kiss cam is a gimmick at the Holly Daze Festival." Molly faltered. "W-we were just playing along."

"I see." The columnist didn't believe Molly, Owen could tell.

Neither did the photographer. "Nonetheless, I still want pictures of you and Owen."

He thought there'd be no dissuading these two fireballs. Molly must have been of the same opinion, because her shoulders slumped in resignation.

The tour of the stables didn't take long. Afterward, they walked to the nearest vacant cabin for the "couple" shots. There, the photographer instructed Owen and Molly to remove their jackets. She then evaluated them with a critical eye before asking Molly, "Do you mind taking down your hair?"

She tensed. "You said you weren't going to film our faces."

"I'm not. But long hair looks better from the back."

"Okay." She reluctantly removed the clasp holding her soft waves in a knot, and they instantly tumbled into attractive disorder around her shoulders.

"Honey, you have spectacular hair. Take my advice and never wear it up."

Owen concurred one hundred percent with the photographer. He'd touched Molly's hair only once and often recalled the silky texture against his skin.

"Thanks," Molly answered self-consciously and finger-combed a few stray strands. "Where first?"

"I want a shot of you two sitting on the bed."

Molly looked worried. Owen was sure he wore a happy grin. She was fun to be with when she was unsettled.

They followed the photographer into the bedroom where she had them sit on the king-size mattress, side by side and very close.

"Move a little to your right." She gestured with her hand. "That way I can get the window and a bit of the headboard in the shot." After they'd shifted, she told Molly, "Put your head on his shoulder, honey."

Molly hesitated.

"It's just a picture," Owen whispered.

"Right." She tipped her head to the side until it rested on Owen's shoulder.

"There. Not so bad," he said, deciding it was more like incredibly nice.

She swallowed.

"Relax." Behind them, the photographer snapped away.

On impulse, Owen reached up and brushed her hair from her face, though he doubted the photographer saw.

"Fantastic. That one's a keeper!"

Guess she did see.

They rose and Molly ran her palms down the front of her pants.

"That wasn't so hard," Owen whispered.

"I suppose not."

"Let's try a shot in the bathroom." The photographer led the way.

"Bathroom?" Molly's expression went from worried to scared.

"The tub is to die for."

"You can't expect us to get in there together."

"Fully clothed." The photographer laughed. "But I'll shoot from an angle that shows only your heads."

"What if they were toasting with champagne glasses?" the columnist suggested. "And eating something decadent like chocolate-covered strawberries?"

"Even better. Don't suppose you have any?"

"Glasses, no problem. There's some in the kitchen cupboard," Molly replied. "We only have plain strawberries."

"That'll do."

"I'll be right back."

Molly left to fetch the requested items. Owen chatted with the two woman about his officiating duties while she was gone. Molly returned shortly, her face flushed and breath short from hurrying.

"Lovely," the photographer exclaimed, taking the items.

Climbing into the two-person spa tub was awkward.

Owen and Molly hunkered down so his shirt wouldn't show. Molly's hair covered her blouse and draped attractively over her arm. The photographer showed them how to hold the champagne glasses, saying she'd Photoshop the picture later so that it appeared as if the glasses were full.

Owen didn't have a choice. In order to fit his long legs into the tub, Molly had to hook her legs over his. Even fully clad, there was an intimacy to their position. He didn't have to worry about romantic stirrings getting the better of him. The photographer hovering inches away and filming from every angle kept him grounded in reality.

"That should do it for this room." She put her camera away.

Molly released a very long sigh of relief when Owen helped her out of the tub, careful where he placed his hands.

"Where to next?" he asked, plunking his cowboy hat onto his head.

"The veranda?" the photographer suggested. "And then the chapel."

"At least we won't have any more embarrassing close-ups," Molly muttered under her breath.

"Yeah." *Too bad.* Owen had rather liked getting up close and personal with her. He only wished she'd felt the same.

"Oh, look!" the columnist said as they neared the house. "A porch swing. I forgot about that."

"Owen, put your arm around Molly," the photographer insisted when they were seated.

He grinned. Things were continuing to go his way.

"You two are adorable," the columnist said when they were done with the interview and photo shoot. "Wouldn't it be something special if you have your wedding here at Sweetheart Ranch? Wedding coordinator marries wedding officiator. You will call us and let us cover the story. Please."

"Really, we're just coworkers." Molly shifted uncomfortably.

The columnist winked. "My husband and I started out as just coworkers. That was eight years and two sons ago."

"I think the interview went well," Owen commented as he and Molly stood on the veranda watching the reporter and photographer leave.

"Yes. Except for the pictures. I really wish they'd used a different couple. As it is, I'm already getting flack for the kiss cam video."

"No one will recognize us in the article. She promised."

Molly made a soft sound of distress. "And what if they do?"

"They'll realize what those ladies and the hundreds of people who voted for our kiss cam video have. And what you keep trying to deny." He reached for her. "Mutual attraction."

"Owen."

"I'm leaving soon, Molly." He held her by the shoulders. "Before I do, I'd like to know for certain whether or not I have a chance with you. If not right away, then when circumstances are right. Which won't be long." He'd see to it.

Before she could answer, they were distracted by a compact car pulling into the drive with a big red bow on the bumper and a reindeer head on the antenna.

"My afternoon appointment's here."

Owen released her, but he wasn't going to let her off that easy. One way or another, she was giving him an answer.

MOLLY HAD BEEN going full steam ahead since the moment her feet hit the floor that morning. Her grandmother and Homer were due home tomorrow afternoon. On top of that, the ranch had no less than seven weddings scheduled during the next three days, including two on Christmas Eve and two more on Christmas itself, all spaced approximately two hours apart.

She'd agreed to the two on Christmas day because they were very small, no more than the bride and groom and a few guests. One of the brides was five months pregnant with her first baby, making it hard for Molly to refuse. The added revenue would look good on the books, too.

Thank goodness her grandmother would be on hand to help by then. As far as having any kind of O'Malley celebration Christmas morning, there'd be little opportunity. Bridget was planning a nice, crack-of-dawn family breakfast for them, but they'd wait to open presents until that evening, when they could finally relax.

"Sorry I'm late." Nora bustled into the foyer and joined Molly at the reception counter. She'd been working almost as many hours as Molly and Bridget. "Owen was late returning from his last-minute meeting at Craft-Right. I couldn't leave the rug rats."

Molly stopped in the middle of updating a client's file. She wasn't aware of the meeting. "Is he officially employed then?"

"He didn't say, and I didn't ask. He'll tell us when he's ready." Nora grabbed the stack of incoming mail and started sorting it. "He was wearing a big smile when he returned. If that makes a difference."

"Oh. Okay. Good."

Owen smiled a lot. Molly tried not to read anything into Nora's remark.

"Hey, did you see your kiss cam video is still at number one?" Nora asked. "You and Owen can make a date of the prize."

Did people have nothing better to do than watch and vote on kiss cam videos? "For the last time, there was nothing to the kiss."

"Uh-huh." Nora chuckled sarcastically. "And I'm running for mayor."

"Are you?"

"Don't play dumb with me." She sent Molly an impatient look. "Either go out with him or give him his walking papers. Just put him out of his misery."

He'd said much the same thing to Molly yesterday.

Ignoring Nora, she flipped a page in the clients' file. Fortunately, the older woman dropped the subject and placed a call to the florist to check on a delivery. Seemed there was a shortage of green hydrangeas, a must-have for one of the brides.

"Did your grandmother say what time she and Homer expect to arrive tomorrow?"

Molly had been so engrossed in thought Nora had had to repeat herself. "Afternoon. But that depends on freeway traffic and how many stops they make."

"Is Emily moving into Homer's house or is he moving here?"

Where they'd live hadn't occurred to Molly. She'd assumed her grandmother would continue residing at Sweetheart Ranch. She was the owner after all. But what if Homer didn't like the idea of cohabitating with a bunch of females? The newlyweds also might want more privacy.

"I don't know. She didn't say."

"She spent a lot of years in this house with your grandfather. The idea of another man occupying the same space might not appeal to her. Too many memories."

"True. It might not appeal to Homer, either. He could feel in competition with Grandpa." Molly had loved her grandfather with all her heart and still missed him. That didn't prevent her from seeing the situation from Homer's perspective.

Many items in the house had been acquired when Molly's grandfather was alive—many of them built by his own hands—and were a constant reminder. While Molly and her family loved those reminders, Homer might feel uncomfortable.

"They'll work it out, I'm sure." Nora checked the wall calendar. "What about your mom and stepdad? When are they due?"

"Christmas Eve day. But we won't be able to spend much time with them because of the weddings." Molly rolled her eyes. "Doug is irritated."

"Why?"

"Every cabin is reserved, and they have to stay at the inn."

"Your mother will love that. She practically grew up there."

"Yes. But Doug doesn't want to pay." Molly lowered her voice. "Not when there are perfectly good cabins where they could stay for free."

"Did he actually say that?"

Molly shrugged. "Mom put a different spin on it, but I could tell."

"Don't make trouble for your mom where there isn't any," Nora cautioned.

She was right. "I can't help it," Molly lamented. "I wanted more for Mom than to settle."

"She wanted more for you, too."

The observation gave Molly pause. Had her mother not liked her former fiancés? She'd always believed the opposite, that her mother was fond of them, or at least considered them good prospects. She should have noticed the small signs that her mother didn't fully support Molly's decisions to rush into marriage.

And rush she had, convinced if she didn't quickly seal the deal, the man would slip through her fingers. Funny how she'd lost them both anyway in the end.

"They weren't right for me. I see that now." What Molly really saw was she hadn't been right for them.

"You're just lucky you didn't go through with the marriages. Hard as it was for you, ending an engagement is far easier than coping with a messy divorce. That could be why your mother stays with Doug."

"You can bet it's *one* of the reasons."

What, Molly wondered, would her mother think of Owen? She didn't have to ask, she knew. Her mother would adore him and his children on the spot. He'd remind her of Molly's father, less in looks and more in personality.

She'd be right, of course. Owen *was* a lot like

her father and, if not for those excuses she'd been manufacturing, he was the kind of man Molly had sworn she wanted to marry.

The revelation gave her a start. As did the chiming doorbell.

"Grab the phone if it rings, will you?" she asked Nora, pushing out of her chair.

The visitor turned out to be a deliveryman with no less than eight packages. Most had Molly's name on them. Buried with work, she'd done her last-minute Christmas shopping online. Not five minutes later, the florist arrived, followed soon after by a group of schoolchildren selling candy for their sports team.

Molly sped from one room to the next. She should have been paying better attention. She nearly collided with Owen as she came around the blind corner into the kitchen. A delicious aroma of gingerbread filled the air. For one crazy second, Molly thought it came from Owen, only to realize Bridget was baking more delicacies.

"Whoa! Slow down there." He grabbed her arms.

"Oops, I didn't see you." Ignoring her sister's nosy stare, Molly dipped her head and extracted herself. The next second, she turned back around. "Any chance I can get you to hang the silver bells from the ceiling in the chapel?"

"Silver bells?" An amused grin spread across Owen's face. "Like in the song?"

"Just like in the song." She stopped to give him an inquiring glance. "Where are the kids?"

"No need to worry. Tracee is watching them. Watching Cody, mostly, and making sure he stays quiet while the girls nap."

She dispatched him to the garage for the six-foot ladder. Upon his return, they quickly established a routine. She held the ladder to steady it and handed Owen the plastic, glitter-covered bells. He hung them where she directed, and they finished in no time.

"We make a good team," she said without thinking.

"In more ways than one."

Ah, that sexy quality to his voice always turned her insides to mush. She required a full three seconds for his statement to sink in. In some—no, many—ways they did make a good team. What should she do about that?

Unable to wait, and hoping she wasn't ruining any plans of his to make a big announcement, she asked, "Did Craft-Right accept your counteroffer?"

He collapsed the ladder, making it easier to carry. "The board is reviewing it. I should hear by tomorrow. Christmas Eve at the latest."

"I'm surprised."

"That they're considering my terms?"

"No. That they aren't waiting until after Christmas. A lot of companies shut down or significantly slow down this time of year."

"The president said they wanted to lock their decision down before everyone took off."

"How'd they react?"

"Positive, I'd say."

"That's good, right? The job will be more to your liking."

Grinning, he handed her the box of screw-in fasteners. "It is good. For you and me."

Against her will, she returned his grin. "You're nothing if not persistent."

"As promised. I happen to think you're worth it."

Before he could weaken her defenses further, she said, "By the way, our first wedding on Christmas Eve is turning into a major production. The Millers would like you to drive the bride to the house in the carriage. The groom is riding up on horseback. They've hired a videographer to film the entire thing. Oh, and *Southwest Bride Magazine* will be here to take pictures."

"They will?"

"Yeah. The columnist called this morning with some follow-up questions. When I mentioned this particular wedding, she insisted on pictures. How could I say no? Now Grandma can be included in the article."

"That's great."

"I'm glad she'll have a chance to meet your children before they leave," Molly said.

"Me, too."

"You ready?"

Owen shook his head. "I haven't so much as cracked open a suitcase."

"I meant, are you ready for the children to leave?"

His demeanor changed, becoming introspective. "Not at all. It's been a great month, and I'm going to hate not having them around."

"There's always the kitten."

"Don't remind me. Marisa's beside herself, refusing to part with Pinkie Pie."

"Molly!" Bridget hollered from the kitchen. "Nora and I need you."

"I'm being summoned."

"Before you go." Owen slid his fingers into her loose hair. "Join me and the kids at the campfire tonight after supper. While they're roasting marshmallows we can talk."

Was that a good idea? Clearly, he wanted to discuss their potential relationship. How she answered in this moment would dictate where they went from here. Yes, she was willing to move forward. No, not a speck of hope for them.

Molly considered a few more seconds before answering, "I'll see you then."

CHAPTER FOURTEEN

OWEN LEANED AGAINST the veranda railing and observed the O'Malley family reunion, his uncle Homer and Emily the center of attention. The RV had pulled into the ranch not five minutes earlier. At the first sound of an approaching vehicle, Molly had torn free from Owen's arms and run through the house to the front door.

Not that they'd been kissing or snuggling or anything remotely intimate. No, Owen had been helping Molly down from the attic stairs. Located in a nook above the second floor, the small storage area contained mostly holiday decorations and keepsakes.

Molly had been determined to locate a doll cradle her grandparents had given her one Christmas when she was Marisa's age. Last evening at the campfire, Molly had told the little girl about the cradle, and she'd been instantly enthralled.

He knew the cradle was special to Molly and warned her that letting Marisa play with it might end badly. Molly was insistent, however, and

Owen didn't argue. He liked that she wanted to share something special from her childhood with his daughter.

Beating Owen and Bridget out the door, Molly had flung herself at Emily the second she emerged from the RV's passenger side door. The next instant, she'd burst into tears and was only now starting to collect herself.

"You're finally home," Molly said between sniffles. "Now it feels like Christmas!"

Emily beamed. "And we're glad to be here."

We're. Not *I'm*. Owen noticed Molly's smile falter a fraction before resuming. He didn't think the reason was a dislike of Uncle Homer. Not in the least. But her grandmother no longer belonged exclusively to the O'Malleys. That would probably require some getting used to for Molly. She was very close to her family.

"Who are they?" Cody asked. He stood beside Owen along with both his sisters.

"Miss Molly's grandmother and my uncle Homer. You remember him." The kids had met Owen's great-uncle once several months earlier. That was long ago for them, and they may not remember him.

Nora waited on Owen's other side, holding back while Molly and Bridget took turns fussing over their grandmother.

"We'll just give them another minute," she said to Owen.

Bridget muscled past Molly to embrace her grandmother. Once there, she didn't let go. "We missed you so much." When she was, at last, through, she turned to Uncle Homer and enveloped him in a warm hug. "Welcome to the family."

"You're not mad at me?" he asked with a chagrined smile. "For stealing your grandmother?"

"We were a little at first," Molly admitted before hugging him, too. "Only because you didn't tell us."

"But we're over it," Bridget assured him when his expression faltered. "And can't wait to celebrate after the vow renewal ceremony."

"We cleared New Year's Day. Yours is the only wedding scheduled," Molly interjected. "And even though we're working Christmas day we're going to have the best celebration that night. The whole family."

"Please don't tell me you turned away paying customers. Didn't I teach you better than that?" Emily sighed, only to loop an arm around Molly's waist and tug her close. "Thank you, darling. That was very thoughtful of you." She let her arm drop and looked about. "Now, where's everyone else hiding?" Spotting Owen,

Nora and the kids, she exclaimed, "There you are!"

Nora scampered down the veranda steps, displaying remarkable agility for a woman her age. She'd been the only one who stopped first to grab a coat and the flaps billowed like wings.

"Didn't think you had it in you, old girl," Nora said. She and Emily clung to each other. "Proved me wrong."

"Please say you're happy for me."

"Over the moon. You got yourself a good one."

"I did!"

Uncle Homer climbed the veranda steps after letting Nora first scold him and then kiss him soundly on the cheek. When he went to shake Owen's hand, Owen pulled him into a bear hug. "Congratulations. She's a great gal. How'd you get so lucky?"

"I'm blessed, no question about it." Before he averted his gaze, Owen caught a glimpse of tears in his great-uncle's eyes. "I appreciate you covering for me, son."

"It was my pleasure and my honor."

"How are the youngins doing?" Uncle Homer bent to address the kids. "You three have been keeping your dad on his toes, I hear."

Willa shied away from him and gripped Owen's leg. Marisa nodded solemnly.

Only Cody responded. "I'm being good."

"Santa will be leaving you lots of presents, then."

"I asked him for a bike. A two-wheeler."

Uncle Homer patted Cody on the shoulder and straightened. "That's a fine gift." He winked at Owen. "I hope you get it."

"We'll see" was all Owen would say. Finding a place to hide the kids' presents where they wouldn't find them had proved a challenge until Molly suggested a closet in the clubhouse. One large enough for a bike.

"When are you thinking of leaving?" Uncle Homer asked.

"Jeanne is coming by Christmas morning to pick up the kids. The next day, I suppose. Molly invited me to Christmas dinner."

Two days from now. He'd be alone and dreaded the moment. In one short month he'd gone from having a lousy relationship with his kids and his youngest barely recognizing him to Cody, Marisa and Willa being his entire world. What would he do with himself?

Of course, he'd have a kitten for company. Rather than impose on Jeanne, he'd decided to keep Pinkie Pie. And, if Craft-Right accepted his counteroffer, a job. He'd yet to hear and was trying not to worry.

Had he made too many demands? Was the

board having trouble getting together for a meeting?

"Any chance you can stay on through New Year's?" Uncle Homer asked. "Emily and I decided during our trip that she's moving in with me. We need a few days to pack her stuff and make room in my house. Also have to clean out and service the RV. I was hoping to take this week off. But if you need to get home, I understand."

Owen's glance cut to Molly. Remaining on at Sweetheart Ranch wasn't in his plans. On the other hand, plans could be changed.

"Happy to help any way I can." He'd be free even if he went to work for Craft-Right. The job didn't start until mid January. "The house can sit empty a while longer. But let's check with Molly first. She may have assumed I'd be gone and reserved my cabin."

"What about your cabin?" Emily asked, making her way toward them. When she reached the veranda, she and Owen hugged.

Homer beamed at his bride. "Owen's willing to remain through the first of the year and give me time off to get you moved."

"I don't want to inconvenience you or take a cabin that could be making you money," Owen insisted. "I can stay at the inn."

"Nonsense. I won't hear of it." She knelt down,

putting herself on the same level as the kids. "Who are these adorable munchkins? Surely not yours? I heard they were little tyrants. All I see are three perfect angels."

"I'm Cody." Because the girls were still being shy, he pointed and said, "This is my sister Marisa and my baby sister Willa. Who are you?"

Emily rubbed her chin in thought. "Hmm. I guess I'm your step-great-great aunt? No, that can't be right. Too confusing and makes me sound *really* old. How about you just call me Grandma Em? Everybody else does."

"But you're not my grandma."

"Technically, no. We can fudge a little, it won't hurt."

"I like fudge." Cody brightened.

"Me, too. Let's see if there's any in the house."

The prospect of treats combined with the cold weather was enough to drive everyone inside. Owen waited for Molly by the door. Without asking, she bent and picked up Willa, who happily went to her. Owen held Marisa's hand and remained ready to chase after Cody if necessary.

As often happened with big gatherings, people congregated in the kitchen. Especially in this house, where one of the residents was a trained pastry chef. Not only was a plate of fudge waiting on the counter, there were also cookies and dessert breads. Molly prepared a fresh pot of coffee and instant hot chocolate for the kids. Good cheer prevailed now that the O'Malleys were back together.

Owen enjoyed participating and wanted to continue doing so. Not just as Uncle Homer's closest relative.

"I have plenty of leftover chili," Bridget announced while they snacked. "You will eat dinner with us, yes?"

"Nothing I'd like better," Emily said, "but Homer and I have so much to do and are just exhausted. I'm going to grab a few things from my room, and then we're heading to his house. I'll be back bright and early in the morning."

"We haven't had a chance to really visit." Molly's smile drooped. "I want to hear about your trip."

"We can do that tomorrow after your mom and Doug get here. She said to expect them by lunchtime."

"The first wedding's at three and the second one at five thirty. That won't give us much time."

"We'll figure something out," Emily said, pulling her into an affectionate embrace. "I love you, sweetie."

After snacks and coffee, they went outside to see off Uncle Homer and Emily. Owen's kids were curious about a traveling home, and Uncle

Homer offered to give a tour of the inside. Owen passed—he'd seen the RV's interior before.

Emily remained behind with him. "Do you have a sec?"

"Absolutely." He assumed she wanted to discuss work. He was wrong.

"I hear things are getting serious between you and Molly."

"She told you?"

"No, no, no. Bridget did. Molly's too close-mouthed."

"I'm not sure *serious* is the word. I'd say 'ready to try serious.' If things work out." He and Molly had discussed as much at the campfire last night.

"She's vulnerable, Owen. I'm not convinced she's fully recovered from her last relationship."

"I'm in no hurry."

"I'm glad." Emily visibly relaxed. "For you as much as her. She can be her own worst enemy. When Molly wants something, she wants it with an intensity and excitement that prompts her to go overboard. Too often, she winds up losing the very thing she desperately wanted. That happened not only with her engagements, also with her jobs."

"She's mentioned a little about her past."

"Yeah? Well, whatever she said, double it. No, triple it."

This time, he didn't hold back and laughed.

Emily did, too, only to sober. "All kidding aside. I don't care what I said earlier about you being family, you hurt her, you give her one moment's grief, and I'll hunt you down."

"I'd cut off my arm before hurting Molly."

She reached up and patted his cheek. "I quite like you, Owen."

"I like you, too, Emily."

The tour evidently ended, for everyone piled out of the RV. Emily left Owen then to rejoin her husband and granddaughters. Owen figured no one had any idea about their conversation. Seemed he was wrong again.

"What did Grandma want?" Molly asked once the kids had gone inside with Nora, and they were alone.

"We were just chatting."

"About?"

"She threatened me with my life if I hurt you."

"Funny. Wait. Are you kidding?"

"Come inside. It's cold, and you must be freezing."

They crossed the threshold and entered the foyer. The twinkling Christmas tree greeted them, bathing them in a rainbow of colors and enhancing the festive mood Owen was already feeling.

She tugged on his arm, bringing him to a standstill. "Tell me what Grandma said."

"She heard from Bridget we were getting close."

Molly groaned. "Blabbermouth."

"Your family loves you." He took Molly's hand and linked their fingers. "It's natural for them to worry. I told your grandma that we were taking things slow."

Molly nodded.

With no one nearby, he dared to pull her against him and stroke her back. "Everything is going to work out for us, honey."

Owen kissed her then, holding nothing back. When Molly raised on tiptoes to deepen the kiss, he experienced a shift inside him. It was the missing pieces of his life falling into place. Surely that was a sign of what was to come.

THE EXCITEMENT OF Emily and Uncle Homer returning was repeated with the arrival of Molly's parents bright and early the next morning, way ahead of schedule. After a very quick introduction, Owen left the O'Malley clan alone to catch up before Molly, Bridget and Emily flew into wedding countdown frenzy.

They all had a full day ahead, including Owen. He'd need to begin grooming and harnessing the horses by noon in order to deliver the bride to the house in time for the wedding. That left him a few hours between now and then to take the kids on a spur-of-the-moment shopping trip.

Last night Marisa had lamented that she had no Christmas present for her mother. Honestly, Owen hadn't given it much thought. Okay, no thought whatsoever. Jeanne had always handled that parenting duty. But because it was important to his oldest daughter that she have a present for her mother, he decided to see what could be done. This morning was his only opportunity.

Cody didn't seem to care one way or the other about a present for Jeanne, and Willa was too young to understand. They were, however, excited to be away from the ranch. The arrival of Molly's family combined with the anticipation of seeing their mother tomorrow had them bouncing off the walls with excess energy.

As Owen and the kids strolled the sidewalks of Mustang Valley in search of a store, he tried not to think about Craft-Right. He'd yet to hear from Monty regarding his counteroffer and hoped no news was good news. But with each passing hour, his confidence waned.

Being a small, rural town deep of the throes of celebrating the holidays, there was a new activity to entice the kids around every corner. Carolers singing jolly songs. A woman walking a dog wearing an elf costume. A volunteer ringing a bell and standing by a red bucket.

"Look, Daddy!" Cody exclaimed. "A charity."

"You're right." Proud of his son, Owen gave the kids each several dollar bills to drop in the bucket.

"Let's go to the feed store" was Cody's next suggestion. He kept attempting to run ahead and was constantly being called back by Owen.

"Yay!" Marisa cried. "We can buy Pinkie Pie a present, too."

Under any other circumstances, Owen would have jumped at the chance to chat with Fred. He'd miss the jovial proprietor when he left.

"I doubt there's anything in there for your mom."

Jeanne was more girlie-girl than cowgirl. Now, Owen? Practically everything on his Christmas list could be found in Fred's store, from a horseshoe money clip to a new hoof pick to a boot shining kit.

He and the kids continued their stroll. Owen knew from his previous visits to the local market there wouldn't be anything in there other than postcards with pictures of jackalopes and cheesy plastic trinkets featuring a cartoon saguaro cactus or the state flag.

At the corner, he noticed a sandwich board sign advertising The Last-Minute Shopper Sale with an arrow pointing at the local church on the corner. The same church where Uncle Homer used to preach.

"Come on, kids." Owen grabbed the girls' hands and prodded Cody along. "This way."

Keeping the kids focused and on task wasn't easy. Who knew there'd be so many toys and games?

Eventually, they found a vendor selling wooden music boxes. Marisa went back and forth and, after much debate, selected a music box painted with flowers and that played "Beautiful Dreamer." Cody settled on an assortment of scented hand soaps from the neighboring table and Owen chose a knitted scarf and matching mittens for Willa to give Jeanne. That prompted him to buy a hand-sewn quilt—a belated wedding gift for Emily and Homer.

Satisfied, he was more than ready to head home. Near the exit they passed a table selling jewelry. A necklace hanging from a display brought him to a halt.

"Hey, guys, wait a minute."

"Not this stuff again," Cody complained when Owen led them to the table. He'd had his fill of shopping for the fairer sex.

The girls were fascinated by the jewelry and wanted to fondle every piece.

The necklace that Owen had noticed was a

pair of interlocking gold hearts with a semiprecious stone at the center, probably a garnet. The hearts made him think of Sweetheart Ranch and of Molly.

Was it too early in their relationship for exchanging gifts? Was a necklace too personal? Like Marisa a few minutes earlier, he deliberated for several minutes. What if she hadn't bought him a gift? What if she had, and he arrived empty-handed? She was planning on bringing presents for the kids early tomorrow morning before they left. Giving her a gift when she had none for him would create an awkward situation.

"I'll take this," he told the vendor and handed her the necklace.

She smiled cheerfully. "Would you like that in a box?"

"Please."

They'd no sooner left the church grounds than Cody said, "Daddy, I'm hungry."

It was almost eleven. One hour remained before Owen absolutely must get to work. "Okay. Let's go." They'd pass the market en route to the truck.

He and the kids were approaching the market's double glass-door entrance when Molly and her parents emerged from inside. Everyone stared at each other for several seconds before Molly spoke.

"Hi, Owen. I didn't realize you were coming here."

He held up his bags. "Some last-minute shopping at the gift sale down the road. We worked up an appetite."

Molly's mom, Caroline, bent to address the kids. Her expression dissolved into one of pure delight. "Did you have fun with your dad?"

"It was okay," Cody said. "We got my mom some presents."

She showered the kids with a bright smile. "How very special. Are you excited about Christmas?"

"Santa's coming to the cabin. We wrote him a letter and told him we'd be here instead of our house."

"That was smart of you."

"It was Molly's idea," Owen said.

"And a good one."

"Come on, Caroline," Doug groused. "The inn won't hold our reservation forever."

Her smile froze for a fraction of a second before she straightened. "We… I…actually, needed a few necessities from the market."

Owen noticed a six-pack of bottled water and a grocery sack. He also noticed Molly casting Doug a thinly disguised, albeit brief, irritated glance.

"I won't keep you," Owen said. "I'm in a hurry myself."

"Owen's driving the bride from the stables to the house in the carriage," Molly said. "This is our biggest, most involved wedding to date." She looked at her mother. "I told you the columnist and photographer from *Southwest Bride Magazine* will be there, didn't I?"

"You did!" Caroline's smile returned. "What a wonderful opportunity. I am so proud of you and Bridget and Mom. I can't believe I'm related to such accomplished women."

"Enough already." Doug tugged on his wife's arm. "You two can gab later." He shook his head at Owen and said in a tone intended to recruit Owen to his side, "I don't envy you, putting up with a bunch of women for a whole month."

"I've enjoyed every minute of it." He sought out Molly, whose eyes conveyed her appreciation.

"Hey, Molly," Doug said. "Why don't you ride home with Owen here? That'll save your mom and me a trip and you can get to work sooner."

"Do you mind, Owen?" She looked relieved— maybe because she was escaping her stepdad, or perhaps she was happy about spending extra time with him. He hoped the latter.

Owen instantly chided himself for being ungracious toward Doug. The suggestion was actually a good one and convenient for Molly's parents.

"Nothing I'd like better," he said.

More goodbyes, and then Molly joined Owen and the kids in the store where the kids pleaded for junk food and got trail mix instead.

Afterward, the five of them walked to the public parking lot half a block away. Molly helped Owen load the kids in the truck's backseat. Two car seats side by side with a booster chair were a snug fit.

"Your mom is great," Owen commented when they were on the road. "You look a lot like her. Both you and Bridget."

Molly smiled at him. She seemed considerably more relaxed now than at the market. "I'm taking that as a compliment."

"You should. She's an attractive woman."

"I know Doug can be trying. Thanks for putting up with him."

"He's not bad."

"I think sometimes I'm too critical of him."

That was a big admission for Molly, and Owen took his eyes off traffic for a quick second to study her.

"My dad, he was such an incredible guy. I could never figure out why my mom settled for someone...not so incredible."

"Maybe people like your dad don't come

around very often, and your mother realized that. Or she purposely chose someone unlike him. To preserve his memory."

Molly drew back, her mouth open. "I hadn't thought of that before. You might be on to something." She leaned back against the seat. "I really believed I was engaged to men just like him. I was wrong." She turned to face him. "I've learned something about myself recently. In part because of you."

"What's that?"

"My former fiancés *were* like my dad on the surface. They both had good jobs, wanted a family, were attractive. What should have mattered, and what I overlooked, was how little they resembled him on the inside where it counted. He was kindhearted, generous and had a strong moral compass. He always put others first."

"Wish I'd met him."

She reached across the console and laid a hand on Owen's knee. "I wish you'd met him, too. You'd have been friends."

"I'm taking *that* as a compliment."

"You should."

Something passed between Owen and Molly then. More than a touch. More than words. More than emotions. It was a connection like nothing Owen had felt before—strong and sure and to his very core. He was sorry when the ranch came into view and sorrier still when the ride was over.

He parked in front of the house, letting the engine idle. As if they'd done it a hundred times, Molly leaned toward him and planted a soft kiss on his mouth. "See you in a little bit."

He couldn't let her go without cupping her face with his hand and tracing his thumbs along the smooth hollows of her cheeks. "I'll be the one driving the carriage."

"I'll be the one looking for you."

Yes! Owen had been waiting almost a month to hear her say that.

He leaned in for a second kiss. At the same moment, his phone chimed. Simultaneously, the number for Craft-Right appeared on his dashboard's display and the Bluetooth kicked in. A loud ringing filled the cab's interior, and his pulse quickened.

"It's Monty Hickman." He pulled back. "I need to get this."

Owen grabbed his phone and pressed the button on the dashboard display that transferred the call from the Bluetooth. He opened the truck door and hopped out, worried the kids might raise a ruckus. Not the professional image he wished to present.

"Hello. Owen Caufield here." He shut the door. While he listened to what Monty had to say,

Molly waited by the front of the truck, giving him privacy.

When Monty was done, Owen thanked the man, a mixture of emotions coursing through him. Until Monty had delivered the board's decision, Owen wasn't entirely sure he'd wanted the job or not.

"Well?" Molly tentatively approached, her expression expectant. "Do we break out the champagne?"

Owen pocketed his phone. "The board rejected my counteroffer. I either accept their terms or they give the job to someone else. I told Monty thanks, but no."

CHAPTER FIFTEEN

MOLLY MOVED THE punch bowl from the center of the table to the right side, only to change her mind and move it back. Deciding the red ribbons on the silver candle holders were drooping, she fiddled with them until they looked worse than before.

"Gosh darn it." Face it, her concentration was shot.

Owen hadn't gotten the job at Craft-Right. More accurately, he'd turned down the job because the board rejected his counteroffer.

He'd handled the news reasonably well. Quite well, in fact. Possibly too well. He'd told her not to worry, that he needed to start harnessing the horses, and promptly left for the stables.

Molly was the one distraught. She'd been hoping he'd get the job for his sake. Owen placed tremendous value on being able to provide well for his children and also on his ability to bring a lot to the table in their relationship. Being unemployed didn't sit well with him, more so every day.

She wished she could go to him. That wasn't

possible, however. Everything had to be just right for today's wedding, down to the tiniest detail. Not only for the couple and their guests but for the columnist and photographer from *Southwest Bride Magazine*.

"Stupid ribbons," Molly mumbled to herself.

"Are you okay, honey?"

She spun to see her mother entering the parlor. Apparently back early from the inn, she'd been in the kitchen helping Bridget with the punch and cake for the reception.

"Terrific," Molly lied.

"You sure?" Her mother approached and studied Molly critically. "You've been staring at those candlesticks for a full minute without moving."

Had she?

Molly gave herself a mental shake. "I have a lot on my plate."

"Yes, you do." Her mother reached out and stroked Molly's hair like she often had when Molly was a child. "What's really wrong? I've known you your whole life. I can tell when something's bothering you."

She willed herself to remain in control. It was tempting to throw herself into her mother's arms and pour her heart out. Now wasn't the time. The bride was due to arrive at two thirty.

"Nothing."

"Honey, tell me."

Molly's determination deserted her. "Owen didn't get the job at Craft-Right."

"I'm sorry to hear that. I know he was counting on it."

Homer had mentioned Owen's job opportunity during what little catching up the family had managed earlier that morning.

"He was," Molly concurred.

"And you were, too. Right?"

"How did you—"

"Know you're seeing each other?" Her mother pinched Molly's cheek affectionately. "Even if I hadn't spotted the chemistry sizzling between the two of you, your grandmother mentioned it and Bridget showed me the kiss cam video."

She should have figured as much.

"You and Owen won, you know."

"We did?"

Molly had been so preoccupied, she'd forgotten to check the announcement of the winner. Unable to resist, she dug her phone from her pocket and checked the website. There was the announcement, big as life.

"I don't think there was a doubt," her mother said. "Maybe you and he can talk things out during the dinner."

Molly replaced her phone. Her first impulse was to hold back, wait for a better heart-to-heart opportunity, one where a wedding ceremony wasn't imminent. But upon seeing her mother's tender expression, the words spilled out, and Molly couldn't stop them.

"I resisted him from the start. Put up every barrier imaginable and concocted countless excuses. He won me over, Mom. I fell for him. Despite my determination not to."

"I understand. It was the same for me with your dad."

"I was starting to think we had a chance even though we're both dealing with a lot and each have twenty irons in the fire. Then he didn't get the job." Molly sighed. "I'm a terrible person."

"No, you're not. You just wanted to eliminate one of those irons. That's natural."

"I feel like we've lost a lot of ground. Here we were ready to move ahead, and now we're back to square one with me feeling like I'm interfering with his priorities."

"It's true that Owen's a package deal," her mother said. "He comes with three big responsibilities, ages five and under."

"I love the children. They're adorable."

"Hey, they had me at hello." Her mother came over and squeezed Molly's shoulder. "If you and Owen truly care for each other, you'll find a way. You have another week before he leaves. Give yourselves a chance to talk before jumping to any decision. He may surprise you with what he has to say."

"There's something else." Molly hesitated, not wanting to voice her secret fear aloud.

"What?"

"I think it might be possible Owen's glad he didn't get the job a Craft-Right."

Shock registered on her mother's face. "Why would he be glad?"

"Maybe *relieved* is a better word. He made some comments the other day about not wanting to go back to sales."

"What kind of comments?"

"Nothing specific. I guess it's more a feeling I have."

"I recommend you not worry until you've had a chance to talk to him."

Her mother's advice was good and worth following. Molly did have a habit of working herself into a sweat unnecessarily.

The mantel clock chiming reminded them that duty called. Sweetheart Ranch had their biggest wedding to date to pull off. Now wasn't the time to let personal problems that may not even be problems get in the way.

Molly reached for the punch bowl. "Should this go here or in the middle of the table?"

"What do you think?"

"At the end. To avoid congestion."

"See?" Her mother smiled. "You're learning."

"I actually haven't disliked covering for Grandma while she and Homer were on their trip. I was convinced at first that I couldn't manage on my own. Then I surprised myself. Yeah, I've made some mistakes. I've also done well, like with the cross-promotion brochure."

"I'd say Mom knew what she was doing all along, choosing you to replace her and putting your feet to the fire."

"Grandma told me she wants us all to go shopping the first of next week. To pick out her vow renewal dress." The thought of the family outing cheered Molly. "She's having me design and send out e-invitations. Can you believe that? Grandma using technology to invite people?"

"I'm still not over her eloping. My mom, running off like a teenager." Molly's mother smiled wistfully. "I guess when you're in love, you throw caution to the wind."

Molly thought about her grandmother and Homer. They'd been so sure, they'd defied convention and rushed off on a moment's notice. How she longed to be like them. Not to run off with Owen but to date him. Her past, however, continued to whisper warnings in her ear.

Unable to postpone any longer, Molly and her mother applied the finishing touches to the parlor before moving to the chapel. The bride and her party arrived promptly at two thirty. She was in a hurry to change into her dress, complete her hair and makeup, and get to the stables where the carriage waited, all before the groom made his appearance.

Thank goodness Molly's mother was there to help as the next minute the columnist and photographer arrived, along with the singer hired to perform during the service; the videographer; and the groom's brother/best man, who pulled a trailer with the groom's horse. While Grandma Em took charge of the magazine reps, Molly's mom drove the bride to the stables. Molly sent the groom's brother to the other side of the ranch, away from the stables, to park and unload the horse. She directed the singer where to set up and discussed vantage points with the videographer.

Despite a prediction for rain by late afternoon, the weather cooperated. The sun peeked out from between drifting clouds, and the breeze remained mild. Molly crossed her fingers that Mother Nature would continue being generous with her favors until after their second wedding at five thirty.

Molly's mother had barely returned when the first of many vehicles drove onto the ranch, one containing the groom and his parents. Molly wasn't prepared for a dog to be included in the group. It seemed the groom's mother didn't go anywhere without her poodle mix, Buster.

Momentarily flummoxed, she decided not to make a scene in front of the magazine reps about only service animals being allowed and no pets. After all, she'd let Owen keep the kitten. Besides, the wedding would be over and everyone gone in a couple of hours. What could go wrong as long as the woman kept the dog on a leash?

The next thing Molly knew, it was time for the wedding to start. As had been arranged, everyone stood on the veranda while the groom rode up on his horse. Then they waited for the bride to show in the carriage. Dark maroon and hunter green crepe paper streamers had been wrapped around the railings and columns, and matching pairs of paper bells hung from the top railing at three-foot intervals. All fluttered prettily in the breeze, giving the place a holiday feel perfect for a Christmas Eve wedding and adding to the festive gathering.

Molly, her mother and grandmother huddled beside the swing, out of the way but ready to step in should the need arise. The columnist and photographer watched from their place near the gate while the videographer tracked the groom's progress.

Every pair of eyes was riveted on the bend in the road when the carriage came into view, accompanied by the sound of hooves and jingle bells. Molly was convinced each person held their breath in collective anticipation.

Amos and Moses walked at a brisk but controlled pace, heads held high as if they understood the importance of their role. The bride sat in the carriage, waving and wearing a huge smile. The mild breeze continued to cooperate and lifted her veil just the right amount so that it floated elegantly behind her. The sight they made as Owen brought the carriage to a stop in front of the house was pure enchantment.

"Whoa, boys." He pulled on the reins.

The bride, her beautiful features radiating joy, started to rise. Gasps of delight traveled throughout the guests. The groom stared, his goofy grin endearing.

Molly couldn't be happier. Everything was going exactly as planned.

And then disaster struck.

BUSTER CATAPULTED FROM the arms of the groom's mother. Hitting the veranda floor with a yelp, he bolted toward the horses, yapping frantically with his leash dragging behind him. Reaching them, he skidded to a halt and faced the giant beasts a hundred times his size, alternately barking, growling and snapping.

Normally calm, the horses began snorting and prancing. Owen commanded them to stand. Holding the reins tight, he reached for the lever to his right. Before he could engage the hand brake, Buster dove in and bit Amos on the front right leg, growling furiously. In retaliation, Amos reared slightly, and then attempted to stomp the dog to pieces. The groom's mother screamed. Rather than run away, Buster became incensed and lunged at Amos a second time, missing his hoof by a mere inch.

As everyone watched in alarm and horror, Amos first bucked and then charged ahead, going from a standstill to a full gallop and dragging Moses with him. Buster was nearly crushed under the front left carriage wheel. Amid cries of alarm, Molly pushed her way through to the front of the gathering, emerging beside the groom.

"Do something!" he hollered.

She ran down the steps and after the carriage, though how she could help she had no clue. Thankfully, Owen brought the horses to a bumpy stop about a hundred yards ahead.

"Grab the dog," Molly hollered.

Short of breath and heart pounding, she caught up with the carriage and was vastly relieved to find the bride unharmed, though obviously shaken.

"Are you all right?" she asked, holding on to the carriage door, her voice choppy.

"I think so," the bride replied weakly.

The groom reached them, equally out of breath as Molly. "My God, Valerie, are you hurt?"

"No." She patted her head. "Where's my veil?"

Molly looked around, dismayed to see it had been lost during the brief runaway and lay in the road several yards behind them. "I'll get it for you." On wobbly legs, she hurried to where the veil lay and picked it up, cringing when she saw dirty streaks on the formerly pristine white lace.

Returning to the carriage, she was glad to see the bride significantly more composed. Also that the groom's father had collected troublemaker Buster. He was safe in the arms of his owner who clutched him to her chest.

The groom was attempting to explain what had happened, and his bride was having none of it.

"You're saying that stupid dog of your mother's is the reason the horses went nuts?" Her expression twisted into one of incredulity.

"Mom's dog isn't stupid. He's protective of her."

Her already flushed face turned beet red. "Are you seriously taking your mother's side over mine?"

"Baby. I'm sorry." He tried to climb into the carriage, but she stopped him with a raised hand.

"No. Stay there."

"How 'bout I turn these boys around and we head back to the house?" Owen said over his shoulder. What he didn't add, but Molly was sure he'd been thinking, was, *before anything worse happens*.

Ultimately, the bride climbed down from the carriage and walked to the house, her dress bunched in her hands so as not to drag in the dirt. The groom trailed behind her like an errant child, desperately trying to make amends for his blunder.

"I'm heading to the stables," Owen said to Molly. "I'll meet you inside."

"And I'll try to restore order."

He grinned. "You think she's still going to marry him after all this?"

"Please, no jokes," Molly begged. Nothing about what had happened was funny to her.

As she started up the walkway to the house, a strong gust of wind came out of nowhere and whipped past them. Fortunately, the bride had a hold of her veil or she would have lost it again. The crepe paper decorations were a different matter. Several streamers and two pairs of bells were caught by the gust and spun like pinwheels across the front yard.

"No!" the bride cried out and promptly exploded into a torrent of tears. She was immediately surrounded by supporters, but their best efforts to soothe her were useless. She couldn't be consoled.

Molly was at a loss. There was no way to undo what had happened. Getting angry at the groom's mother would only make the situation worse. Perhaps the best course of action was to let the bride's meltdown play out before intervening.

It was then Molly noticed both the magazine photographer and the videographer capturing every moment and she wanted to scream with frustration. How could she have forgotten about them? Just imagining the negative recounting in the magazine—who was she kidding, Sweetheart Ranch would probably be cut from the top ten list—and a video of the runaway carriage going viral online had her longing for a dark cave in which to hide.

"Don't cry," the bride's mother crooned, "you'll ruin your makeup."

"I don't care! I don't even want to get married anymore."

"Baby." The groom put an arm around her, squishing her veil. "Don't say that."

She shrugged off his arm with a "Leave me alone."

"Buster didn't mean to scare the horses." The mother of the groom took a step forward.

"Keep that mangy mutt away from me." The bride's laser glare sent her future mother-in-law slinking back to her former place.

Molly squeezed her eyes shut and silently prayed for the day to be over. The next moment, her grandmother cut through to small crowd.

"Valerie, you poor dear." She took the bride's arm and patted it comfortingly. "How about I take you inside and help you tidy up? You don't want any pictures with your hair mussed and your makeup smeared." She addressed the gathering. "I'm sorry, but the dog needs to stay outside. Someone will have to remain behind with him."

"But Buster doesn't like the cold," the mother of the groom objected.

"I'll bring a blanket."

"Thank you." The bride gazed gratefully at Grandma Em.

"The groom and everyone else, please follow Molly to the chapel. Valerie, maid of honor and Mom—" she pointed to each person as she spoke "—you all come with me to the bride's dressing room. We've got some work to do."

The three women willingly accompanied Grandma Em into the house. Molly corralled the rest of the group with her mother's help and escorted them to the chapel. The columnist and photographer came, too, as well as the videographer. Molly silently groaned with every photo snapped and each time the video camera was directed at her.

Was this the end of Sweetheart Ranch, all because of a disobedient dog Molly had allowed to stay?

CHAPTER SIXTEEN

MOLLY CONSIDERED IT a Christmas Eve gift from above that the first wedding went relatively smoothly once the bride's hair, makeup and veil were restored. The only other glitch wasn't really a glitch at all. Because of the delayed start, the second wedding had to be pushed back. But then bride number two's cousin was late, so the delay didn't affect much.

To Molly's surprise, the columnist and photographer asked to stick around for the second wedding. She wondered if they were secretly hoping for a repeat disaster—she'd heard they were very entertained by the runaway carriage. Thankfully, wedding number two proceeded flawlessly.

The second bride had been so thrilled at the prospect of potentially appearing in what she loudly proclaimed was her favorite wedding magazine she'd not only consented to pictures being taken, she'd personally orchestrated every one.

Molly carried a stack of forks to the kitchen,

glad that bride number two had promised to pass on her positive experience to all her friends. Molly had been too nervous to check the ranch's social media page, though her phone had vibrated several times, alerting her to new comments or posts.

Her mother entered the kitchen right behind Molly, bringing the last of the punch cups. She and Molly had volunteered to clean up, allowing Grandma Em to attend a candlelight church service with Homer and Bridget.

"Did you notice Owen talking to the columnist?" Molly's mother began rinsing dishes.

"No, when was that?"

"She stopped him on his way out."

"Hmm." Molly's mind instantly concocted multiple scenarios. "I thought they left during the reception."

She and her grandmother had seen the magazine reps off, leaving them with the best impression of Sweetheart Ranch they could. Grandma Em's many years dealing with dissatisfied customers at the inn had come in handy.

Even though the columnist had complimented them on their handling of the runaway carriage and distraught bride, Molly agonized over the catastrophe appearing in the article.

"What did they talk about? I wonder," she mused aloud.

"The columnist asked him where he'd gotten his ceremony. I overheard them when I was taking down whatever crepe paper decorations didn't blow away in the wind," she added. "The columnist said she'd never heard a service like Owen's."

Neither had Molly.

"You have to admit, it was nice."

"It was," she agreed.

Owen had used the same ceremony for both weddings. Altering his usual introduction, he'd included a part about how the Egyptians were believed to be the first culture to exchange rings of love and that they also believed a vein or nerve ran directly from the ring finger to the heart. With his sexy, lopsided grin and down-home speaking style, he'd made it sound romantic.

He'd made amazing progress since that first ceremony. He'd become polished and professional and could easily make a career of officiating weddings if he chose.

"He was a big help with damage control after the carriage ride fiasco, don't you think?" Molly's mother asked.

Molly nodded. "Lesson learned. No dogs ever again. Unless they're part of the ceremony and stay inside."

Her mother's phone rang. She went to her

purse on the counter and grabbed it. "Doug needs the car," she said, hanging up.

Molly refrained from complaining. She may not fully understand her mother's marriage to Doug, but she was committed to being more tolerant of him. Owen's recent remarks were responsible for her enlightened perspective. "Go on. There's not much left."

"You sure?"

Molly could see her mother was torn. "Get some rest. We have another busy day tomorrow."

They hugged goodbye at the door and Molly returned to the parlor, intending to make a final pass and retrieve any missed items. She became distracted when her phone vibrated for the third time in the past few minutes. Now that she was alone, she risked checking the ranch's social media page, bracing herself for the worst.

Good thing she had. There at the top was a scathing post from the groom's mother, Buster's owner. Molly barely took note of the recent rave review from a wedding the previous weekend.

"'The house is gorgeous and the cake divine but skip the carriage ride,'" Molly read out loud, her blood running alternately hot and cold as her pulse pounded. "'The horses ran off with my new daughter-in-law before the poor girl had a chance to get out of the carriage. Almost ruined the wedding.'" Unable to read any more,

Molly closed the app on her phone. "You failed to mention your dog yapping his head off and biting Amos's leg."

Her anger changed targets, from the groom's mother to herself. Why hadn't she insisted Buster not be allowed near the wedding? She'd known better. Even Grandma Em had questioned Molly's decision.

Grandma Em, Molly thought glumly. In an effort to prove herself capable, she'd let down someone she loved and who had depended on her.

Worse, she'd let herself down. Molly had worked hard to help launch Sweetheart Ranch and build the family business. Just look how far they'd come in a month. Now their future might be in danger all because of one bad decision.

Molly let herself wallow for another minute before deciding the parlor was clean enough. Returning to the kitchen, she stopped short upon seeing Owen at the counter, pouring himself a mug of leftover coffee.

"I thought you were at the cabin," she said. "It's late."

"Nora's with the kids." Setting down his mug, he yanked on his coat, popping open the snaps one at a time. "I just came from checking the horses one last time. Gave them a thorough once-over in case something other than the dog caused them to spook."

"And?"

"Nothing." He shook his head. "I honestly thought those two were impossible to rile. Apparently not when it comes to being barked at by a twelve-pound dog."

"More than barked at. Buster bit Amos."

Owen laughed. "Not that you can tell. Tiny teeth apparently aren't enough to penetrate his thick hide."

"Mom said you talked to the columnist before she and the photographer left."

"For a few minutes." He sipped at his coffee.

"What did she say?"

"Not much. They've been to a lot of weddings and assured me they'd seen worse disasters."

"I can't imagine anything worse. I dread seeing the article when it comes out."

He settled himself beside Molly at the counter, their arms and legs brushing. "I wouldn't lose any sleep over it."

She was aware of his presence, but it didn't slow her racing thoughts and tangled emotions like usual. "Easy for you to say. This ranch isn't your livelihood and your entire world."

"But it's yours. And because I care about you, its success matters to me."

"What if we fail?"

"You won't. Not over one incident."

"Just look at that restaurant chain in the news. It went under all because their CEO made an inappropriate remark caught on video." Molly's phone vibrated again. She didn't dare look, afraid of what she'd read.

"Don't take this wrong, please, but is there any chance you're overreacting? Nothing bad happened after Tasha and Wayne's wedding when their son live streamed Marisa shoving her."

Molly's muscles tensed. "My concerns are valid."

"I'm not saying they aren't. Only that you shouldn't drive yourself crazy with needless worry."

Despite her mother saying much the same to her earlier, Molly bristled.

"Is this your way of trying to make me feel better? Because I'm feeling worse by the minute." Annoyed, she took out her phone and checked the newest comment. "See here." She showed him her phone. "This person writes that she was considering having her wedding here but after reading about the runaway she's going to book her wedding at that Victorian house in Gilbert."

"She's one person."

"One person can start an avalanche."

"Post a reply," Owen suggested. "Businesses

do it all the time. When I was at Waverly, we received plenty of complaints. Customers seemed to appreciate a personal response that addressed the problem."

"How can I do that without blaming the groom's mother? People will hate us."

"Be sincere. Apologize. Say the horses were frightened by a dog but don't mention who owned the dog."

"It's not that simple, Owen."

"It's not that difficult," he countered.

Says him. She dumped the rest of the coffee down the sink and rinsed out the pot. "I get that I can be…overzealous sometimes. Allow my emotions to get the best of me. But this is serious and, in my opinion, worth getting upset about."

"Take a deep breath." He placed a hand on her arm. "Relax. Tomorrow things won't look so terrible."

She stiffened at what she perceived to be a condescending tone.

He let his hand drop. "Sorry. I'm trying, Molly."

Her anger marginally abated. "I wish you'd support me rather than criticize me or contradict me."

"I thought I was supporting you."

"Telling me to take a breath and relax or that

I'm overreacting isn't being supportive. It's patronizing."

"I don't see it that way but okay."

She'd hurt him and possibly angered him. She could tell by the way his mouth flattened to a narrow line.

"What I need from you is sympathy and understanding. Even if you think I'm going off the deep end."

"I was offering advice," he said.

"In a way that dismisses my concerns."

He drained his coffee and set the mug in the sink. "You're upset."

"With good cause."

"And you want to pick a fight."

Did she? Possibly. Her worry about their future on top of the wedding calamity had her nerves wound tight as a drum.

She strived to keep her voice level. "I'm not a child, Owen. I don't pick fights. I was expressing my concerns, talking through my problems as a means of finding solutions."

"Okay. I didn't get that."

No, he hadn't. Not in the least. Which caused her to wonder how little he knew her, and she him.

Losing the battle with the doubts and concerns she'd been resisting, she blurted, "I'm not sure dating is a good idea. Every time we've encountered a problem, we've come at it from opposite sides. Your children, the kitten, the carriage runaway, the negative reviews. It's like we're complete opposites."

She expected him to disagree, only he didn't. "You may be right."

His response threw her for a loop. Always in the past, she was the one putting on the brakes and he was the one wanting to move forward. "What changed your mind?"

"Not getting the job at Craft-Right."

She mulled that over for a moment. "I understand. I do. You've been clear about your need to be employed and the reasons it's important. What I don't understand is why you threw away a perfectly good opportunity."

"I didn't."

"I saw your face, Owen. You were relieved when Craft-Right rejected your counteroffer. I'm willing to bet that's what you hoped for."

Again, he didn't disagree with her. "Every time I thought about returning to the same old grind, my stomach turned to cement."

She'd been there herself and felt sorry for him. She was also angry, however, and, in her opinion, with good reason.

"You should have told me," she said. "Instead, you persuaded me to give us a chance even when

I was reluctant, and then pulled the rug out from under me without any warning."

"I'm not sure I knew myself until yesterday how much I didn't want the job and for purely selfish reasons." He looked truly miserable and remorseful. "What kind of a dad does that make me? Putting myself first?"

"I don't have children, I can't answer that. I do know you're devoted to Cody, Marisa and Willa, and you'll do whatever's necessary to see they lack for nothing."

He met her gaze, and the sorrow and remorse in his eyes quelled her anger. "I've screwed up, haven't I? Big time."

Somehow, she found the courage to speak what was on both their minds. "You're not just out of a job, you're at a career crossroads. Until you decide on a direction, we have to put our relationship on hold. We don't have a choice. Continuing would be unfair to your children, to yourself and to me."

"Hold? Or is that your polite way of giving me the boot?" His sad grin broke her heart.

"The choice is yours."

"I don't think I have but one."

She blinked back tears. He might have done the same, she wasn't positive.

"Nora's waiting on me." He glanced at the clock. "We're packing the kids' stuff so they'll be ready to leave in the morning when Jeanne arrives."

He turned to leave. Molly could sense his withdrawal, both emotional and physical, like heat escaping through an open window. It matched her own. She considered calling him back, but that would just make their already painful parting infinitely worse.

"See you in the morning." He left without looking back at her.

The sound of the door closing echoed inside Molly's empty chest. She sank into a kitchen chair and let her head fall into her waiting hands.

MOLLY STUMBLED INTO the kitchen over an hour later than usual, her eyes gritty from lack of sleep and her spirits so low she feared she'd trip over them. If not for the two small weddings that afternoon, she'd have stayed in bed all day with her head buried beneath the covers.

"Merry Christmas," Bridget announced. "You missed breakfast. Cinnamon French toast."

"Oops." That would account for the delicious aroma lingering in the kitchen. "My alarm didn't go off."

"Good thing we're opening presents tonight after the weddings."

"Yeah." Not that Molly was looking forward to it now that Owen probably wouldn't be there.

Too tired to see where she was going, she felt her way blindly to the refrigerator for some orange juice.

"There's leftover French toast in the microwave if you want," Bridget said.

"Thanks." Molly gulped her juice, the sweet taste boosting her lagging energy. "Where's Mom and Grandma? I didn't see them."

"Saying goodbye to Owen's children. Their mother will be here soon. They're stopping at her parents' house before driving to Lake Powell."

"That's a long day for three young children. A car trip on top of a visit to their grandparents."

"Which is why I'm making fun snacks for them to take along. Hopefully it'll cut down on the squabbling. You know how cranky Cody and Marisa can get when confined together in a small space."

Yes, Molly did. She supposed that happened after a month, getting to know a person's habits and quirks and likes and dislikes. Owen organized the money in his wallet by denomination and listened to sports talk radio in his truck.

"I'm going to miss them," Molly confessed.

"Me, too." Bridget stopped filling small plastic sandwich bags with carrot sticks, celery sticks and pretzel sticks. "I bet you're going to miss their dad, too."

"I already do." The words slipped out before Molly could stop them.

"Were you able to spend any alone time together last night?"

"A little. And all we did was disagree."

"No!" Bridget wiped her hands on a towel and came over to join Molly at the table where she'd taken a seat. "What about? Not him turning down the job at Craft-Right?"

"That and other things." Molly recounted to Bridget how she and Owen had reached a mutual agreement to call off dating. "He's burned-out on sales. That's the real reason he said no to Craft-Right."

"Huh."

"Translate *huh* for me."

"You're not going to like it." Bridget stood and retrieved a storage container holding cookie bars.

"Tell me anyway."

"This is strictly my opinion."

"Argh!" Molly wanted to scream. "Say it already."

"You didn't support him in his time of need just like you accused him of not supporting you when the groom's mother posted a bad review on our social media page."

Yikes. When Bridget put it that way...

Molly's chest ached. She knew she could have

handled the disagreement with Owen better. Even so, she stuck to her guns. "I don't know how we can have a relationship until he figures out what the heck he wants to do with his life."

"Him finding a job is important," Bridget conceded. "He has three kids to support."

"Right. And he should focus on that while I focus on the ranch."

"Have you checked our social media page this morning?"

"No. My phone's upstairs charging." Truthfully, Molly lacked the courage to look.

Bridget picked up her tablet from the counter. After a moment of scrolling, she announced, "There's a glowing post from our second bride yesterday." Bridget read a snippet. "Wow. Very nice. Twenty more weddings and that lousy post will be so far down the list no one will notice it."

Molly was less sure. When she ordered anything online, she always searched for and read the bad reviews. "Owen suggested I respond to the groom's mother and apologize."

"That's a good idea."

"What if it backfires and makes things worse?"

Bridget resumed packing snacks. "Your decision. But I happen to think this is one of the many ways you and Owen are a good match.

He provides the voice of reason when you go off the rails."

Off the rails. Not a flattering description of herself. She really did need to work on more self-control.

"I'll post later today," she muttered. When her head was clearer.

Bridget sat down beside her. "You feeling okay after everything, because, frankly, you look terrible."

"It's not like we had anything to begin with." Other than a few, no, several, wonderful kisses and a potential chance for happiness that she'd tossed away.

Her attempt to infuse lightness into her voice didn't fly, and Bridget called her on it.

"You don't have to pretend with me. Of course you're hurting. You cared for him. A lot from what I saw."

Molly still did and would for a long time to come.

"Don't write the two of you off yet," Bridget said. "You'll be seeing him again. He's Homer's only relative in Arizona. Grandma's sure to invite him for holiday dinners. Him and the kids."

Molly hadn't thought of that and didn't know whether to be glad or dismayed.

"Change is inevitable. Now might not have been the best time for the two of you, but who knows how different things will be in six months or a year?"

But would Owen's feelings for Molly remain the same? Neither of them had left the door open to start fresh.

"We need to hurry." Bridget stood and pulled Molly to her feet. "If we're going to take our presents over to Owen's kids before their mom arrives."

Molly wasn't sure she was up to seeing Owen, but nothing on Earth would stop her from saying goodbye to the kids.

Should she take the present she'd purchased for Owen, an I-Hart-Catering gift certificate? He'd really liked their food. Molly would decide while she dressed and applied a bit of makeup, too.

"Can I have a few minutes?"

"Sure. Meet you down here in fifteen."

Silly as it was, Molly used every one of those minutes plus three more to make herself presentable. Well, she had looked terrible as Bridget so kindly mentioned.

The pair of them cut through the clubhouse courtyard and trudged along the road. Molly grappled with the presents while Bridget carried an eco-friendly grocery bag filled with her treats, paper cups and a jug of lemonade. Naturally, she'd packed enough for three families.

Even before they reached the cabin door, they heard Marisa crying from inside. Owen could also be heard appealing to her, his voice not loud but firm.

Molly and Bridget paused on the stoop, trading looks.

"Should we leave?" Molly asked in a low voice.

"If we do, we might miss them."

Gritting her teeth, Molly raised her hand and knocked. Perhaps the presents would calm whatever storm was raging in the cabin.

Owen answered the door, Willa in his arms and strain visible on his face. "Hi."

"Mawee!" Willa held out her arms.

Molly freed a hand to clasp Willa's. "We can come back," she told Owen.

He took in the presents she held. "No, it's okay. Come on in."

Cody and Marisa stood in the middle of the living room. Suitcases, bags and boxes were stacked in a small mountain near the door. Marisa held Pinkie Pie in a death grip, the poor kitten yowling and squirming. The harder it fought, the louder Marisa cried.

"Is everything okay?" Molly asked, momentarily forgetting about her and Owen's disagreement.

He visibly reined in his temper. "Marisa wants

to take Pinkie Pie with them on their trip. Her mother and I have both vetoed the idea. She decided to sneak the kitten out inside her coat."

"Pinkie Pie's going home with you, right?" Molly asked.

"That's not making a difference with Marisa."

"We have snacks," Bridget announced brightly and held up the bag. "And presents."

Cody bounded over. "I want presents."

Molly set the load she'd been carrying onto the couch. Except for Owen's gift—that she kept in her coat pocket.

"Don't open them yet," Owen warned and lowered Willa to the floor. "Wait for your sisters."

Cody pouted for two seconds. After that, he became engrossed with reading the name tags. "This one's for me!" he shouted and grabbed a box to shake it.

Marisa didn't move. She continued to stare down at the kitten in her hands.

Molly sympathized with the little girl. Without thinking, she sunk to her knees in front of her. "Kitties don't like riding in cars. It scares them. Plus, they can get sick and throw up."

Marisa squeezed Pinkie Pie tighter, and the poor kitten's eyes bulged with fright or anger or both. "Who will take care of her?"

"Your daddy. He promised he would and he's very good at keeping his promises."

The little girl's lower lip trembled and her slight body shuddered.

"Tell you what. I'll make sure he sends a picture of Pinkie Pie every day to your mom's phone so you can see for yourself that she's fine and misses you."

Marisa appeared to consider this, and her grip on the kitten marginally lessened.

Molly quickly reached in and took hold of the kitten. "I'll put her in the bedroom, okay? She'll be safe there."

Marisa reluctantly let go, and Molly stood.

Owen sent her a grateful look that instantly warmed to something more. She didn't want to consider what that something more was and glanced away. With her feelings residing close to the surface, he was sure to read them.

When Molly returned from the bedroom it was to find that Bridget and Cody had distributed the presents. For the next fifteen minutes, everyone's troubles disappeared while gifts were opened. Molly was glad she'd held on to Owen's gift certificate, for the only presents she and Bridget received were from the children. Matching oven mitts for Bridget and a desk caddy for Molly.

They were cleaning up the torn wrapping

paper and discarded ribbon when a minivan pulled up in front of the cabin.

"It's your mom!" Owen announced with obvious relief. "She's here."

The children went wild with excitement, clamoring to be the one to open the door.

"Let's go," Molly whispered to Bridget. Jeanne might not want others horning in on her reunion.

"Don't go yet," Owen said when they started for the door.

Did he want them there? Molly hadn't considered that this moment might be difficult for him. Jeanne was arriving with her boyfriend. It had been Willa's attachment to the man that had prompted Owen to quit his job and come to Sweetheart Ranch.

The door flew open. Molly wasn't sure which child had won the battle.

"Mommy, Mommy!"

The trio immediately mobbed Jeanne. She bent and drew them into one big hug. "There you are. I missed you so much."

"Santa came last night," Cody announced. "He left us presents."

"There are presents for you at Grandma and Grandpa's, too."

"Do you want to see Pinkie Pie?" Marisa asked.

"Of course. Before we leave."

It was difficult to hear above the children's raised voices. Eventually Molly realized Owen was making introductions all around.

"Nice to meet you." Molly was suddenly shaking Jeanne's hand. It wasn't a horrible experience. Well, Owen's marriage had ended long ago, and Jeanne had undeniably moved on.

Her boyfriend remained behind, smiling stiffly and nodding. Willa didn't go to him. She didn't appear to notice him in the least. Cody and Marisa had responded when he initially greeted them but not a word since. All they talked about was their dad and the fun they'd had at the ranch.

Molly thought she noticed the strain on Owen's face diminishing.

"I love the ranch," Jeanne said. "It's beautiful."

"Thanks." Molly smiled. "We love it, too."

They spent a few more minutes chatting before Molly and Bridget made their excuses.

"We'll walk you out," Owen said. "We have to load the car anyway." He issued instructions to the children which were promptly followed.

"My, my, Owen," Jeanne commented as they walked out. "I've never seen the kids so cooperative. Maybe I should let you take them for a month more often."

"I hope you will."

Both Molly and Bridget embraced the children. Willa began to cry when Molly kissed her forehead and told her, "I'll see you soon."

Marisa buried her face in Molly's side. Cody hugged her waist.

Molly and Bridget left then, silently agreeing that the final goodbyes should be shared exclusively between Owen and his children.

It was only when they entered the kitchen that Molly realized she had tears in her eyes.

CHAPTER SEVENTEEN

Owen placed the empty suitcase on the bed and unzipped it. His other suitcase sat on the floor. Two days from now, on January 1, he would officiate the vow renewal ceremony for his uncle Homer and Emily. The next morning, he'd depart Sweetheart Ranch for his house in the northeast valley. A house that would now feel cold and empty after living in close quarters with his three active offspring. A house he'd bought out of necessity after he and Jeanne divorced and had no emotional attachment to whatsoever.

There wasn't much for him to pack. But with no wedding scheduled today and five tomorrow—New Year's Eve was another popular day for tying the knot—he'd decided to get a head start on the task. Besides, if he waited until the last minute, he might have a hard time. A big part of him didn't want to leave, that part being his whole heart.

This was not how he'd envisioned spending his last days at the ranch. He and Molly should be looking forward to their first date, not being polite but reserved with each other.

She'd come to his rescue Christmas morning. She and Bridget. The presents they'd brought for the kids helped distract them from the emotional goodbye with Owen and Pinkie Pie.

At a loss for what to say, he'd kept his mouth shut. Molly was right, Owen hadn't wanted the job at Craft-Right and should have been honest with her. If he had, things might have gone very differently. Then they could have had a serious discussion about him being at a career crossroads. God, he hated the idea. It left him on shaky ground when Owen had always been so sure of himself and what he wanted in life.

A small orange blur appeared from nowhere and leaped onto the bed. Pinkie Pie. The kitten stopped in her tracks, hissed at the empty suitcase, and then proceeded to hop into it. Sniffing a strap, she batted at it before lying down and claiming this new territory as hers.

"I suppose I need to buy you a travel crate." Owen scratched the cat's head, and she instantly started purring. "Maybe Fred sells them at the feed store."

The kitten was cute, and Owen had become quite fond of her over the past five days since his kids left.

"Misery makes strange bedfellows," he said. A scary thought occurred to him. "Please, don't tell me I'm turning into my mother, the cat lady."

He opened the bottom dresser drawer and examined its sparse contents. A check of the laundry basket he'd been using as a clothes hamper revealed most everything he'd brought with him was dirty. He sorted lights from darks while Pinkie Pie watched. He'd throw a load into the washing machine on his next trip outside.

Finishing with that, he grabbed his phone and snapped a picture of the kitten dozing in the suitcase, texting it to Jeanne for Marisa to see. His daughter was amassing quite a collection of pictures. Owen had been diligent about keeping his word.

The top dresser drawer didn't yield much more than the bottom one. Owen packed a belt and socks and kerchiefs he wouldn't need before leaving. Beneath an undershirt, he found the package containing the necklace he'd bought at the church gift sale to give Molly at Christmas. That hadn't turned out as planned, either.

Instead of finding an opportunity to give her the necklace, he'd avoided her. Owen was having enough trouble keeping himself together. Baring his soul was more than he could handle right now.

He should have just stuck the package in the suitcase and not opened it, for the air left his lungs upon seeing the interlocking hearts. All the emotions he'd worked to keep at bay in the aftermath of his and Molly's falling-out rose up to choke him.

He sat on the bed next to the suitcase. "Not my best moment, Pinkie Pie."

The kitten studied him through half-closed eyes, purring loudly. At least one of them was content.

"Molly's a catch. Women like her don't come around very often. And what did I do? Made one mistake after the other with her from the moment I arrived. Nicely done."

He'd been so focused on his own needs and goals, he'd ignored hers. The same thing he'd done to Jeanne and to his kids, Owen realized.

"You'd think I would've learned the first time."

Instead of putting the necklace back into the box, he slipped it into his pocket. Something told him that he'd be carrying it with him for a while.

At least he'd accomplished one thing. His relationship with his kids was the best it had ever been. He now talked to them every day, either on the phone or by video chat. Willa not as much as Cody and Marisa. His youngest didn't understand video chats and mostly pointed at the phone's screen saying, "Look, Daddy, look."

The kids were coming to stay with him the weekend after he left Sweetheart Ranch and alternate weekends after that, including when his parents visited. Owen would attend every Saturday soccer game, every Tap for Tots dance recital, every birthday party, every Easter egg hunt, along with kindergarten and preschool registration, and swim lessons in the summer.

He should be happy, only the opposite was true. He missed Molly, her A-type personality having grown on him. He still didn't think he'd patronized her. What he had done was give too little importance to her concerns because he himself didn't consider them a big deal. That was wrong and not what friends did for each other. Certainly not what a *boyfriend* did.

The negative comments on the ranch's social media page that had upset Molly so much had yet to amount to anything significant. Owen took no pleasure in being right and was simply glad the ranch hadn't been negatively affected. The phone continued to ring, and January was shaping up to be a busy month.

Owen wished he could say the same for himself. The business world had come to a standstill this week between Christmas and New Year's. There was nothing decent posted on the various employment websites he'd registered with, and his headhunter had taken the entire week off.

Hopefully, the job market would improve soon. Owen had enough money remaining from his Waverly severance package to last a good two months. After that, he'd be forced to dip into his investment account. And while he might be able to petition the court for a reduction in his child support payments, he refused to go that route. His kids wouldn't suffer for his choices.

Owen pushed to his feet, feeling the walls closing in on him. "Pinkie Pie, I'm out of here. You finish the packing, okay?"

Startled by his sudden movement, the kitten leaped to the floor and scurried out the bedroom door, slipping on the smooth hardwood floor in the hall as her paws scrambled for traction.

"You just can't get good help these days."

He carried the laundry basket with him to the storage room beside the clubhouse where the guest washer and dryer were located. Next, he strode to his truck and climbed in. A trip to town for a pet crate was merely an excuse for a change of scenery.

On the drive to the feed store, he decided to purchase some hay and oats as well. Molly had told Owen yesterday that Big Jim's wife was doing better, thanks to rest and medications. He was willing to return to work until Molly found a permanent replacement, after which he'd retire altogether so that he and his wife could travel and remodel their house. Owen wanted to lighten the older man's load by leaving the stables clean and in good order.

He parked behind the building near the rear entrance and lowered the tailgate on his truck in preparation of loading hay bales and sacks of grain. He entered through the heavy metal door, hailing Fred who was in his customary place behind the counter.

The proprietor had yet to take down his holiday decorations. The entire town was still celebrating from what Owen had seen on the drive here. Everyone but Owen. He hadn't felt the Christmas spirit since his argument with Molly.

He and Fred completed the sale with Fred putting the bill on the ranch's account, with the exception of the pet crate, which Owen paid for. Rabbit pen, actually. Fred didn't carry pet travel crates, but Owen figured the rabbit pen would suffice for Pinkie Pie's short journey.

"Are you coming to the reception?" Owen asked while Fred accompanied him to the back area where livestock feed was stored.

"Wouldn't miss it."

Many of the town's residents had been invited. Between Uncle Homer's years preaching at the church and Emily having owned the local inn, they had a lot of friends in Mustang Valley.

"Great." Owen helped lift sacks of grain onto the handcart and wheeled it outside to his truck. "Glad I'll get to see you one last time before I leave town and you move to Minnesota."

"The wife's starting to doubt that'll ever happen." Fred paused to shrug and wipe his damp brow. "I've had the store for sale these past three months and not a single serious offer."

"Hard to believe."

"I agree. I have a ready-made clientele. Mustang Valley is a horse and cattle town and nearly everyone shops here. No competition, either. The next closest feed store is in Rio Verde, darn near twenty miles away."

They finished loading the hay bales and grain sacks. Owen closed the tailgate and put the rabbit cage in the backseat of his truck. He was thinking Pinkie Pie would hate it.

"The smartest thing I did was add Western apparel and merchandise." Fred leaned against the upright handcart. "You'd be surprised how many hats and boots and shirts I sell every week."

Owen admired the man. "That was good strategy. You saw a need and filled it."

"I could've done more these last couple of years. Been getting tired," Fred admitted.

"Can I ask how much you want for the store?"

Fred named the price. "I'm willing to finance the buyer at reasonable terms. Not sure why I can't generate interest. The economy's been bouncing back recently in this part of Arizona."

"It takes an owner who's experienced in

horses and horse people and with a strong sales background."

"Someone like you." Fred winked at Owen. "This place could be yours. If you have a hankering."

"I just might," Owen heard himself saying.

Fred grinned. "Why don't you come back inside and let's talk. I'll show you the sales package my broker put together. It includes my financials for the last two years. You can see for yourself how I've done. A smart, motivated man like you could do better."

They chatted for over two hours. In between customers, Fred not only showed Owen the sales package and financials, he explained the store operation and took him on an in-depth tour. Before Owen left, they phoned Fred's broker and set a time to meet the next morning—the woman was willing to work on a holiday if it meant writing an offer on the store.

Owen hadn't felt this excited since he won his last rodeo championship. He didn't so much drive back to Sweetheart Ranch as sail. A call to his investment advisor ended with them arranging a meeting on January 2 to review Owen's financial portfolio. He had enough money for the down payment on the store and the first year's payments if he liquidated a portion of his retirement account and sold his house.

With careful budgeting and modest living, the monthly income from the store would cover his expenses. He already had a dozen ideas on how to expand the store and increase revenue. Employer-paid benefits was something he'd unfortunately lose. The trade-off was he'd be happy at his job. Hopefully, Jeanne would be willing to add the kids to her health plan. He thought she would, once he offered to increase his child support payments.

Was it possible? Could the life Owen had previously wrecked be coming together? His relationship with his kids was improving for sure and potentially his work—if the store purchase came to fruition. The only missing piece was Molly.

What would she think of having him as a neighbor? He'd find out soon enough. News tended to travel fast in small towns. No doubt him buying Fred's store would be the topic of conversation at Uncle Homer and Emily's reception.

THE CHAPEL WAS standing room only for Grandma Em and Homer's vow renewal ceremony. Twice as many people would be at the reception. Perhaps even three times. The side table in the parlor was already covered in envelopes. The happy couple had insisted they had everything they'd ever need and requested donations be made to the outreach programs at Homer's church in lieu of gifts.

Both Molly and Bridget had labored to the point of exhaustion to make every one of Grandma Em's wishes a reality. Bridget had baked herself into a frenzy, but the results were spectacular. The traditional four-tier wedding cake was topped with a pair of engraved champagne glasses and decorated with live red roses. Molly had personally tied countless miniature silk bows for the guests to wear.

She was truly ecstatic for her grandmother and Homer. Too bad she couldn't say the same for herself.

Unlucky in love once again. Though she and Owen hadn't progressed to the point of being in love, they'd been headed there, of that Molly was convinced. What other explanation was there for her deep despair since their disagreement?

She blamed seeing him on a daily basis. Hard to get over someone who was there whenever she turned around.

Surely things would be different once he left Sweetheart Ranch. She'd moved on fairly easily after her former engagements ended. Then again, she'd wanted to move on. Not so with Owen. She spent most of her waking hours wishing she could go back in time. If he gave her the tiniest indication he was open to a reconciliation, she'd leap on the chance. But he didn't, and her despair continued to linger.

While Bridget and Molly's mother helped Grandma Em with her outfit, Molly and Owen acted as cohosts, greeting guests and trying to find places for them in the crowded chapel. Frequently, their glances connected from across the crowded room. It couldn't be helped.

During one exchange, he'd appeared as forlorn as she, and she wondered if he, too, was regretting their decision to call it quits.

No, she had to stop thinking like that. Owen was her past not her future, and attempting to read more into his expressions than was there would be counterproductive.

"Grandma's ready." Bridget came up behind Molly and squeezed her affectionately. "She asked Nora to walk her down the aisle and Mom to be her matron of honor. You should have been there and seen the three of them crying and hugging."

"That's sweet." Molly worried about her own ability to keep the tears at bay during the ceremony.

"The photographer caught it all."

They'd decided at the last minute to hire a professional photographer rather than rely on friends to take pictures. It was Molly's idea. She remembered receiving a wedding album as a bridal shower gift and her joy at the prospect of filling it with pictures. She also recalled acute sadness when she'd returned all the shower gifts after her fiancé had called off the wedding.

"Owen looks like a kid who just learned Santa Claus isn't real."

"What?" Molly spun to face her sister.

"He's a mess." Bridget evaluated Molly closely. "He's not the only one. You aren't exactly kicking up your heels."

"I'm hanging in there."

"You were wrong to let him go. Or should I say, you let him go for the wrong reasons."

"No more armchair psychology, please. Not today."

Bridget ignored her. "You're so darn afraid of being dumped again, you dumped him first."

The jolt ripped through Molly from her head to her toes. It was the truth breaking loose from where she'd buried it.

"I don't want to make another mistake," she admitted in a broken voice.

"Owen's not a mistake."

"You can't be sure. Look at Mom and Doug."

Both Molly and Bridget's gazes sought out their stepfather who was keeping to himself in a corner and pretty much ignoring everyone there.

Every couple of minutes he would check his cell phone.

"Owen couldn't be more opposite from Doug." Bridget rested a hand on Molly's arm.

"I'm high maintenance. What if I wind up like Jeanne? She was always making demands on him. That's one of the reasons their marriage failed."

"Again, complete opposites." Bridget sighed. "Did you ever notice that all the obstacles in front of you and Owen were put there by you?"

"Being afraid of making another mistake isn't an excuse."

"Oh, baby sister. Don't let a little thing like fear get in your way."

Molly was abruptly recruited to attend to a minor problem with the sound system and went gratefully. Not because she'd rather avoid the uncomfortable conversation with her sister but because today was all about her grandmother and Homer. They deserved her complete attention.

With a little nudge here and there and a kindly phrased, "Can you move over just a little?" Molly was able to either seat everyone or find them a place to stand behind the pews. A small path was left for the wedding party to make their much-anticipated entrance.

Owen made his way to the altar. He'd donned his usual Western-cut sports jacket. In place of a bolo tie, he'd chosen an old-fashioned black string necktie like those worn by characters in old Westerns. More than one woman commented on his good looks.

If Molly hadn't been so determined to stay strong, she'd have melted at the sight of him.

Minutes before the ceremony was due to begin, Molly and Bridget took their seats in the first pew reserved for the bride's family. Grandma Em's younger sister had made the trip as well as two of her cousins and Molly's aunt and uncle. And, of course, there was Doug. The cabins were filled with out-of-town family and friends. Owen had graciously agreed to let Homer's best man, a buddy from his army days, sleep on his sofa bed.

"No worries," Owen had said, "I'll be gone tomorrow, and he can have the cabin to himself."

Molly forced herself not to think about Owen's departure as she waited for Mendelssohn's "Wedding March" to start playing. Fat lot of good it did her, since she couldn't stop looking at him standing at the altar. At his right waited Homer, wearing a dark blue suit and a huge grin, *his* best man beside him.

The first few strands of the familiar melody filled the chapel, and Molly's mother appeared, holding a small bouquet of festive winter flowers and escorted by Nora's oldest grandson, who was all of nine. He accompanied her to the altar and then, giggling, scurried over to sit with his family. The photographer floated around the room, taking pictures.

And then the bride appeared on Nora's arm. Those who were seated rose to their feet, their expressions tender and warm. Upon reaching the altar, Nora released Grandma Em. Molly's mother then took Grandma Em's bouquet so that she could hold hands with Homer. The moment was pure magic.

Owen smiled at the elated couple and began reciting. "Who gives this woman to be married to this man?"

The timbre of his voice, Molly noted, was strong and sure, as if he'd been officiating weddings his entire life rather than the last five weeks. All things considered, he'd been a wonderful substitute minister for Homer and wrangler for Big Jim. He'd treated his job at the ranch as if it was the most important one he'd ever held.

Molly watched transfixed as he talked about the six cornerstones of marriage: commitment, honesty, communication, respect, forgiveness and unconditional love. There was something about his manner and delivery that convinced her he wasn't just saying the words, he believed them.

"Marriage is not simply a sacred institution.

For many people, it's the closest, most intimate, most important relationship they will ever have with another person. It deserves no less than our best efforts and our greatest sacrifices, as I know Homer and Emily are willing to give."

Owen glanced up, and this time his gaze connected with Molly where it remained, absolutely unwavering. She knew then that he was speaking not only to Homer and Grandma Em but to her, too.

"As the poet James Kavanaugh said, 'To love is not to possess, to own or imprison, nor to lose one's self in another. Love is to join and separate, to walk alone and together, to find a laughing freedom that lonely isolation does not permit. It is finally to be able to be who we really are.'"

Finally to be able to be who we really are.

The phrase resonated with Molly. She was impulsive. High maintenance. A little OCD, as Bridget had said. Convinced she was always right. Yet Owen had come to care for her despite her many quirks. He'd let her be who she really was and didn't want to change her.

Whatever flaws he possessed, whatever differences they had, weren't important. Commitment, honesty, communication, respect, forgiveness and unconditional love. The cornerstones of marriage as Owen had recited. Those were what truly mattered.

When Molly next looked at Owen, he was staring down at the paper in his hands. After that, he launched into the exchange of vows, and her hopes sank. If there had been an opportunity to communicate her revelation to him, she'd missed it.

With loud and exuberant gusto, Owen pronounced Grandma Em and Homer man and wife. Though it was their second wedding in five weeks, Homer kissed Grandma Em as any newly married man would kiss his beautiful bride.

Molly watched the two of them through misty eyes. They hadn't let fear or difficulties prevent them from going after what they wanted.

She could learn a lot from them.

Frank Sinatra's "The Best Is Yet to Come" filled the chapel as Homer and Grandma Em strolled hand in hand back down the aisle. Molly and Bridget joined them and the rest of the wedding party in the foyer to form a short receiving line that included Owen at the end.

Nora squeezed in between Molly and her mother. Leaning sideways, she said to Molly in a loud whisper, "Did you hear the news? Owen is buying Fred's feed store. He's not leaving town after all. Going to live right here."

Molly whirled to gape at him, her jaw slack. "Is it true? Are you buying the feed store?"

"I signed the papers yesterday."

"Does this mean—" She couldn't finish. Couldn't think.

Owen formed his hands into the shape of a heart and held them in front of his chest.

"Oh, my," Nora crooned. "I do believe the man is taken with you."

Molly felt herself throwing doubts aside and rushing headlong toward what could only be love.

CHAPTER EIGHTEEN

THE PARLOR COULDN'T contain all the people attending Homer and Emily's reception. As a result, some gathered in the foyer and others in the kitchen. Several brave souls ventured into the cold to stand on the veranda.

The photographer took both candid and posed pictures. Owen had been asked to join in various shots of the wedding party and their family and friends. He wouldn't have minded standing next to Molly, but the photographer insisted on putting him to Homer's right with the Foxworthy clan and Molly to Emily's left with the O'Malleys.

He kept trying to get a good look at her and determine if she'd understood the subtle messages he'd conveyed during the ceremony and while in the receiving line. But she was continually snatched away, leaving him more determined than ever to get her alone for just a few minutes. That was all he needed to tell her he'd meant every word he'd spoken during the vow renewal ceremony and would prove it if she let him.

News of him buying the feed store had spread quickly—every few minutes someone stopped him to wish him well. No one was satisfied with the short version of how he came to buy the store and insisted on details. Owen would politely break away as soon as he could and continue his attempts to locate Molly.

Where was she? It was as if she'd disappeared.

Finally, she emerged from the bride's dressing room with Emily. They must have gone in there to freshen up after the long and involved photo session.

"Cake and champagne are being served in the parlor," someone called out.

Owen was involuntarily swept along by a large group of guests converging on the parlor, his frustration at continually missing Molly mounting.

Uncle Homer's best man made a toast once the champagne was served—sparkling cider for those underage. Several people shared amusing stories of Homer and Emily. Cake was cut, more photos taken, and hugs and kisses exchanged.

Owen had officiated dozens of weddings during his stay at Sweetheart Ranch. None were happier than this one.

He'd almost given up on ever finding a moment alone with Molly, when he felt a tug on his sports coat sleeve. He sensed her presence before he'd even turned. Discovering her standing so close was like seeing a blazing sun breaking over the horizon at dawn.

"I was wondering—"

He grabbed her hand and dragged her along with him before she could finish, navigating their way through the throng. Now that he had her, he wasn't about to let her escape before she heard him out.

"Where are we going?" she asked.

"The chapel." It was the only public room in the house he could think of where they might find a modicum of privacy.

To his relief, the chapel was empty. No sooner did they sit in the first pew than Owen enveloped both of Molly's hands in his.

"I've missed this," he said.

"Holding hands?"

"Being with you. And before you start telling me how different we are and that I need to get my life together—"

"I'm not going to tell you," she said quietly.

No? Well, in that case, Owen didn't beat around the bush. "I know buying the feed store is risky. Working for Craft-Right or a company like them is the safer choice. But I'd hate it."

"I agree. You'd have done well at Craft-Right, Owen. You'll do better owning the feed store."

"I think so, too. It's the kind of business tailor-made for me. And once I sell my house, I'll find an inexpensive place in town. I want to put as much money into expanding the feed store as I can. Fred had a lot of ideas. I have more."

"I'd love to hear about them."

"Yeah?"

"I have a lot of ideas about expanding Sweetheart Ranch. We can swap."

"Sure." He tamped down his disappointment. She was interested only from a business standpoint.

"Congratulations, Owen. I'm excited for you."

"Are you okay with me staying in Mustang Valley? Be honest."

She stared at their joined hands. "Actually…"

He cut her off. "I want another chance. Hear me out before you say no."

She nodded. "Okay."

"I've made a lot of mistakes with you. Ones I regret. It was a learning process. Fortunately, I'm a quick study."

"I made mistakes, too. I've realized these last few days, or should I say I've had it pointed out to me, that I was afraid of being hurt again. I still am."

"I swear, Molly, I'll do my best not to let that happen."

"I believe you. If I didn't, I wouldn't be here with you."

A light came to her eyes, and the hope he'd been holding at bay broke free, filling his chest. "Is that a yes?"

"It's a let's see what happens. No promises."

"Sorry, not good enough."

Her smile began to fade. "I beg your pardon?"

"It's New Year's Day. A time for resolutions. I'm making several of them and intend to keep every one." He reached into the inside pocket of his jacket and removed the package containing the double-heart necklace he'd planned on giving her at Christmas. "Open it."

"Owen, I wasn't… I don't have—"

"Shh." He placed the package in her hand. "Just do it."

She gasped softly upon seeing the necklace. "It's beautiful. Thank you."

He closed his hand over hers, the necklace nestled between their palms. "Molly O'Malley, I promise to treat you with respect and to always listen with an open heart and mind. I promise to value your opinions and not dismiss them. I promise to make you laugh and to be a shoulder for you to cry on. I promise to keep things interesting and exciting, to delight in our differences and cherish our similarities. I promise to learn from you and grow into a better version of myself. Lastly, I promise to kiss you every day."

"Oh, really?" She arched her brows.

"Many times every day."

Her expression softened. "That almost sounds like a wedding vow."

"I've been reciting a lot of those lately." He lowered his mouth to hers. "You should know, I date with purpose, not casually. I want for this to go somewhere and last a long time. If you're not on board, now's the time to say something."

"I'm on board."

That was all he needed to hear. Owen jumped to his feet and led her out of the chapel, through the foyer, and to the front door. The crowd there had moved to the parlor leaving Owen and Molly alone.

"What are you doing?" she asked, laughing.

He pointed to the mistletoe hanging above them.

"You could have kissed me in the chapel."

"This is better. More meaningful."

He wrapped his arms around her and lifted her onto her tiptoes, then off her feet entirely. Their kiss was gentle and sweet at first but soon escalated in intensity, a reflection of their feelings for each other.

Something filled him then, an emotion that had been missing for too long. Contentment. Molly's soft sigh spoke of that same contentment, and he pulled her closer.

When he finally released her moments later, he couldn't stop smiling. Neither could she.

Laying her head against his chest, she sighed expansively. Owen was content to remain where they were, holding her indefinitely. Too soon they were interrupted by a pair of departing guests.

Owen didn't mind. Later, when they were the only ones left downstairs, he'd kiss her again. And again.

EPILOGUE

"Turn him to the left, son. That's right. Don't let him walk away with you."

Owen called out instructions to Cody, who sat atop Moses. The draft horse's large size dwarfed the young boy, giving the pair a comical appearance.

"I wanna ride, Daddy." Marisa stood beside Owen, tugging on his jacket sleeve. "You said I could."

Willa added her vote to the mix. "Me, too!"

At almost three, she was quickly catching up to her siblings. Owen couldn't believe how much they'd grown this past year. Before long, he'd be teaching them to drive a car rather than ride.

"All right." Owen lifted the girls one at a time onto Popeye, the pony he'd purchased back in April. "Hold on tight."

This particular riding lesson was taking place in front of the ranch house on a lazy and unseasonably warm Christmas afternoon. After picking the kids up at their mother's, Owen had brought them home to Mustang Valley for the next couple of days. He, Molly and the rest of her family had postponed opening presents until the kids arrived. They'd insisted on trying out the new chaps and cowboy hats "Santa" had left for them with Owen. Since Molly, her sister and grandmother were busy getting ready for a small evening wedding, keeping the kids busy with Moses and Popeye and out of the way had seemed like a good idea.

Owen couldn't help thinking back on all the changes from a year ago. He'd found a house to rent after the sale of the feed store had gone through. The owner of the house was willing to sell it to Owen, and they'd recently entered discussions. He'd been waiting to buy the house until the store was making what he considered a decent profit, and he'd reached that point in October, well ahead of the schedule he'd set for himself.

Pinkie Pie had settled in nicely, turning out to be a good cat. Except for when the kids were staying with him, she lived at the store, earning her kibbles by keeping mice out of the grain and entertaining the customers.

Entrepreneurship. Owen had been heading down that path since he quit the rodeo circuit. He just hadn't seen it until coming to Mustang Valley—and until Molly had pointed out to him that he was at a career crossroads. Luckily, he'd wised up before losing her altogether.

When he wasn't at the store or one of the kids' events, he helped out at Sweetheart Ranch. With their hectic schedules and free time at a premium, it was an arrangement that enabled Owen and Molly to see each other as much as possible.

Who was he kidding? He just wanted to be with her whenever and however. That, he supposed, was what happened when someone fell deeply and completely in love like he had with Molly. He'd been ready to commit to more almost from when they'd started dating. She, however, had insisted on waiting, citing that they had a lot on their respective plates with the feed store and the ranch.

So, Owen had bid his time. Until today. The Christmas gift he'd given her earlier had been a decoy. His real gift was in his jacket pocket where it would stay until the moment was right.

He was confident her family would approve. His, too. Owen's parents had taken to Molly immediately during their visit last February and became good friends with her over Thanksgiving when they visited again.

With business booming, Molly existed in a near constant state of panic. Even so, she always set aside two evenings during the week when she'd let herself relax. Whenever possible, she went with Owen to Cody's soccer practice or the girls' dance classes. The kids adored her, and she doted on them.

Life, Owen thought, didn't get much better than this. Well, it could be, he amended and patted his jacket pocket.

While shooting a video with his phone of the kids riding, the door to the ranch house suddenly flew open, and Molly came running down the veranda steps, shirttails flying and her face flushed.

"Owen! Owen! Look at this." Reaching him, she took hold of his hands. "You'll never guess who just called. The editor from *Southwest Bride Magazine*."

"On Christmas day?"

"She apologized for disturbing us, but apparently the final edition's been approved, and she wanted us to know." Molly grinned excitedly. "They named Sweetheart Ranch as their editor's choice for this year's best wedding venue."

"You're kidding. That's great, sweetheart." He pulled her into a fierce hug.

The flattering article featuring Sweetheart Ranch from last February had impacted the ranch greatly, bringing in a slew of new customers from all over the country. And while not singlehandedly responsible for the ranch's impressive growth this past year, it had contributed greatly. Molly's cross-promotion efforts with other local businesses, including Owen's store, had also paid off. She wasn't just a success at her job, she was a powerhouse.

"What's going on, Daddy?" Marisa nudged Popeye into a trot and rode over to them. Behind her, Willa held on, squealing with delight.

"Molly got some really good news."

Cody, too, rode over. "Does this mean we can have cake?" For him, all celebrations were good for one thing: dessert.

"Maybe later." Owen turned back to Molly. "You should send a copy of the excerpt from the magazine to your former clients and everyone on your mailing list."

"And hang a framed copy in the foyer!"

"Molly," Bridget called from the veranda. "You need to come inside. The bride just phoned. There's a small problem with the ceremony, and Grandma needs your advice."

"Oh, boy." Molly started to go. "It never ends."

Owen tugged on her hand. "Don't go yet. I have something for you."

"Now?" She patted his cheek. "Can't it wait?"

"I've waited long enough. Two months, to be precise. That's how long I've been planning this."

"Planning what?" The look of confusion on her face instantly cleared when he removed the small velvet box from his jacket pocket, and her hands flew to her mouth. "Is that what I think it is?"

"Molly O'Malley, I love you with all my heart." He flipped the lid on the box to reveal a diamond solitaire ring that sparkled in the bright sunlight. "You are more than the woman I want to spend the rest of my life with, you're—"

"Yes!" She let out a gasp. "I'll marry you."

"I haven't finished."

"You don't have to. I accept."

Owen laughed. So much for the flowery speech he'd prepared. Removing the ring from the box, he slipped it on her finger.

"I love it!" she exclaimed, holding her hand and admiring the ring.

"What about me?"

She threw herself at him. "That, my darling, goes without saying."

He held her close and nuzzled her ear. "This is only the beginning for us."

As he pressed his lips to hers, he dimly heard Cody saying, "Ew…" and Bridget hollering in the distance, "Hurry up, no time for that."

He ignored them. Molly did, too.

* * * * *

*In the small Texas burg of Rambling Rose, real estate
investor Callum Fortune is making a big splash.
The last thing he needs is any personal complications
slowing his pace—least of all nurse Becky Averill,
a beautiful widow with twin baby girls!*

*Read on for a sneak preview of
Fortune's Fresh Start
by Michelle Major, the first book in
The Fortunes of Texas: Rambling Rose continuity.*

"I didn't mean to rush off the other day after the ribbon
cutting," he told her as they approached the door that led
to the childcare center. "I think I interrupted a potential
invitation for dinner, and I've been regretting it ever
since."

Becky blinked. In truth, she would have never had the
guts to invite Callum for dinner. She'd been planning to
offer to cook or bake for him and drop it off at his office
as a thank-you. The idea of having him over to her small
house did funny things to her insides.

"Oh," she said again.

"Maybe I misinterpreted," Callum said quickly,
looking as flummoxed as she felt. "Or imagined the
whole thing. You meant to thank me with a bottle of wine
or some cookies or—"

"Dinner." She grinned at him. Somehow his
discomposure gave her the confidence to say the word.

He appeared so perfect and out of her league, but at the moment he simply seemed like a normal, nervous guy not sure what to say next.

She decided to make it easy for him. For both of them. "Would you come for dinner tomorrow night? The girls go to bed early, so if you could be there around seven, we could have a more leisurely meal and a chance to talk."

His shoulders visibly relaxed. "I'd like that. Dinner with a friend. Can I bring anything?"

"Just yourself," she told him.

He pulled his cell phone from his pocket and handed it to her so she could enter her contact information. It took a few tries to get it right because her fingers trembled slightly.

He grinned at her as he took the phone again. "I'm looking forward to tomorrow, Becky."

"Me, too," she breathed, then gave a little wave as he said goodbye. She took a few steadying breaths before heading in to pick up the twins. *Don't turn it into something more than it is*, she cautioned herself.

It was a thank-you, not a date. Her babies would be asleep in the next room. Definitely not a date.

But her stammering heart didn't seem to get the message.

Don't miss
Fortune's Fresh Start *by Michelle Major,*
available January 2020 wherever
Harlequin® Special Edition books and ebooks are sold.

Harlequin.com

Looking for more satisfying love stories
with community and family at their core?

**Check out Harlequin® Special Edition
and Love Inspired® books!**

New books available every month!

CONNECT WITH US AT:

Facebook.com/groups/HarlequinConnection

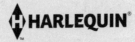

Facebook.com/HarlequinBooks

Twitter.com/HarlequinBooks

Instagram.com/HarlequinBooks

Pinterest.com/HarlequinBooks

ReaderService.com

HARLEQUIN®

**ROMANCE WHEN
YOU NEED IT**

HFGENRE2018

"There's an open bottle of very expensive scotch on
the counter, just waiting for someone to enjoy it." She
laughed again, softly this time. "And I'd *really* like to
hear the story of how Danger Dan turned into a lawman."

Dan grimaced. He hated that stupid nickname Ryan had
made up, even if he *had* earned it back then. Especially
coming from Mack.

"Is your husband waiting upstairs?" Dan wasn't sure
where that question came from, but, to be fair, all Mack
had ever talked about was leaving Gallant Lake, having a
big wedding and a bigger house. The girl had goals, and
from what he'd heard, she'd reached every one of them.

"I don't have a husband anymore." She brushed past
him and headed toward the counter. "So are you joining
me or not?"

Dan glanced at his watch, not sure how to digest that
information. "I'm off duty in fifteen minutes."

Her long hair swung back and forth as she walked ahead of him. So did her hips. *Damn.*

"And you're all about following the rules now? You really have changed, haven't you? Pity. I guess I'm drinking my first glass alone. You'll just have to catch up."

He frowned. Mackenzie had been strong-willed, but never sassy. Never the type to sneak into her father's store alone for an after-hours drink. Not the type to taunt him. Not the type to break the rules.

Looked like he wasn't the only one who'd changed since high school.

Don't miss
Her Homecoming Wish *by Jo McNally,*
available February 2020 wherever
Harlequin® Special Edition books and ebooks are sold.

Harlequin.com